Mary E. Galloway Giffen, J. C. Galloway

Life and Letters of Mrs. Mary Galloway Giffen

Who Was the Pioneer Missionary of the Associate Reformed Church....

Mary E. Galloway Giffen, J. C. Galloway

Life and Letters of Mrs. Mary Galloway Giffen
Who Was the Pioneer Missionary of the Associate Reformed Church....

ISBN/EAN: 9783337016494

Printed in Europe, USA, Canada, Australia, Japan

Cover: Foto ©Raphael Reischuk / pixelio.de

More available books at **www.hansebooks.com**

LIFE AND LETTERS

OF

Mrs. Mary Galloway Giffen,

WHO WAS THE

PIONEER MISSIONARY

OF THE

Associate Reformed Church, South,

AND SERVED NEARLY SEVEN YEARS.

COMPILED BY

Rev. J. C. Galloway, A. M.

LOUISVILLE, GA.
1882.

INDEX.

PREFACE.

MANY of the letters which have found a place in this volume first appeared in the *Associate Reformed Presbyterian*, yet many others will be found which have not heretofore been submitted to the public.

The principal difficulty encountered in the preparation of this volume was that of *selection* and *condensation*. The published letters alone, of Mrs. Giffen's would have made half-a-dozen volumes the size of this. In some of the chapters the contents are made up of selections from half a score of letters, written at as many different times. In itself this was not desirable, but the limits of the present work demanded it. For this reason many letters of as great merit, and just as deserving of perpetuity as any herein contained, have been omitted.

It is greatly to be regretted that Mrs. Giffen *kept no diary*. In such a biography as this, leaves from the diary usually fill no unimportant part and are of absorbing interest. Deservedly so. But if the information to be gained from the pages of a diary could be dispensed with in any case, we think the present a case in point. Her letters are so frank and unreserved in their style, and so clearly mirror her every thought and feeling, that the want of a diary will not be very sensibly felt.

In assigning the writer the preparation of this Memoir, the leaders of the church desired thereby to stimulate and perpetuate in the church the spirit of missions, so signally illustrated in Mrs. Giffen. Perhaps it was also their fond hope that Mrs. Giffen's mantle might fall upon the shoulders of some of the living.

LOUISVILLE, GA.,
    April 23rd, 1882.

LIFE AND LETTERS

OF

MRS. MARY GALLOWAY GIFFEN.

CHAPTER I.

BIRTH AND CHILDHOOD—DEVELOPMENT OF YOUTHFUL
CHARACTER—SCHOOL DAYS—AMBITION AS A PUPIL—
GRADUATION.

MRS. MARY GALLOWAY GIFFEN was born in Newberry county, S. C., December the 8th, 1842. She was the second daughter of Rev. Jonathan and Mrs. Martha Speer Galloway. At the time of her birth her father was pastor of all the Associate Reformed churches in the county of Newberry, and so remained for fifteen years. In consequence of the failure of his health he gave up his pastoral charge. Loving his work as he did, with all his heart and soul, his forced retirement from the active work of the ministry brought him many a heart pang. The rest of his life he devoted to the education and the religious training of his children. He lived long enough to see them all complete their education and become with him members of the church on earth.

It is usually true that those characteristics which distinguish one in mature life, are seen in their dawning, in the first years of life. This was true of Mrs. Giffen. Those characteristics which were so marked in after life were seen even in the bud. In childhood her contented, cheerful, sunny disposition was very manifest. To this was added a spirit of intense activity—activity of feet, hands and mind. The loss or denial of childish toys and trifles, which usually brings such grief to a child, were generally of slight concern to her. Ordinarily her sports were not of that kind which affords most delight to children of the same age. While they might be contented to gather the roses which grew just by the door-step, she loved to wander away in search of some amusement which better suited her taste. She would be missed, and the question raised "where is Mary?" Soon she could be heard singing in the distance; then perhaps be discovered in the topmost bough of some convenient apple-tree, swaying to and fro, singing as merrily as some bird of the forest, and like it just as unconscious of danger. This insensibility to fear she carried with her through life. In all those situations were woman is usually paralyzed by the presence of danger she manifested little concern. Even when they were overtaken by a mighty tempest on the Atlantic, she says: "There was mingled with it no feeling of fear, only a sense of the keenest enjoyment, and a most vivid and powerful realization of the might of Him who made the sea, and walks upon its waves."

Soon after she was able to read a great passion for books discovered itself. Everything in her reach that the mind of a child could comprehend was literally devoured. As the capacities of her mind unfolded themselves she seemed to thirst for knowledge, The narrative and biography of profane history she loved, and the wonderful stories and simple narratives of the Bible fascinated her. But at that time they were read and studied not for their devotional spirit, but because her mind craved the knowledge thus gained. Books were to her what the sunlight and the dew are to the flower. Unlike most eager and rapid readers, what she once read became her permanent property. It was not unusual in her school-days to find her surrounded by her companions, while she delineated the character and the achievements of some hero of history, giving names and dates and personal expressions and judgments with much of the clearness and distinctness which characterized her writings in after life.

She had a great wealth of affection. Those whom she loved, she loved with an intensity and devotion such as few natures are capable of feeling. So strong was this feeling that those who knew her best were often surprised. Her father and mother, brothers and sisters she almost idolized, —so that their fortunes and misfortunes lay very close to her heart. From her friends she withheld nothing—what was hers was theirs; so that it was often said of her, "she could not do too much for those whom she loved."

"Excellence of character is not secured by birth or blood," but it seems most likely that in Mrs. Giffen was reproduced some of the prominent traits of character which were manifested in both her paternal and maternal ancestors. It is often true that certain peculiarities of mind and body will overleap a generation or two and develop themselves in just as pronounced a way as in the originals. The subject of this sketch doubtless derived the brilliancy and versatility of her mind from her mother's family—the *Speers*. But in every other particular she strikingly resembled her paternal grandmother—Mrs. Mary Millen Galloway. This grandmother was endowed with more than ordinary mental vigor, and piety. Her school-days were prior to the war of the Revolution when school books could not often be obtained at any price. But even when a very small girl she attended school and made fair progress by simply listening to the recitations of those who were fortunate enough to have a book. This same energy and determination of will characterized her through life. Though she was an ardent lover of books and read all the religious and theological books she could obtain, yet "she looked well to the ways of her house," and the wants of her very large family. Although she was the mother of nine sons and two daughters who grew to maturity, and living in an age when every vestige of clothing had to be carded and spun, and woven and fashioned by her own hands, still she found time to read a portion of some instructive book each day. Much of her reading was done from an open book lying at the head of her wheel—from this she read as she worked. In this way she acquired much important information. As she possessed in a high degree the faculty of communicating to others the treasures of her own mind, her children were indebted to her for most of their religious education, and for that training in the distinctive principles of the Associate Reformed church, to which she so tenaciously clung. The father in true patriarchal style would sit by, in his large arm chair, and endorse the mother's instruction. When the congregation at Bullock's Creek, York county, S. C., abandoned the use of Psalms and substituted hymns, she persuaded her husband to remove their membership to Hopewell in Chester county. And when her youngest child—Mrs. Giffen's father—was baptized, she carried him on horseback, to Hopewell, a distance of twenty miles. After a generation had passed away, and her children were old and grey-headed, they never spoke of her except in the tenderest accents. They "rose up and called her blessed," and the heart of her husband "safely trusted in her."

The resemblance between grandmother and grand-daughter—Mrs. Mary Millen Galloway and Mrs. Mary Galloway Giffen—was very complete in nearly every point. Not only was the physical similarity almost perfect, but in mental ability, and quick readiness of action the one was almost a reproduction of the other. In the same way the affectionate and sympathetic nature of the grandmother, purified and sanctified by grace, was no less clearly developed in the granddaughter, who a century later gave up kindred and home for the Master's service.

The foregoing brief sketch of Mrs. Giffen's ancestry and early life will better enable us to understand her career as a school-girl. Since it was not the privilege of the writer to have any personal knowledge of what took place during those years, the following letter from Prof. Wm. Hood, under whose tuition she received almost all her education, will be read with very deep interest:

" REV. J. C. GALLOWAY—DEAR SIR:

Having learned that you intend to publish a sketch of the life of your sister, Mrs. Mary E. Giffen, along with letters written while she was a missionary in Egypt, I desire in testimony of my appreciation of her merits to furnish you some data of her life while she was a school-girl.

It was my privilege to be her instructor, both in the village and county schools of Newberry, S. C., during a part of the years 1854, 1855, 1858 and 1859. In consequence of this relation to her I am probably better acquainted with the early developments of her mind than any one outside of her own immediate family. In fact it is likely that I had advantages which even members of her own family did not enjoy of judging, not only of the character and capabilities of her mind at this period, but also of her social qualities, and the womanly graces that marked her intercourse with strangers.

The years mentioned, with the intervening ones, cover a term of six years and include her life during that most interesting period when the frank and confiding little girl shades by beautiful, but almost imperceptible gradations into young womanhood. During a part of the two years just mentioned, in addition to my opportunity to know her in all the phases of life in the school-room, I boarded in your father's family, and was therefore allowed to see and understand her more fully. Whether in study or amusement, at school or at home, she manifested the same striking individuality of character, quick, positive, comprehending at a glance the circumstances around her, and as an act of instinct discovering the means of execution.

It has been said that " the boy is father to the man." This saying was never more fully exemplified than in the life of your sister. No one could know her at all intimately without feeling forced to study her character. Never have I seen a character unfold more evenly, nor more in accordance with antecedent tendencies,—no abrupt changes, no retrogrades, no relaxations—but a symmetrical, uniform and rapid progression with high and heroic purposes in view. In the time specified she completed all the studies from the arithmetic and English grammar to the higher branches, including Latin, required for admission to a class nearly completing the curriculum in the College where she graduated. In all the study involved in this large amount of work, I do not think she ever appeared with a recitation indifferently prepared. She was eminently prompt in all that she undertook, energetic and ambitious of progress almost to impatience at times. Partial views of a subject or topic of study never satisfied her, and her inquiries as to the bearing of the terms and principles of the sciences under review, were so discriminating as to show thorough work at every step. She eagerly pressed forward for final results, but never allowed her zeal to obscure the importance of details. The details might be tedious, but to her mind problems were structures in which every part and piece of timber must be laid true, and made fast in its place to insure the strength and completeness of the whole.

Thus while she was daily building up her own life into the truest type of noble womanhood, she was dealing methodically with everything she touched, which moulds and strengthens intellectual development. No encouragments were needed except what she derived from daily triumphs over obstacles in the path of study, and no stimulus except what the subject to be mastered furnished. To learn at once and thoroughly was her ambition; and her reward was the consciousness that what she attempted she was able to perform. She rather sought than avoided the difficult parts of science. The deeper the fountain the purer the waters, and a draft from the bottom cooler than the surface. No investigation intimidated. Every line of thought was a vein of gold that grew richer at each advance.

Her memory was equal to her energy and courage. I often thought that she lost less of what she read than any pupil it was ever my privilege to teach. Frequently have I had occasion to request her assistance to refer to matters contained in an author I knew she had read. It always seemed to afford her pleasure to undertake the search, and she never failed to find, with remarkable facility, the subject, sentiment, and even the words in question.

Of course it was only natural that the influence of a pupil of such habits, should be very great on her schoolmates. She was conspicuous in a class of a number of young ladies, all of whom I would be pleased to mention, were I not writing of the lamented dead alone, on whose example in study and attractive proprieties in all the relations of the school-room, I relied as a main support, in the later years of her connection with it. She appreciated the value of order in all that appertained to the management of a school, and heartily co-operated in securing it. I recall with pleasure the many gentle admonitions I have heard her give the less thoughtful among her schoolmates, the happy inspiration of her example to them, and accept it all as thus early foreshadowing the eminent success won by herself in that profession in the still later days of her illustrious life.

I could recall and record many incidents illustrative of all that I have said of her, and much more than I can indulge myself in saying, were it consistent with the object of this short sketch.

Should you find anything to be of service to you in this notice of so short a span in a life rendered sublime by the sacrifice of its temporal comforts, in obedience to the Master's call for more laborers in his ripened fields, and all too short when measured by our hopes in her work, and love for herself—make such use of it as may best suit your plans in the publication you have undertaken."

To all the other attributes of Mrs. Giffen's mind we must add that of an exalted ambition. If she found herself excelled by a classmate in any department of study, or in any single recitation, her mortification was very great, but her classmate would never discover it from any act or word of her's. Quietly, but with invincible resolution, she wrought the harder for the disputed position, and the sharpened zest and increased toil rarely failed to secure the coveted prize. If a reward was offered by her teachers instantly the resolution was formed: "I must have that prize." Others might keep abreast if they could, but she suffered no one to go in advance. This was the creed which governed her school days. But as the years passed on and her intellect developed and expanded, she rose above the merely ambitious desire to excel. Her reading and study were now for the pleasure and satisfaction that it afforded her in acquainting herself with the thoughts of the wise and good and great among men in all past time.

But it must not be supposed that all this was gained without great exertion. It was true of her, as of the rest of ordinary mankind, "there is no excellence without great labor." When engaged on some difficult problem or in the ambitious desire to excel, the hour of midnight often found her bending over her task.

When the failing health of her father necessitated his retirement from the active work of the ministry, and the resignation of his pastorate, he turned his attention to the education of his children. This work had always lain very near to his heart, and to accomplish this best, in the winter of 1859 he removed his family to Due West. Here Mrs. Giffin entered the Junior class in the female college, half advanced. The same unflagging energy and close application which had so signally marked her earlier years of study, were just as manifest in these closing months. Indeed so thorough and so successful were her efforts at this period that her school record shows that there were not above three or four recitations during the entire term, which were not *perfect*. She enjoyed the advantages of a collegiate instruction for a very brief term—not more than sixteen months. Perhaps five years would cover the entire period of her school life. But as "labor overcomes

all things," Mrs. Giffen received on her graduation day
the highest honors conferred by the institution from which
she graduated.

At the age of eighteen, when she left college she had
read almost all the popular classical authors, and in addition to these a very wide range of other literature, of such
a character that few young ladies have the capacity or the
taste to investigate. After graduation she was very desir-
ous of pursuing a more extended and thorough course of
study than that afforded by the ordinary institutions of
learning, but finding this impracticable, she immediately
entered upon a very comprehensive course of reading.
She had access to several extensive public libraries, and in
these she literally reveled. No miser amid his heaps of
gold and silver ever handled his coveted treasure with the
delight and unalloyed happiness which she felt in commun-
ing with the master minds of the literary world.

In a few months she had read all the greater English
poets, and had arranged and classified in her mind, the
contents of each one in regard to their intrinsic merits, or
peculiar style. But of them all the transcendent genius
and lofty imagination of Byron most fascinated her.

Of all her studies, however, none so interested and in-
structed her as history—whether of individuals or nations.
She dearly loved to trace the efforts and struggles of each
one, as they appeared and disappeared on the stage of the
world's history, rose to dazzling greatness, or sunk into
nothingness. Here she gained her deepest insight into human
motives and character, and learned her profoundest lessons
in regard to the problem of life.

Nor were the prose writings of the best authors in any
degree neglected. But her reading in the realm of ficti-
tious literature was conducted with great caution, and in

MRS. MARY GALLOWAY GIFFEN. 17

the exercise of a most discriminating judgment. She gave
her attention only to such as were pure, refining, and ele-
vated in its tone. The imbecility, insipidity and mawkish
sentimentality which constitutes so large a part of the warp
and woof of modern literature was offensive to her, and just
as she would repel indecent conduct and offensive words in
her presence, so did she repel such literature. And when she
was betrayed into the reading of a book of questionable tendency, she either laid it aside at once when discovered, or else
continued its perusal with that offended sense of delicacy
and modesty which a well-bred lady feels in the presence
of what is indelicate and immodest. On one occasion a
friend sent her a copy of George Eliot's *Middlemarch*, ac-
companying it with a note of most enthusiastic commenda-
tion. She had not read many pages before she discovered
its detestable morality, laid it aside in deep disgust and
never opened it again.

Nor did she neglect purely philosophical studies and in-
vestigations, for her mind was not one-sided. All her mental
faculties were evenly and equally developed: or, as another
has phrased it, her mind was "circularly developed." She
did not suffer from the infirmity so common to so many
truly great minds—that of being strong and powerfully
developed in some lines of mental activity and capacity,
and weak as a child in other departments. Hence she
mastered a difficult equation in algebra, or solved a
problem in geometry with the same ease and facility
with which she translated a page in Virgil or
Horace. But her mathematical faculty was best developed, and in its exercise she most delighted and
most excelled. Yet she took a peculiar delight in
what was especially imaginative, and as her writings
will testify, often allowed her fancy to soar aloft in

the boldest flights of imagery. At the same time she could
descend into the most purely practical and severe forms of
study and thought with equal facility. For example witness her letter on the mathematical proportions and scientific construction of the great pyramid illustrating the theory
of Piazzi Smyth, "astronomer royal," of Scotland; then in
vivid contrast her description of her feelings and thoughts as
she stood on the top of that mountain of stone. At this
period of her life the taste for purely mental culture, was
so absorbing, and was carried to such a degree, that her
friends became alarmed lest the intellectual part of her
nature would swallow up the religious. The greed of her
intellect was circumscribed only by her surroundings.
What she read was quickly assimilated, what she once
made her's was never lost, and it was as easily retained as
the facility with which it was obtained.

During all these years she must have had some religious
impressions and convictions, for her Christian training was
all that a pious, faithful and devoted father and mother
and mother could make it. Yet judging from her well-
known open and decisive character, and the entire ignorance
of her most intimate friends in regard to it, these impressions
could not have been very permanent or profound. They at
least produced no marked change in the tenor of her life.
The purely intellectual seemed to have dominated her
whole nature.

CHAPTER II.

DEATH OF HER BROTHER—CONVERSION—EFFORT AT
MISSION WORK—CAREER AS A TEACHER—LETTERS
FROM TEXAS—MISSION TO THE GERMANS.

AT the time of Mrs. Giffen's graduation the country was
darkened by the shadows of a coming civil war. All was
commotion and confusion. Men seemed frenzied with excitement and political passion. The artisan left his bench,
the student his text book, and the farmer his plow. The
tramp of armed men was everywhere heard, and the country seemed one vast mustering camp. Still so insatiable
was her thirst for the fountains of knowledge, that even in
these untoward circumstances she pursued her studies pri-
vately for many months. But as the great conflict deepened, and the church-yards began to fill with the dead
brought back from the fields of carnage, the spell seemed
to be broken, and she turned to the sober prosaic duties of
the hour. But no one gifted with her boundless energy
could long remain inactive, and she now turned her attention to the vocation of the teacher, and took charge of a
private school in Georgia. Here her large-heartedness,
her attractive social qualities, and brilliant conversational
powers made her many friends. All with whom she was
brought in contact were won to her, and became fast and firm
friends, and even to this day "Miss Galloway" has a large
place in their affections." But at the end of the year she
returned home, for the country had become so convulsed
by the throes of the gigantic conflict, that almost all the
liberal professions were suspended, and men and women
gazed with bated breath upon red battle-fields and smoking
cities.

Perhaps a year before this Mrs. Giffen's eldest brother,—Calvin M. Galloway—a "beardless youth," enlisted in the Confederate army. Between these two there existed a pure and deathless affection. She loved him with a wealth of affection that few brothers ever receive, and few sisters are capable of giving. And he fully returned it. At the time of his enlistment he was a member of the Freshman class in Erskine College, and was a youth of uncommon promise, closely resembling in intellect and affections his now sainted sister. The correspondence between them was close and full. Every week the mail bore away a thick letter, filled with such hopes and messages as such a sister alone could give. When the telegraph flashed the news "a great battle has been fought," her heart seemed to stand still until a letter in his well known handwriting brought relief. At that time every family had a daily newspaper. Mrs. Giffen was an accomplished reader, and during those dark days of "agony long drawn out," the chiefest event of the day was the gathering of the household around the fireside for the perusal of the paper. By universal consent Mrs. Giffen was installed as reader, and one of the brightest memories of that dark time is the recollection of her clear ringing voice, as she read column after column of "The very latest from the front."

The weary days and months dragged on, and at last the armies confronted each other at Spottsylvania Court House. At day-break, on the 12th of May, 1864, the Confederate line holding the extreme point of a projecting angle was overrun and captured by the Federals, "twenty lines of battle deep." To restore the line McGowan's South Carolina brigade was sent in this angle. After fighting all day, in that carnival of death, with a cool courage that extorted admiration even from strangers, this loved brother fell "in the fore front of the battle."

It fell to my lot to bring home the sad tidings, "Calvin is missing." And when she ran to meet me at the gate, and I told her the terrible truth, I will never forget how looked her white and agonized face. It was a blow that seemed to drive back the whole tenor of her life. Her nature was convulsed from center to circumference. The blow, so keen-edged and severe to a disposition like hers— an affection so deep and pure, and a sensibility so extreme —was like taking her own life.

His death produced a complete *revolution* in her feelings. Although he was smitten down in an instant and never spoke after, she had no doubts and alarms about his future, for he had been for some time in connection with the church of his father and mother. But at this time she was not. This event turned the whole current of her life into an entirely different channel. It aroused deep and searching questions about her own future. The idea of a final, total separation from this loved one, seemed to be more than she could endure, and on the wings of affection her spirit followed his into the spirit land. "Shall I *never* see him again? Am I to be *forever* separated from him? I cannot even bear the thought. He cannot come to me but I can go to him." And then and there with all the energy and purpose that characterized her life, she resolved, "I will go to him. God helping me I will see his face once more, and see it in that land where war is unknown," and "whose sod has never yet been pierced for a grave." To this solemn resolve God added his blessing, and in her case literally fulfilled the promise, "they that seek Me early shall find Me." Thus does God bring good out of evil, and make man's extremity His opportunity. Her Bible had been much read before this, but now it was read with an entirely new meaning. It became her constant companion, her daily and hourly study. With the Bible, and some Commentary in her hand she daily sought the quiet and solitude of a neighboring grove, and seemed intent only upon communion with her Saviour. In addition to this she used all other helps and theological writings which were at hand. The writer well remembers her serene and satisfied demeanor when this course of reading was finished. Her manner and actions plainly indicated that the light from above was shining full upon her, that there were now no distracting doubts and fears—all was clear and peaceful.

But it was the study of such works as the " Life of Mrs. Judson," Mrs. Harriet Newell, and Mrs. Graham, that most interested and delighted her, and which most largely shaped her future life. The cultivation of her religious life was now as earnestly and diligently pursued as had been her intellectual nature. She seemed intent upon educating equally in religious truth, both her heart and mind, that she might not only feel in her soul all the tender and loving force of " the truth as it is in Jesus," but also have a thoroughly intellectual and theoretical knowledge of the way of life. This she attained in a very eminent degree.

Mrs. Giffen's religious experience was, in one respect, very striking. If she was ever troubled with those seasons of weakness and darkness which often make up no small portion of the lives even of very eminent Christians, her friends never knew it. And we think that such was not the case. The reason for this doubtless lay in the fact that her knowledge of religious truth was very clear, positive and comprehensive, so that when once grounded in a truth, nothing moved her. Most of the distress and perplexity which Christians experience arises from imperfect apprehension of the truth, and the want of positive and settled convictions. All these sources of weakness were wanting in Mrs. Giffen's religious character, hence her Christian race was firm and vigorous, like "the path of the just which shineth more and more unto the perfect day."

Up to this time she had lived principally to gratify her intellectual tastes, for her sisters and brothers, and for the devoted friends whom she had won. But now under the impulse of the new Divine life stirring within her, and largely also because of reading such biographies as those of Payson and Brainerd, Mrs. Judson and Mrs. Newell, her soul was strongly drawn out to her unfortunate sisters in heathen countries. Since she now knew something of the power of the love of God, in her own heart, and the joy which His Spirit gave, she was filled with a great longing to go forth and toil in those lands that were covered with the shadow of moral death, where "there is no vision and the people perish." Time only seemed to feed the holy flame that was burning within her.

At this time, however, the country was still distracted by civil war, and it was therefore impossible to enter upon work of that character. As soon however as national quiet was restored, and communication was again established between the Northern and Southern churches, she attempted to put her resolution into effect, and formally consecrate her life to the Master in the great cause of missions. To this end, at her request, my father directed a communication to Rev. J. B. Dales, D. D., Secretary of the Board of Foreign Missions of the United Presbyterian church, asking if that Board would be willing to send out a single lady into the foreign field. To this inquiry the answer came, "we have more applicants than we have the means to support." Application was made to this Board because at this time the Associate Reformed church had no Board of Missions. This attempt was made in the latter part of the year 1865. Notwithstanding this failure she still clung to her purpose. In the summer of the following year, in company with her brother, she sought and held a conference with Dr. Bonner. It was long and earnest. China was the field which she had selected when she first formed the resolution to devote her life to missionary labor, and at this time she was seeking his advice in regard to entering at once this field. As the conference drew to a close she said : " Then you do not favor the undertaking?" His answer was cheerful in tone, but discouraging in effect. "Wait a while—wait a while, and let us see." Perhaps his sagacious mind foresaw what actually occurred ten years later, when she entered the work as the honored missionary of her own church, and in the field of that church's own choosing—a thing then impossible.

Cut off again in this direction she accepted the result cheerfully, as she always did any inevitable result, saying, " I will devote my life to teaching in this country." This she did with marked success, for whatever she did was done with her might. Her thorough capacity, rare power in reaching the hearts of her pupils and high social qualities rendered her very acceptable as a teacher. Not once during her career as a teacher did she leave a situation with the consent of the trustees. During this period of her life she visited many sections of the Southern States, and in every instance left behind an enviable reputation.

Rev. D. G. Phillips, D. D., for several years associated with her in the class-room, thus writes : " Her mind was pre-eminently analytical, and very tenacious, possessing in a wonderful degree the power of abstraction. She could hold it on an isolated thought until she had weighed it, labeled it, and stored it away for future use. Another peculiarity was her love for the study of dry text books; and it was this love for dry and severe forms of study, which made her both an exact and profound scholar. As a teacher her effort was to train the mind of the pupil to *think*. She often quoted to her pupils the language of Dr. Thornwell—"ability to think is worth a thousand thoughts." With a masculine energy she grappled with abstruse ideas, and inquired into facts, and the nature, laws and relations of things. She found more pleasure in calculating the sides, angles, height and age of one of the Pyramids, than in the beauties and niceties of polite literature."

"In 1871, I opened an Academy, and in looking around for some one competent to take charge of the advanced classes, in French and mathematics, and at the same time give instruction in both vocal and instrumental music—a combination of talents not easily found—my mind at once turned to Mrs. Giffen, who already had a reputation as an expert teacher. She accepted at once and entered into the work with the feeling, " 'Tis not in mortals to command success, but we'll do more—deserve it," she did both, and left in this section memories fragrant as " ointment poured forth." As a teacher she needed neither government nor discipline in her school. There was a kind of magnetism in her method which served for both, and caught and held the attention of her pupils. Her method of instruction was strictly analytical. If teaching a child its alphabet, she began by teaching it to fix its mouth, and make the sign of the sound before uttering the sound. Or if hearing a recitation in Quadratic Equations, she required the pupil to analyze the statement, and tell how the work should proceed, and what the result should be, before making a letter on the board. Thus all her pupils were taught first to think and then to demonstrate the correctness of the thought. Thus the mind was trained to make and keep all its faculties subordinate to the will. As proof of her efficiency, several of her pupils who afterward stood high in their college course, and received college honors, attribute their success to the methods of study she taught them."

"With her education was not cramming an already distended and active mind with great thoughts and well digested ideas, but a drawing out and cultivating the latent powers of the mind, and enabling it to think great thoughts, and digest great ideas. Patient and painstaking her first object was to get the attention of the pupil fixed on the labor before it, and her abundant resources were always adequate to that task. Herein lay her strength. It was impossible for a pupil to recite to her one hour without being (so to express it) *inveigled* into thinking. Even then she never allowed herself to seem to think for her pupil. If he could not master a difficulty, and called for assistance she and he would think it out together and in such a way that he should feel that it was a mutual victory. Here she acquired the title of "*the* teacher" by way of preeminence. She lives in the hearts of many pupils whom she taught, on two continents, to many of whom she will be able at the great day, to point and say "the children whom thou hast given me."

She had much of that subtile influence which we will call the power of personal magnetism, and sometimes it was exerted in a wonderful way. Take an example of this:

She had been teaching in Middle Tennessee, in a high school, and the term had closed. The last day was devoted to the usual public examination of the various

classes. The morning exercises had progressed very satis-
factorily until noon. The school being located in the
country, at the intermission, some of the young lady pupils
gathered in the music-room to have a last talk with " Miss
Mary," for her friends enjoyed few things more than her
rare conversational powers. They expressed their regrets
that the efforts of the trustees could not induce her to remain another year, and they knew they would not have
another whom they would love as they did her ; and now
she was going away, and they would see her face no more.
Soon some of them were in tears and others were sobbing
aloud. She remonstrated and endeavored again and again
to restore quiet, telling them that the remaining exercises
of the day would soon come on, and that they were unfit-
ting themselves for their duties in these. But it availed
nothing ; and the sobbing soon extended outside of the
music-room and affected the entire school. Others beside
herself interfered and endeavored to restore quiet, but all
efforts proved unavailing. Several of the young ladies
became rigid and insensible and in this condition were
carried to the nearest dwelling. The visiting committee
perceiving the position of affairs, advised that the exercises be closed at once and all return to their homes.

This was done.

Time passed on and the year 1873 found her in the great
State of Texas, whither she had gone at the solicitation of
very dear friends, whom she had met years before. The
idea of making such a distant journey—across the Southern States, over the Gulf, and far into the interior of Texas
—a State at that time regarded as the paradise of vagabonds
and cut-throats, rather appalled some of her less courageous
friends. After residing here for several months and
making a thorough study of Texas, her people and her

material resources, she wrote a series of letters for the *Presbyterian*. These were known as the famous "Texas Letters," and were well received by the public. The author was unknown at this time, and there was much discussion as to whether the writer was a gentleman or lady. Some contended that the mental breadth and grasp of the subject and the bold, vigorous style indisputably proclaimed the writer a gentleman. Others were equally sure that the keen powers of observation and delicate feminine touches manifested in these articles discovered the hand of a woman.

The lamented Dr. Bonner, editor of the *Presbyterian*, in writing to Mrs. Giffen in acknowledgment of these articles says : " I must confess that I have treated you badly in not writing to you long ago. You have been very kind in writing for me—have written a dozen articles of very great interest, and yet this is the first time I have sat down to thank you. But let me assure you that my seeming neglect has not been on account of indifference. I can never forget one who has always been so kind to me, but especially the kindness shown me in Augusta when I was sick—that will always have a place in my memory. But I do thank you most sincerely for your excellent letters from Texas. Without any intention of flattering I must say that I regard them as equal to the best correspondence of the metropolitan papers. This is the verdict of all intelligent readers. Whenever you can write without interfering too much with other pursuits, I hope you will use your pen for the benefit of the readers of the *Presbyterian*. I assure you the favor will be appreciated.

" Old Mr. Stevenson, of Generostee, came up to me last Sabbath evening as I was leaving and said : ' I do not know who it is that writes from Texas, but the writer ex-

presses exactly what I have long felt, but could not express
—about 'forgiving and not forgetting.' He is a good old
man, and says as he gets nearer and nearer to his end he
feels more and more interest in the cause of Union, especially with the United Presbyterians."

But the cause of Associate Reformed Presbyterianism in
that distant region received much attention at her hands.
She was devotedly attached to the church of her fathers,
and it grieved her to find how many of its members had
found homes in that great State, but had no church organization of their own. Indeed at that time there was only
one minister of the Associate Reformed Church in the
State. By personal observation, by diligent inquiry,
and by every other avenue of knowledge open to her,
she gathered up all the information which might be
useful to the church in forming a correct judgment
of the wants of this field, and in prosecuting her
work there. After her return home she continued to
agitate the subject at every favorable opportunity, stren-
uously urging the claims and the needs of the Texas
churches. One after another of the leaders of the church
took up the cause, and the force of missionaries was increased year by year, until Texas had a Presbytery of her
own.

But the spirit of missions had not died within her.
During her stay in this region she made a visit to the
south-western part of the State. While there, like Paul
at Athens, her "spirit was stirred within" her when she
saw the country given up to Catholicism. Its mummeries
and superstitions, its ignorance, its Sabbath desecration,
and its entrenched hold upon its degraded adherents—all
these things produced a profound impression upon her. It
was her first contact with the system and it engendered a

repulsive horror which never forsook her. And now her old yearning to deliver misguided souls from their ignorance and darkness—to do active work for the Master—returned upon her with all its former power and intensity. "Shall I permit these people to perish and lift no hand for their deliverance? God saw fit to prevent me from going to a heathen land to labor, and now he has brought me face to face with as deep a destitution of vital truth as exists in many parts of the heathen world. Is not this an indication that he wished me to labor here? With his help I will do what I can."

With this purpose in view she addressed a letter to the writer—then a student in the Seminary—asking him to join her in a mission to the German Catholics of South-western Texas. This mission she proposed to sustain by *her own efforts*, for at that time the Synod was hardly pressed for the means to sustain the vital enterprises of its home work. To procure the money necessary to support the mission she proposed to labor in the school-room during the week, but devoting Saturday and Sabbath to active mission work. That she would largely have succeeded in supporting the mission in this way had it been undertaken, few question who were aware of the energy and persever-ance which she brought to bear upon the accomplishment of a darling purpose.

But the plan was never carried out. To have entered this work at that time would have required the writer to sacrifice a large part of his theological education, and this his wisest friends discouraged. The scheme was, therefore reluctantly abandoned.

During the fall of the same year—1873—the Synod met at Mt. Zion, Mo. The delegate from the U. P. Church warmly urged the Synod to co-operate with that body in the work of missions, saying: "You have a young lady who is spoiling for a mission." His impressions in this respect were derived from Mrs. Giffen's "Texas Letters."

In the following year a very decided spirit of missions manifested itself throughout the church, culminating in the formal offer of Rev. W. A. Wilson, to enter the foreign field. This offer was eagerly accepted by the Board of Missions, and Egypt, a field of co-operative labor with the United Presbyterian church was selected as the initial point of labor. The whole church hailed this step with unfeigned rejoicing as the omen of a better and brighter day for our Zion, feeling that our reproach among the thousands of Israel was now taken away. But as had so often happened in the past, so now the church was doomed to disappointment. Unforeseen family affliction compelled the resignation of the newly-appointed missionary.

The history of the mission efforts and failures of the Associate Reformed Church South is rather a curious one. Verily it would seem that God severely tried the faith of the church in this matter. About the year 1838, the Synod passed an order requiring all her congregations to take up collections for Foreign Missions. The first effort was to co-operate with the Reformed Presbyterian (Covenanter) Church North, in their missions to India, by giving pecuniary aid. To this work three or four very liberal donations were made, in acknowledgment of which some of their heathen converts and students of divinity were named for the leading members of the Synod—viz.: John Hemphill, Wm. Blackstocks, and Isaac Grier.

After a few years Synod determined to establish a mission of her own in Liberia, and for this purpose appointed a Board of Missions. This Board determimed to establish a Mission School in Liberia, and through Rev. W. R. Hemphill held a correspondence with a Mr. Erskine, colored, of the North, but without accomplishing any results. They then employed a Mr. Ware, colored, of Liberia, to teach their mission school. This resulted in failure either comparative or complete. It was then resolved to educate a colored minister for the Liberian mission. In response to a call to the "pious and liberal of the church to furnish suitable persons to be educated," Dr. Geo. W. Pressly, Mr. James Robinson and the Misses Murphy each devoted a boy. After a short trial, Rev. N. M. Gordon, to whom they had been committed for education, sent them all back as incompetent, both mentally and morally. About the year 1848, Revs. Messrs. W. W. Patton and J. M. Young were sent out to explore Texas. At this time Texas was regarded as a foreign field. On horseback they traversed Texas in every direction for several months. This resulted in sending out Rev. W. M. Sharp, who proceeded to Brenham, Texas, and there endeavored to establish a mission. But like the others this also failed.

Succeeding these efforts and failures the church, for some time, was much engaged in bootless discussions and dissentions on "The Marriage Question," "Union" with the G. A. Presbyterians South, to the great detriment of her missionary zeal and effort. During the next ten years Home Missions gained the ascendancy.

But in the year 1858, a permanent Board of Foreign Missions was established, which entered actively and spiritedly upon their work. Egypt and South America were the fields prominently before the Board, a majority favoring Egypt. When arrangements were well nigh completed for putting workers into the field, "the war between the States" effectually suspended operations. When this unhappy struggle was terminated, the Church was so pros-

trated by its results that for a half a score of years it could
barely stagger along under the burden of its own immediate necessities.   And when its mission spirit revived again
in 1874, it experienced another keen disappointment.

<hr>

CHAPTER III.

OFFERS HERSELF TO THE BOARD—IS ACCEPTED—FARE-
    WELL   MEETINGS—JOURNEY   TO   PHILADELPHIA—
    EMBARKATION.

THE retirement of Rev. Mr. Wilson still left the church
without a missionary.   The attention of the Board was
then centered on Mrs. Giffen.   Early in the fall of 1874
Dr. Bonner, then Secretary of the Board of Foreign Missions, held a conference with her in regard to offering
herself as a missionary.   As President of the Due West
Female College he had been her teacher during the last
months of her college life, and thoroughly understood her
nature and capacity.   He was also a very warm personal
friend.   In this conference all his powers of persuasive
earnestness as well as his great personal influence were
brought to bear to induce a decision favorable to missions.
It should be stated that in this conference Dr. Bonner
was not acting as the official representative of the Board,
although it was aware of and approved his action.

But she seemed disinclined to *offer* herself, most probably
because of the fact that the Church had no missionaries in
the field, and being a frail woman shrank from the responsibility of being the "pioneer missionary," and because of

the fact that the church preferred to send out a *man* as
her "first missionary." She felt that if the sequel proved
that she had a call to go and teach in a heathen land the
call would come to her in a more formal way, from the
authorities of the church. This would relieve her from
all appearance of self-seeking, of thrusting herself on the
church, for she was well aware of its preference. But
with all these influences brought to bear on her we may
be sure the fire burned hotly within. Day by day and
week by week she waited to see what God had in store for
her. It was no light thing for her highly sensitive and
deeply affectionate nature to leave all, country and friends,
father and mother—all that life holds that is dear to a
woman's heart, to enter a mission of another church, and
that church entirely confined to a different section of the
country, and to be wholly thrown with persons not one of
whom she had ever seen or known; to stand upon the
threshold of a new and strange life, filled with hardship
and self-denial, in a semi-heathen land, that land seven
thousand miles away and two oceans rolling between, and
only a frail, lonely woman—such a situation would bring
up questionings deep and solemn.

But the call did come, and with a clearness and force
which swept down all obstacles. In December, 1874, two
months after this conference, Dr. J. B. Dales, Secretary of
the Board of Foreign Missions of the United Presbyterian
Church of N. A., addressed a communication to Dr. Bonner,
Secretary of the Board of Missions of the Associate Reformed Church South, stating that his Board would soon send
out two young men to the field in Egypt, and asking if the
Church South had not some one whom it was willing to
send to the same field, and urging in a very cordial way if
the Synod would not co-operate with them in their Foreign

Mission work. With this letter in his hand, Dr. Bonner immediately paid Mrs. Giffen a visit, and warmly urged her to offer herself and go in company with these newly-appointed missionaries to the Egyptian field. She answered that if " it was the concurrent wish of the Board," she would willingly go. The time was short, a meeting was called that day and she was unanimously appointed.

This appointment was heartily endorsed by a large majority of the Church, and especially did it kindle the zeal and enthusiasm of the noble women of the Church, and they held up her hands with a sympathy and devotion worthy of all honor. But there were a few cavillers who said : " Why all this excitement and enthusiasm; it is *only a woman*. Why send her; she can't preach the Gospel ? " This last remark once happened to be made in the presence of Dr. Jas. P. Pressly. He instantly replied : " Indeed she will."

As the time for her departure drew near the Board arranged for a series of " Farewell Meetings " in the vicinity and along the route until the limits of the Church were passed. The object of these meetings was to create an interest and excite an enthusiasm for the person of the missionary and her work. But they were a fearful ordeal for the missionary.

The most noteworthy of these occurred in Due West, the home of Mrs. Giffen, and was reported in the succeeding issue of the *Presbyterian*, part of which report is here given :

FAREWELL MEETING AT DUE WEST.

This meeting came off on Wednesday night of last week, the 27th of January. A more affecting scene we have never witnessed, unless it was in a case where a catastrophe or a death was involved. A procession was formed on the street, headed by Dr. Grier and members of the Missionary Society of the Female College, then by the officers and members of the Board of Foreign Missions, the officers and male members of the Missionary Society of Due West, followed by the Missionary and the committee of ladies who had been appointed to accompany her that night, then by the lady members of the Due West Missionary Society, then by students and citizens. In a few moments the church was crowded from the pulpit back to the doors, with a considerable number of both whites and colored in the gallery. The officers of the Board and of the Due West Missionary Society, the professors and the speakers took their seats in the open space near the pulpit, while immediately in front of them in the first pew the missionary and her attendants arranged themselves. The first thing that attracted the attention of the audience on taking their seats were the writing and other significant characters which were seen upon the wall above the pulpit. In crimson capital letters were, " Lo, I am with you alway," in a semi-circle, encased in a beautiful wreath. Beneath this there was the representation of *a shield*, not the word. On the left were the words, " Take the "—on the right, " of faith," so that it read, " Take the shield of faith." Within the lines indicating the shield were in gilt letters, " M. E. Galloway, our first missionary." Below this was the word " Farewell," in large illuminated letters.

The duty of presiding over the meeting was assigned to Dr. Boyce, chairman of the Board of Foreign Missions. The exercises were opened by singing a part of the 45th Psalm, the following being one of the verses:

> " O daughter take good heed,
> Incline and give good ear,
> Thou must forget thy kindred all,
> And father's house most dear."

Dr. J. P. Pressly then offered an appropriate and an affecting prayer. The chairman of the Board of Foreign Missions then addressed the missionary.

The address of the chairman was followed by that of Rev. W. L. Pressly, pastor, in his own behalf, and in that of the congregation. It was peculiarly touching and affecting.

Then followed addresses and resolutions by the pupils of the female college, and the students of the seminary. Rev. J. O. Lindsay, of the Old School Presbyterian church, then forcibly and eloquently presented the encouragements to mission work, and was followed by the farewell address of the missionary, written by Mrs. M. A. Lindsay, and read by Rev. W. M. Grier, D. D. :

THE MISSIONARY'S FAREWELL.

" Yet once more bless me, father,
　With tender words of love,
They'll often soothe and comfort
　When far away I rove ; ·
And whether you or I shall first
　Death's narrow stream pass o'er,
'Tis sweet to know that we will meet
　On the eternal shore.
Then bid me go in peace, father,
　His wondrous love to tell.
· And may He be your guide and stay,
　Farewell ! Farewell !

Call me your own dear child, mother,
　And fold me to your breast,
The sweetest place in all the world,
　For wearied heads to rest.
Your heart is throbbing sore, mother,
　And mine is filled with pain,

How will it often yearn to see
  This dear, dear face again!
My mother: what you are to me
  No faltering lip can tell;
Yet I must go. My mother dear,
  Farewell! Farewell!

Brothers, true-hearted, loyal ones,
  Your sisters' joy and pride,
I've watched you grew to manhood,
  Three brothers, side by side.
Ye, too, will leave the parent roof,
  Yet on and upward press,
And though you meet with loss and cross
  Our father's God will bless.
Perhaps—nay, 'tis too sweet a hope—
  That one of you may dwell
With your sister in the heathen land.
  Farewell! Farewell!

Sisters, you'll often miss me,
  And bitter tears will shed,
Almost as if the exile
  Were numbered with the dead.
Yet not too sadly mourn me,
  Our parents you will cheer,
You'll help them every burden
  And every grief to bear.
Sweet memories will haunt us,
  Like Ocean's murmuring shell,
And we in dreams will often meet.
  Farewell! Farewell!

My home, excepting God's own courts,
  No other spot so sweet.
My church, within whose sacred shrine
  Heaven bends our souls to greet.
My friends—oh bear me in your hearts;
  If you will for me pray,

Then I shall go from "strength to strength
  Rejoicing on my way."
My native land—no other clime
  May wield my magic spell,
And until death I'll cherish thee.
  Farewell! Farewell!"

Dr. Bonner, in behalf of the missionary, tenderly returned thanks to the audience for the interest manifested
in the missionary personally, and in the cause which she
represented, and asked that prayer might continually be
made for her that she might be sustained in her distant
field, and a "wide and effectual door opened" for her, in
her labors for the Master.

The impressive ceremonies were then concluded by
prayer, and singing these words:

The Lord thee keeps, the Lord thy shade
  On thy right hand doth stay;
The moon by night thee shall not smite,
  Nor yet the sun by day.

The Lord shall keep thy soul; he shall
  Preserve thee from all ill.
Henceforth thy going out and in
  God keep forever will.

THE PARTING.

"The programme, with one exception, was now filled up,
and that was the most touching part of all—the leave-
taking, the bidding adieu, the last kiss, the last embrace.
As one crowd after another of men, women and children,
of Seminary students, and of students in the male and
female colleges, of classmates and other friends, came forward to bid farewell with the missionary—some pronounc-
ing blessings upon her, others taking their leave with long

C

and tender embraces, others with tears in their eyes, and all looking sorrowful, the scene became so affecting as to move the stoutest heart."

For himself the writer would say that he never witnessed or passed through a similar scene. There are some occasions in life when we witness and experience emotions which no pen can portray. This was one of those instances. The awful silence was unbroken save by the voice of the speaker, and here and there a suppressed sob. A great weight seemed to be pressing down upon the souls of all, and men and women sat in their pews in a crushed and hopeless way. When the interest of the occasion reached its culmination, there were few faces in that large assembly that did not bear traces of recent tears. And when the audience broke up and found their way out into the cool night air they looked like men shaking off the incubus of some fearful nightmare. I hope never again while life lasts to pass through such a scene or experience similar feelings.

It was during the solemn and impressive services of this meeting that Rev. N. E. Pressly, now missionary to Mexico, formed the high and holy purpose to devote his life to the mission cause.

Perhaps of all present Mrs. Giffen shed not a tear. She sat rigid and stony-faced, as if feeling were dead, and hope perished. Two years afterward she said:

"To-night is the second anniversary of the farewell meeting at home. I wonder if any of you will remember it. The recollection of that night always throws a shadow over my feelings. I do not think any one in this mission was ever just so situated except Mrs. Lansing, and therefore this one was not just like other farewell missionary meetings. There were moments while it was in progress when it seemed that human nature could not bear any more, and I now feel that if a visit home had to be purchased at the expense of such another leave-taking, I would freely choose *never to go home.* I have often felt that as far as earth is concerned, I have experienced what it is to die."

The next day—January 28th, 1875,—brought the last day of her stay under her father's roof, and she passed out over the threshold for the last time on earth. The parting with the family was as sad and heart-breaking as such scenes can ever be. When she bade her mother and brothers and sisters farewell, she hoped some day to take them by the hand once more, and look again into their dear faces. But when she bade her father farewell, she knew that it was for the last time, and that she would never see him again until they met before the throne above. · What she suffered in these moments when she looked for the last time upon the scenes of her youth, her friends, her home and her family we may never know. Her pale face and set features showed something of the severity of the strug-
· gle, and she afterward tells us that in these moments she "experienced what it was to die." But before this the cost had been counted, and the sacrifice measured, and now her face was resolutely turned toward the East.

On the morning of the 28th of January, 1875, the missionary party began their journey to Philadelphia, to meet Mrs. Giffen and Alexander, and there embark for Alexandria. Mrs. Giffen was accompanied by Dr. Bonner, secretary of the Board, and by her brother. A series of farewell meetings and receptions to the party had been arranged all along the route. Every mark of honor and kindness that could be bestowed on Mrs. Giffen, both by the citizens of her home and along the way was freely manifested. In Newberry, the place of her birth, her father's old friends received her as if she had been their own child. Her father's old slaves, in procession, escorted her to the depot on her departure, and overwhelmed her with their demonstrations of sincere affection, creating a scene rarely witnessed in the streets. In Winnsboro, the home of her eldest brother, a reception was also tendered, while that held in Charlotte, N. C., closed the series. These meetings were very trying and exhausting to Mrs. Giffen, but since they were deemed essential to the good of the cause were endured with patience and fortitude. Indeed with regard to the entire journey, Dr. Bonner, who had contributed so much to her comfort and encouragement, writes: "Miss Galloway bears the trial of leaving home and friends and country, with a brave heart and is contented and cheerful." But along the route the writer often detected Mrs. Giffen looking first at one, and then the other of our party in a very unusual way. Her glance was so clinging and piercing that she seemed to be graving upon her inmost soul every line and feature of our faces, that nothing might ever be able to mar the faithfulness of the image, putting "memory on its honor," that the impression might be as lasting as its own immortal self.

In Philadelphia our party was received and entertained at the hospitable home of Rev. J. B. Dales, and during our entire stay were the recipients of much distinguished kindness. Here the entire missionary party assembled. The time and place of sailing having been changed, the party on the 9th of February proceeded to Jersey City to be in readiness for departure on the morning of the following day. Here Mrs. Giffen was joined by her eldest brother.

The eventful morning of the 10th dawned clear and bitterly cold, the river full of ice, and the incoming ocean steamers encrusted with ice to the topmost spar. But by eight o'clock all were on board, the sad parting over, the hawsers cast off, and the prow of the ship turned to the ocean. As the steamer rounded the point at Castle Garden, Mrs. Giffen came on deck, waved a last farewell, and we saw her no more. We remained on the pier until the black hull vanished in the distance, and then turned sadly away and left the deserted wharf. And now my imagination pictures that black iron ship as some monster bearing her away to some unknown and undiscoverable country. To-day is seven years since, and of the three who made the journey together to that ship's side two "are not"—the Master called them and they have gone to be with Him. "And I only am left alone to tell thee."

Her last message to her mother, from the ship's side was, "I am afraid I will never write you again from America, and if I would I could weep an ocean of tears, but I do not. Think of me every day, and write me long letters, May God watch over us all, and keep us together in spirit here, and forever together hereafter. All loving thoughts to each one, and a long affectionate farewell."

CHAPTER IV.

MRS. GIFFEN'S FIRST LETTER—THE VOYAGE.

"Last ties are hard to be broken, last words hard to be spoken, and last farewells hard to be taken. They either cut deep, long gashes, and leave the torn trembling fibres to ache and quiver for long days afterward, or they turn you into stone. Perhaps there are few in this wide world who have not experienced something of one or both these forms of a great sorrow; few who would not give some real sympathy to one who looked into dear faces with only this one distinct consciousness, that it *might be* for the last time. Leaving home and friends is or may be very sorrowful on land, but when oceans are to roll between, all that is sad in the one is intensified in the other. And when you come suddenly around some angle and there stands out before you the gloomy old ship which only seems waiting to carry you away, how the current seems to stand still in your veins, how the heart seems to refuse its accustomed throbbings, and how many sad old stories of these remorseless seas come trooping through your quivering brain. There stands the black old hull, which in a moment of little faith you tell yourself may go down with you a thousand fathoms deep into ocean caves; there are the masts and spars where the storm king may revel; and there the sails and rigging where the lightnings may leap, and where over all the mad waves may roll and toss and lash you in blind fury.

So ominously loomed up the *Cuba*, in our sad imagination, as she stood in New York harbor on the evening of the 9th of February. Ungenerously, no doubt, we could not resist the inclination to clothe her with a living personality, a hard, unfeeling, *revengeful* personality. And more horrible than all, is the idea which fills your mind at first sight of what might be called the genius of the ship—its "mast head figure." How terrible to make it *a woman*, a frail, helpless girl, forever hanging there over the rolling sea. There she clings tightly with one hand to the ship, while her waving hair and flowing robes blow on always in the breeze. With one glance aloft and a laugh on her lips she seems forever defying the sea.

How sorrowfully we felt as we crossed the gangway into the ship! To us it was indeed a "bridge of sighs"—with a gulf below which we felt we might never re-cross. And when the last word was spoken and the last kiss taken, how keenly we felt that *all was over.* How much it seemed as if the church-yard breeze were blowing over us, how much as if we had seen and felt our own self laid gently down in our last quiet home, had heard that terrible first shovelful of earth fall heavily on the boards above, had seen the red heap outside grow gradually less and the deep vault fill slowly up, till, smoothed and solemnly shaped, the last footfall had departed and left it for the springing grass and the falling showers.

But the leave-taking in the ship was not altogether *the last.* With a heart full of all sad thoughts we went up on deck to see the last of what was really a beautiful prospect spread out around us. We had supposed you all gone, that no doubt you were by that time away up on Broadway, but to our great joy there you were, all three, still on the wharf. How uninteresting then was all New York spread out around us, how oblivious we were of that brilliant sun gilding a harbor full of rolling ice, how entirely forgetful of all save the one warm thought that those who were now the embodiment of all that I knew or loved on earth still stood on the wharf, still looked after us, still had me in their hearts. And though there did spring up a great longing to know your thoughts, thrust back by the remembrance that we could speak to each other no more, still it was the one bright spot, the one happy moment in that miserable morning. And its brightness and quiet joy have not faded out yet. Though we could but exchange feeble signals, yet how full they were of meaning and how they cheered me up and gave me new hope and vigor for our long journey.

We stayed on the hurricane deck most of the morning, two of our party seeming intensely interested in getting the last sight of their country. In the afternoon we came down to the cabin, gathered around one table, took our first dinner on board, and spent the evening in cheerful, pleasant conversation, though about nine most of us felt decidedly called upon to look up rather more private quarters. By morning the tossing had increased and the moans and groans of sick passengers were rather doleful. Two of our party have escaped entirely or almost so. Miss McD. has not missed a meal, but her *compagnon de voyage* has not fared so nicely. Thursday Mr. A. and myself were ever so sick, and towards night it commenced blowing quite a gale. That of course increased our distress, and all night long we could do nothing but lament our miserable condition, while we did our best to hold ourselves in our berths. It was indeed a "rough night." Every movable thing in the ship tossed and slided, slided and tossed, rattling and clattering back and forth, up and down the whole night long; and the poor sick passengers felt that life *anywhere,* so it was but on land, would be unmixed happiness. You may guess how deeply we sympathized with the man who declared while sea-sick that he had but two purposes in life. One, to set his foot on *terra firma* once more, and the other *to find the man who wrote "Life on the Ocean Wave."* Seriously, it is no laughing matter to be shut up in a state-room, crammed into a miserable little berth, shut out from the light, and with no breath of fresh air, while you are just sure you *never were* so sick in your life before. If we had been on a pleasure excursion things would have looked pretty blue. As it was, we tried to remember that even if we should be sick all the way, even *eleven* days would come to an end sometime, and that

this was one of things we were to bear *for Christ's sake.*
But it wasn't a pleasant night even for the few who have
not been sick at all. We were all the time "shipping seas,"
as they say, wave after wave dashing clear over the decks,
and during part of the night the whole stern of the vessel
was *under water*, compelling them to "lie to" or "heave
to" for a couple of hours. This wouldn't have added
anything to our comfort if we had known it, but of course
we did not know it, and I venture there is not a soul on
board, among the passengers, I mean, who has felt the
least sensation of uneasiness or want of safety since we left
New York. Of course there may be losses at sea in the
safest and most careful of lines, but then there are ac-
cidents at home ; danger and death may come into your
fireside, but He who made the sea and holds it *in the
hollow of His hand* can rule the storm and guide the waves.

Towards evening on Friday the weather grew milder
and the sailing smoother, and Saturday morning our good
friends dragged us out and up into the air, albeit it was
"a hard pill to swallow," for sixty hours of intense suffering left us very weak indeed. The day was fine though,
and we gathered up a little strength. Some of our passengers are now on their seventeenth voyage, while there
are only a few like ourselves who have never crossed before. All agree, however, that if it is possible they will
never try it again in *February*, for though we have made
good progress, owing to the fact that the wind has nearly
always been in our favor, it has nevertheless been, on the
whole, a rough voyage. Saturday night we noticed a
steward putting a heavy iron bar across the cabin doors at
the stern, and fastening it down with heavy wedges. One
of the gentlemen inquired the reason. He said that a
month ago perhaps, on the last voyage from New York to

Liverpool, a heavy gale was blowing and the ship was running before the wind at full speed, sixteen knots per hour. But the waves ran faster still and finally they "stove in" these cabin doors, tore away the "break-waters," rushed down the cabin, and the water was one and a half feet deep on the state-room floor. The fireman shoveled the coal into the engines standing in water waist deep, and all that saved the *Cuba* from going down was that the guards on the main decks gave way and let the water out in that way. That was rather a rough experience but the *Cuba* is afloat yet, and now they make the cabin doors sure every night against a repetition of such an undesirable occurrence.

In bad weather on shipboard it is apt to be right dreary, at least for the first three or four days, but I don't think one remembers the discomforts of a voyage long after it is over. We, two of us at least, have no reason to entertain particularly delightful recollections of the sea; indeed while we were shut up down in our "lower regions," as we call the state-room domains, we felt well convinced that if ever we got over to Egypt we should certainly stay there, for the idea of crossing this old ocean again was not to be entertained for a moment, but with returning health we felt decidedly braver.

Sabbath morning dawned beautifully bright and clear, and, after breakfast, Bibles and prayer books were distributed through the cabin, a desk was arranged, passengers stewards, sailors, and steerage passengers were all assembled, and the captain went through the English service in quite an impressive manner. It really seemed more like Sabbath than one might expect at sea. After service everybody betook himself to the deck except our party. We produced our little stock of books and thought and spoke of how many at home were thinking of and praying for us; they in the churches at home and we "on the rolling deep." Our Sabbath passed quietly away, but towards night another gale sprang up, and another sleepless night came on. Monday morning it was raining and storming, great waves dashing entirely over us and lashing us on all sides. Only one portion of a door could be kept open on the lee-side of the vessel, and oh what a dearth there was of fresh air. But it was well worth being sea-sick, well worth clinging to door facings and swinging to hand-railings to get one glance at that magnificent sea. It was an ocean of swelling mountains, a sea of smoking volcanoes, rolling and tumbling, tossing and heaving, towering up above us as if they would swallow us up and then sinking away as we rode over them. Now they look like rocks on a mountain side, black as the granite of the "everlasting hills," and now they break and change and melt into the softest green, while the "white cap" of foam and spray is crowned over all. It was a sight which must *be seen*, which no pen can describe, and which once enjoyed never can be forgotten. There was mingled with it no feeling of fear, only a sense of the keenest enjoyment and a most vivid and powerful realization of the might of him who made the sea and walks upon its waves. To-day it is still cloudy, but we are getting on well, they say averaging perhaps three hundred miles per twenty-four hours. Our voyage will be about three thousand, two hundred miles, and we hope to get to Queenstown by Friday. So remembering my promise to let you hear from us by that mail I have worked hard to get up sufficient equilibrium to write to-day, but it is decidedly "up hill" business. At every roll of the ship I feel as if my head *remained* at the starting point, or was gradually lengthened to the extreme of the downward inclination, and then was compressed again, the interesting operation continually repeating itself, and table, ink and all seeming to be always running away from you. There is no quiet either; you are either interrupted every moment almost, or you feel an unconquerable inclination to listen to what everybody is saying around you. It is raining again and a heavy "head wind" is blowing. The ship is closed up on all sides and the passengers look for all the world like children shut up in the house at home on a rainy day. We are bouncing around in a most uncomfortable manner, and the spoons and forks, plates and glasses are making most undignified journeys across the cabin floor. Some of the passengers are trying to read, some are singing to a violin accompaniment, some are trying to play chess, but the greater part are talking at the top of their speed. But the main business on the ship is *eating*, or trying to eat. We have breakfast at eight, lunch at twelve, dinner at four, tea at seven, and supper at nine, your correspondent, however, has not taken many meals at the table. There are so many meats and sauces and pastries and such a variety of flavors and odors that I almost wish I might never see meat again, or taste a sauce again. There seems to be brandy in the soup, brandy in the meats, brandy in the puddings, brandy above the table, but especially brandy on the table. Nearly every gentleman, except those of our party, have glass after glass at every meal except breakfast. What a luxury it will be to us to get out of sight of so much drinking. We wonder if it is introductory to what we shall see on the continent. And another luxury will be to get a good appetite again and some good plain food, without any added flavoring. I know I have thought longingly fifty times about that dish of corn bread we got at Taylor's the morning we sailed.

There are very few Americans on board. At our table
we have a very pleasant English lady who entertains us
with very interesting accounts of men and things in her
country. She thinks the Queen "a nice old lady," whom
Providence kindly continues between the Nation and the
Prince of Wales. Her opinion of him could not well be
worse. She declares he does not deserve the name of *a
man*, that he does absolutely nothing but drink and smoke.
A Canadian across the table suggested that that was a good
deal for one man to do.

Tuesday evening " the force of circumstances " compelled
me to leave off rather abruptly, and I did not get up stairs
until late yesterday morning. I was like an escaping con-
vict, detected and remanded to his cell ; but I hope now I
am bravely over it all, but Mr. A. is still quite sick and
weak. In fact he has had the hardest time of anybody on
board, and has now no hope of getting up at all until we
get ashore. Very few persons are ever so much affected
as he has been, or there would not be quite so much travel
over the Atlantic.

Everybody is busy writing, the mail bag is hanging
out to-day and all who are not otherwise employed, or
rather who can stop their writing long enough are guessing
when we shall get to Queenstown, but especially when we
shall reach Liverpool. In fact there is a good deal of
betting on the question, but we are afraid we cannot land
before Sabbath morning. I wish we could get in Saturday night, then we could go and hear Messrs. Moody and
Sankey.

February 23.—The *Cuba* came to anchor in Queenstown
harbor at four o'clock Saturday morning, the 20th. I
mailed you letters the night before, and hope they are now
fast on their way. We should have been in Liverpool by

ten that night, but were compelled to wait until morning
for the tide to put us over the bar. Our last day on shipboard was very unpleasant. A snow storm came on
early and the sea was very rough. This kept some of us
in our berths all day, and some who got above stairs early
could not get down again until late at night. At ten
o'clock Sabbath morning the Custom House officers came
aboard, and we succeeded in getting our baggage "passed"
without any difficulty. A tug-boat then took us up to
Liverpool and we were ashore by eleven. Notwithstanding some of us had been so uncomfortable on the *Cuba*,
still we did not take our leave of her without some emotion. She had carried us safely through quite a storm and
through several rather severe gales, and we looked back to
her from our tug-boat with a deep feeling of gratitude that
a kind Providence had made our ocean home a safe one,
and had brought us across the stormy Atlantic without
anything "to disturb or make us afraid."

We took lodgings at the North Western Hotel, as most
Americans do, it being well situated for getting over the
city, and also being in connection with the London and
North Western railway. We found ourselves very greatly
fatigued, and with some of us the motion of the ship continued a long time after we got on land. However, we
took luncheon and hastened out to Victoria Hall to hear
Messrs. Moody and Sankey.

Monday morning we set out early for our banker's, Hon.
David Stuart, and we must say we were all greatly surprised, as well as pleased, with the marked courtesy and
kindness there shown us. All the members of the firm
were brought in and introduced in a friendly way, and one
of the young gentlemen told us pleasantly that he had been
"baptized in Philadelphia by Dr. Dales." But pleasantest

of all, he sent me in *a letter*. Perhaps not everybody will understand how my very finger's ends tingled with pleasure that any one should so remember me *in Liverpool*, and wonder, too, as to who it could be. Imagine then the *real enjoyment*, to all our party, when I looked at the signature and read the name of one of our Alexandria missionaries, an unknown friend, an affectionate, sympathetic, Christian heart, thinking of us, sharing our sorrow in parting from all we love, and in just as far as she could "bearing our burden." It touched us very deeply, and we felt that a *very warm welcome* did indeed await us in Egypt. Perhaps some will say it was a little kindness—only a letter. To *us* it was very great—"the cup of cold water" to a thirsty heart. We read it more than once, and we took our "sister in Christ" into our inmost heart.

Business being finished, our banker's son kindly begged to show us over the city and escort us to "the shops," as they call the stores here, and quite a kindness it was too. He took us to an immense house, but while we found great variety we are all about agreed that we do not find things very much less in price than at home.

Liverpool is a very *substantial* looking city, everything seeming to be iron or stone. But the objects of greatest curiosity and amusement to the ladies of our party are *the English women and the English horses*. The former are the most perfect specimens of independence, don't-care-ism, and want of taste that we ever saw in our lives. We have not seen two pretty ones yet, and their costumes, both in cut and color, are almost indescribable. Except in silk they scarcely wear black at all, and they mingle up blue, purple and rose color at a shocking rate. They seem every way inferior to the men, unless it be in apparent strength, and ability to help themselves.

The horses are fully as striking—the Norman horses, we mean, which correspond to our dray horses at home. They are of immense size, and their feet and pasture joints are large enough for *elephants*. They step along as softly and carefully and exactly like a man walking on a frozen street. Their shoes, I am sure, must be as large, many of them, as a *peck* measure, and they are attached to drays nearly as large as our "flat" cars on the railroad. These drays really are larger, a good deal larger than the "flats" and box cars on the English railways, and it is almost incredible the immense loads you may see drawn by one of these horses, two being occasionally harnessed to the same dray, but *never* abreast, always one before the other, and never driven, always led. Occasionally, too, we passed one of these immense drays drawn by a *single donkey*, our gentlemen declaring the load to be *forty* times the size of the donkey.

Of course there are many things here which are new, strange and amusing to us, and possibly we may be equally as odd looking to those whom we meet, but, take it all in all, we are not smitten with England by any manner of means. Our hotel was a good one, I suppose. By the way, it is just fronting St. George's Hall, containing, as perhaps you know, one of the most magnificent organs in the world, and having on the facade, I suppose you might say, equestrian statues of Prince Albert and Queen Victoria, each one standing between a pair of huge crouching lions. But all this does not make amends for the miserably poor fare we got at the celebrated North Western. Twenty-five dollars per day would not give you the fare we get at home in our *second class* hotels, perhaps I should even have said third class. After ten days of sea sickness and consequent fasting we really needed good food, but we certainly did not

get it ; and yet we were charged higher than we ever paid at
home. So much for the Great North Western. No doubt
there are more quiet hotels where we could have gotten
better fare for less, but it is true the world over, that if you
ask to be recommended to a hotel every man will send you
to the most expensive of his acquaintance. If he knows a
good second class he won't tell you.

Well, we have availed ourselves of Miss Campbell's
timely suggestions as to what purchases we ought to make
for Egypt, got our goods up to the hotel, and, weary as
we were, packed ever so hard, closed up our trunks and
had them shipped by the "Memphis" direct from Liverpool to Alexandria, so that we shall not be troubled with
anything but "hand baggage" on the Continent. At seven
o'clock this morning we bought our tickets for London,
"second class," as almost every one does except the nobility, one being just about as comfortable and respectable as
the other. The officials took them, punched them, the
guard opened a door, thrust us in in a great hurry, and off
we went to London. The compartment has not anything
like the comfort or elegance of our ordinary cars at home,
there being no heating apparatus except a queer, sheet iron,
"foot warmer," filled with hot water. We were not at all flat-
tered with the accommodations, but behold, when we were
nearly in London, another official thrust in his head for
tickets, and when he had them very graciously informed
us that we were in "first class" cars, and *must* pay the
excess of fare. Of course we complained. It was no fault
of ours. We had showed our tickets, were thrust in where
we were, &c. But no, he politely referred us to the company in London for redress of grievance and pocketed the
extra seven shillings, making the full fare £1, 9s., or about
$7.25. Their whole system of railroading is on the rather

contemptible order. The passenger cars are small, dingy and dirty-looking, even the best of them, their box cars are not larger than a good-sized wagon, the engines are little, puny, ugly-looking things, and even *the whistle* has a babyish squeak. Every one of us made that very remark about it the first time we heard it, so you may accept it for a fact. How much the English might afford to learn from America! But the country of England is beautiful. For many miles out of Liverpool the meadows were as green as in our summer, and the hawthorn hedges give it the appearance of flower beds in a garden almost. Everywhere there were traces of such careful culture, if only we could have seen the growing crops. I suppose, of course, we saw some castles, or at least the residences of some of the nobility, with their towers and turrets, and country seats, perhaps, they were. Some of them were very pretty, indeed, but we could not say as much for the little village which was always near by. The buildings have almost all such an old, dingy look, not redeemed either by the idea that "classic antiquity" was found about there, but generally the first thought suggested was the *smallness* of these old houses, the even *diminutive* looking rooms added where we have large long ells.

There is such a manifest division into rich and poor all through this country, which is very striking. There was snow on the ground, the fall being heavier as we went towards London, still we saw many laborers in the fields, principally plowing, always with double teams, and never abreast, generally there were four horses in a line. A pretty fringe of trees is planted along every little brook and canal, the channels are smoothly and regularly marked out in a pretty, winding way, the drainage appearing perfect and altogether the effect is charming. Cold as it was

we thought so often of the delightful summer days one
might spend "under the trees" along these pretty brooks.

But perhaps the most beautiful thing we saw, was a
range of hills to the north-east of London, white with snow,
glittering in the sunlight and seeming indeed to be part of
the sky. Except in form and brilliancy they did not seem
other or differing from the clouds, but we left them behind
at last and found ourselves running rapidly through the
vast suburbs of London. Rows on rows of handsome
buildings were everywhere to be seen, and noise and bustle
and business were on every hand. Glad indeed were we
when we rolled up in the station after our six hours' ride
of two hundred miles, and the united testimony of our
party was that we never had gone such a distance before
with so little personal comfort. The cold was very disagreeable indeed, notwithstanding they say the mercury
here never falls here very much below freezing point.

In company with several of the other passengers of the
Cuba, we took lodgings at Charing Cross on the Strand. It
is a handsome building but rather worse for us in some important respects than the one to which we objected in Liverpool. The fact is, we entertained ourselves at luncheon
with imagining what our friends in America would think
if they could see us sitting down to such a dinner in London. Of course we get just what we order in all European
hotels, but we have learned to be wary of the orders. By
the advice of our Liverpool banker, the gentlemen went
immediately after to Cook's Tourist to endeavor if possible
to get his tickets through to Egypt and also to secure his
hotel coupons, by which means we shall always have our
lodgings selected, get better meals and have to pay less for
them. After tea we went out for a promenade on the
Strand, and a magnificent street it is. The displays in the

shop windows are beautiful indeed, and many of the fine
buildings have all the signs and fancy adornings in front
ends as stars, diamond-shaped figures, &c., done all in gas
jet, hundreds and hundreds of them blazing and flickering
in beautiful, changing quivering sheen. We walked till
nine o'clock, very much enjoying the handsome windows
and magnificent buildings and now at eleven o'clock we
are in the reading room—there being no ladies' parlor in
these splendid hotels—finishing up our letters. But the
gentlemen say, finished or unfinished after such a fatiguing
day, we must go up stairs.

February 26.—We are just starting on our "last day in
London." Our first intention, however, was to have left
for Paris about half an hour ago, but as we can not get a
steamer from either Naples or Brindisi before the 8th, we
felt at liberty to dispose of the intervening days according
to our own inclinations. It has been snowing heavily ever
since we came into London, and, as it melts almost as soon
as it falls, we have had a terrible time of it trying to get
round to the most interesting points. Yesterday the gentlemen secured our tickets from Cook's Agency. We go
from here to Paris, *via* Dieppe. This will require perhaps
six hours on the Channel, but it is considered the prettiest
route, and it suited us better in several respects.

Monday morning, the 2d, we propose setting out for
Turin, Rome, and Naples, so we have a journey of about
twelve hundred miles by rail ahead of us. I sincerely
hope it may not prove as uncomfortable as the ride from
Liverpool. But it has been a most unfortunate time for
us. At the American Legation, when we told them we
were on our way to Egypt, the Secretary said, "Well,
you'd like to get there pretty fast out of such weather as
this, wouldn't you?"

But I am more and more interested in London every way. I would like to get an American history of England, and go and stay a week in Westminster Abbey, then carry my book along and stay another in the Tower, only one of the gentlemen suggests : " You wouldn't like to sleep there, would you?" I fully agree with him, I would only want to be in either place when there was a good deal of daylight abroad, for sure I am nobody could close his eyes in composure in the dark in either of these wonderful old places. Even when we are quietly in our hotel at night, I am in imagination continually walking round the monuments, and through the chapels, and over the vaults of those great old kings, queens, crusaders, poets, warriors, &c. Nothing has so impressed me as the Abbey and the Tower, and half the night I imagine I am first in one and then in the other. Everywhere you go there is something to deepen this impression. Yesterday we were in the Houses of Parliament, and looking through the corridor leading from the Central Hall to the House of Lords, we stopped before a fine painting of the " Farewell of Lord and Lady Russell." We had seen his tomb, with his full-sized figure in bronze reclining above it in the vaults of the Abbey, and were told by the guide that " he was executed." And in the painting we recognized the stone room at the top of the " White Tower" where he was imprisoned and where the farewell took place. Out in the yard was "the block," and there, I think, he was beheaded. Everywhere you are overwhelmed with *the great, the grand, the old*, and not less by the *blood and suffering* mingled in it all. Here is a woman's tear, trembling on her cheek as if it had but fallen there. By her side is a glittering Queen, or some haughty monarch clad in burnished mail. On the opposite wall the scales may turn completely, and for a sceptre and crown, there are the axe and the block. But I can not linger over the Abbey and the Tower now. When I have had time to breathe, I will tell you more about them both, as also of other things which we have seen.

I wish we could have been in London over Sabbath, so we might have heard Spurgeon preach. In fact I feel as if the Continental cities would none of them prove of so much interest to us as this one. We have learned the streets and go round all distances with perfect ease.

We find it very difficult to accomplish very much here. Nothing is open until half-past ten or eleven o'clock, and then all close at about four. The days are so dark too and foggy that gas is in demand almost all the time, unless for two or three hours at noon.

American travelers tell us we will admire Paris very much more than London. Everything here is so black and dingy. All the monuments in the city squares look black, though they as well as the buildings are very handsome. Nelson's monument in Trafalgar Square is quite imposing. Together with its adjuncts, it occupies a very considerable space. There are two beautiful fountains, four immense crouching lions, and several very large equestrian figures in the square, and all very handsomely enclosed. The shaft is very high, so much so that it seemed to me the old hero might very well weary of his great altitude, forever looking down on all the world below.

Regent street is very handsome, or so we thought driving through yesterday. It is nowhere straight, I think, but serpentine, winding along in grand massive blocks of buildings on either side, crowded with vehicles of all kinds, and the side-walks lined with all classes, shopping, all stopping outside and making their selections in the shop windows before entering. These windows are beautiful, and contain, in many instances, the greater part of the shopkeeper's goods. Samples of everything he has are exhibited there with the prices marked, and there is, therefore, not only a much better opportunity for the purchaser to make judicious selections, but also very much gained to the shopkeeper in the way of his time.

One thing which interests us on the streets is the English shopping Cab, or *Hansom*. They have tops a little like our top buggy, but are nearer the ground. Instead of an *apron* in front, there are folding leaves which shut you in, a glass entirely over the front which you may have either up or down, entirely shutting you in if you wish. Then the driver sits up above it all behind, driving over the top, and communicating with his passengers by a window in the top. They are very convenient and comfortable, and drive very rapidly.

About the most difficult thing in London is *to sleep*. There is so much to excite you in waking hours, that is presuming you are a stranger and devoted to sight-seeing, that it is nearly impossible to shut it out of your mind at night. Should you succeed after a time and forget your fatigue in happy slumber, why then your bliss is not of long duration, for nearly every church or large building of any importance has a tremendous great clock on it, and every hour, half hour and quarter hour is regularly *chimed*. It is right pretty, you think, before retiring. Afterwards it is an unmitigated nuisance.

On the whole though, I suppose we ought to be pretty well satisfied with our stay in London, for though it has been quite fatiguing, yet we are all well, and have really enjoyed most things, the weather and the general gloom always excepted. Perhaps, too, we shall like the English

better when we get to where we can only guess at what people say, without being able to answer them at all.   At any
rate we shall soon see, as in a few hours we propose to set
foot on 'La Belle France.' "

CHAPTER V.

BOLOGNA, ITALY.

" Leaving London and crossing the Channel, we landed
at Dieppe Saturday morning at eleven o'clock, and left in
half an hour for Paris.   Our route ran almost all the way
down the valley of the Seine, through the most pictur-
esquely beautiful country we ever saw.   It exhibited more
careful, economical culture than in England.   In every
spot where a tree or shrub may grow without lessening the
garden ground, there one is planted, and every year's
growth of twigs is carefully cut and bundled into sheaves
as you do wheat, and used, we suppose, for thatching roofs
and kindling fires.   Such prunings, often repeated, give the
trees the general appearance, at this season of pruning, of
low *stumps*, but which in spring would branch out beautifully.   Another favorite style of pruning a different tree is
to let it run up very tall, along the little streams, of which
there are very many, trimming them to the very top.   The
houses are very old and quaint looking, and the little yards
everywhere alive with turkeys and chickens.   And so many
old mills, with moss-covered roofs, and lazily turning old
wheels, where only slight imagination was needed to see in
the white ruffled faces some old poet's "maid of the mill."

The fields were green, and the gardens full of nice things for the table, all of which looked extremely inviting before we got to Paris, for we had only the most meagre of lunches from Friday evening in London to the same time Saturday in Paris. It was cold and disagreeable, too. In fact there was such a storm on the channel that we lay at anchor from eleven Friday night till five Saturday morning. At some places there was a cold rain falling, at others it was snowing, and at Paris everything was white with the snow. Arrived there our vexation increased considerably when we left the cars and could not find a soul who could speak a word of English, and we not three words of French, or rather in a slow way we could make them comprehend our wishes, but could not catch a word of their rapid enunciation. We finally declared ourselves "Innocents Abroad," and soon after fell into the hands of a "shark" who promised to take us to our hotel, and who could speak English enough to deceive us. We got into his 'bus, rather against our wishes, however, rode and rode, and finally found that instead of putting us out at Cook's selection, the St. Petersburg, 35 Rue Caumartin, he had taken us "to my own hotel, I no understan, I tought I say come here, Monsieur no say. I have good house, good room, Monsieur go up and see. Speak English. Gentleman from New York say he have friends come on dat train. I not know, I bring you here. Rue Caumartin very far, I not know, de coachman may," &c., to an indefinite extent. We felt very indignant, were sure we were dealing with an unprincipled, unsafe character, that we had been impudently defrauded, for we had given him the printed card of the hotel to which persons traveling on Cook's Tourist Tickets are sent, and he had distinctly stated at the cars that though he would like to have us at his hotel, yet he would send us to the St.

Petersburg just as well and as cheaply in his 'bus as if we took a cab.

We felt just a little uncomfortable, held a two minutes consultation, picked up our satchels, stepped past "the vociferating fraud" as the gentlemen dubbed our knight of the 'bus, mustered up all our little stock of French, got a cab for "deux francs," and were soon in nice, quiet, comfortable rooms, where we felt secure and at home. The clerk in the office, or bureau as they say, was a pretty little woman who spoke English fluently, and so did the waiter, or *garcon*, in the Salle a Manger.

But we did not go "sight-seeing" in Paris, and therefore I cannot tell you very much about this beautiful city. We went only to Notre Dame, and I must wait till some other time to tell you about that. From there we *walked* back in the rain to our hotel and were so weary that we did not venture out any more. Table d'hote over, we got our Bibles, took possession of the reading room and spent as pleasant a Sabbath evening I venture as any of you at home. Before we knew it was almost eleven o'clock, but we still had plenty of time for sleeping as we knew we could do nothing next morning but get breakfast and get off on the eleven o'clock train for Turin. But for our Cook's tickets I do not see how we should have got on at the stations and along the road. They are printed in pamphlet form both in French and English, and enclosed in a neat little case. They are everywhere recognized with respect, and if we wish to know what train to take, or what direction to go in the station houses, the gentlemen just hold up the tickets to the guards and they point us right. So we got off from Paris more pleasantly than we got into it, but it was still snowing, growing heavier as we approached the Alps. We did not enter them until after night, but they were white from base to summit, and very grand and bold looking against the smoky sky. It was with difficulty though that we saw them at all through the frosted window panes. At Madane we reached the Italian frontier, were waked up and thrust out to go through the Custom House again. At Dieppe passports were not demanded. Here they were asked for provided you did not have a card with your simple address on it, the purpose being merely to learn if you are English or American. If you are, you may "do what you plçase." If you are not, the scrutiny is more rigid. And again in the cars, we soon entered Mount Cenis Tunnel, but of course we could get no impression beyond the mere fact that we were in it, "under the Alps," and on the classic ground of which we had read and dreamed all our lives. We were in quite comfortable carriages, as they call the cars here, that night, and as the darkness forbade, or rather refused to supply much material for poetic dreaming, we soon left Mount Cenis and its "eternal snows" to take care of themselves, while we betook ourselves to *dreaming* of another character. We came by way of Dejon, Macon, &c., and arrived in Turin at nine o'clock next morning, distant from Paris five hundred and one miles. Passing on through Alessandria, Piazcenza, Parma and Modena we found the snow constantly increasing, and on arriving at this old city of Bologna, the guard opened the door of the voiture and mustered up English enough to tell us to "descend," pointing very significantly to the steps of the carriage and then to the door of the station. We "descended," and then to work to find out what for. After some moments we understood that the snow was so deep on the mountains between Bologna and Fairenze, as they call Florence, that trains could not pass over, consequently we must lie over here. Cook's Tourists

do not stop over at Bologna and there was no list of hotels
on his guide-book, so we knew not where to go. Just at
this juncture we were interrogated with, "Americans?"
just as we had so often been in London, and on assenting
we got a perfect stream of *real* nice English. It was from
one of the station guards who had been six years in the
United States. The first question was if we were from the
North. One of the gentlemen said yes, and on he rattled,
telling us where he had been and how much he liked
America. He was in New Orleans, he said, when the war
commenced, and "they got me in the Zouaves and then say
I *volunteered*. Oh! you know Stonewall?" While he
asked the question a glow of pleasure at the recollection
of that honored name spread over his swarthy face. I said,
"O, yes, I was a rebel." "Oh! were you?" and he
laughed with a real hearty ring. "Yes," he said, "I was at
Chancellorsville when Stonewall was killed, and at all those
other battles. At Antietam a grape shot took me here,"
laying his hand on one limb, "and when I got well *I rund
away*." "You *rund away*, did you?" said I. "O yes, I
say this not my country. I got nothing to do with this
quarrel, and I got out of that." For all that there was
genuine pleasure gleaming in his face at talking to Americans and a real glad sort of a "fellow feeling" sparkling in
his eyes when I said I was a rebel too. By this time there
was a swarm of great black Italian eyes glaring into our
faces, and we got our English-speaking friend to get us a
cabriolet and start us off to the "Bologna Hotel." The
snow was very deep in the narrow streets, and every where
"the snow shovelers" were at work clearing out a carriage
way, and banking it up ready for dumping it into the
sewers. They were on the roofs of the houses, too, clearing it off as fast as possible, as it is such a wet, heavy kind

of snow, that they fear the giving way of the roofs. As
we passed "the gates" of the city the guards came and
stopped the cab, looked into our faces and said "Americans?" to the drivers. We suppose they said yes, and drove
on. It is a quaint, queer, old, old-looking city that we
drove through.

So many things had the unmistakable air of the "dark
ages." So many old, old-looking churches and cathedrals
with the "key and mitre" cut in stone over the door, and
great stone figures of Peter standing on the rock and grasp-
ing a bundle of brazen keys. On one there was "Plenary
Indulgence" and other such stuff, in antique Latin, over
the door, and sure I am that old church is as old as Tetzel
himself. At last we were set down at a most forbidding-
looking entrance, with no gas anywhere. The hackman
gave the bell-rope a vigorous jerk, and out came the
proprietor, a waiter, a woman, and a boy. One flew to us,
another flew at the gas, and a third jerked another bell-
rope. The proprietor could speak enough English to understand that we wanted two rooms and dinner. He
started the waiter up stairs with us and then ran to a back
door and with many gesticulations ran out a *long whispered
hus—h—h* to somebody behind the scenes. The stair-cases
were unswept, and both they and the little dark narrow
halls looked as if cut out of the solid rock. But after
getting up stairs the atmosphere seemed changed, and our
rooms looked very inviting but for the cold. However
we would much rather have been in the cars on our way
to Florence. We almost felt as if we were surrounded
with banditti, for these Italians have rather more of a
savage, highway-robber look than one likes, and you have
such an oppressive realization in these narrow, dark, dingy
streets that you are not in a *Christian* country. Grim-

looking old priests glided along in the streets and most un-
pleasantly associated themselves in our minds with the
horrible days of the Inquisition, but we took off our wraps
and concluded to make the best of a bad bargain.   Candles were brought in and we ordered a fire.   The wood,
when it came, consisted of a few little sticks and a great
hamper of *grape prunings* tied up in little bundles, and
burned in a porcelain-covered stove made into a fire-place.
Table d'hote was soon ready, and to our surprise we found the
salle a manger a beautiful room and the dinner the very nicest,
richest meal we had enjoyed this side the Atlantic.   The
proprietor did the service himself and soon convinced us that
the bustling and confusion on our arrival was just a little
" natural flustration " caused by anxiety to do just the
right thing for " the American."   So we ate our dinner in
high, good humor, came up stairs, gathered round our little
stove, listened to the jingling of the bells on the donkeys
in the snow carts, and the strange, wild shouts of the
shovelers, asked each other what we thought of ourselves
in this queer old city of Bologne, and wound up as we
usually do with wondering what our friends at home
would think if they could but peep in on us.

Morning came, and when we went down to breakfast the
proprietor enquired how we slept, expressing his fears that
we might have been disturbed, as they were shovelling
snow from the roof all night.   He told us it was *a metre*
deep, and took us out to show us how it was banked up in
the court-yard.   It is more than three feet deep almost
anywhere, and as the streets are all solidly paved and very
narrow you may guess how the rain and melting snow
streams down them.   Breakfast over, the gentlemen went
over to the station and were told we could leave at five in
the afternoon, though the proprietor stoutly affirmed we

could not. When we *would* go, he could scarcely be *made* to comprehend that the "Americano" would *walk* a mile through that "very much cold" to the station in order to let the ladies see more of the city. But we got off at last, though the half-melted snow was still falling. It was about the strangest walk we ever had. Such eyes as stared at us! How handsome many of them, and how fearfully ugly others were! What a set of vagabonds and ruffians the shovelers looked! and what dark, dingy little shops lined the sidewalks, and last, but not least, what piles on piles of *Bologna sausage!*

In due time we were at the station, and, to our great regret had to convince ourselves that our Italiano had not told us more, than the truth when he declared we could not get over the mountains to-night. Notice to that effect was posted by the authorities in the station, and the guard would not allow us to pass. Our porter had followed us down in the sure hope of taking us back. He told the rebel guard in a dazed kind of a way, that "the Americans *walked* down there," and what was more we walked back again and let him drive his hack alone. The proprietaire met us at the door, not at all discomposed that we had not accepted his statement of the situation, showed us up stairs, ordered us a fire, and announced *table d'hote* in half an hour. It was nicer than the first, and we concluded we might be just as comfortable here as in Rome in such weather. It is a great disappointment though, when we had tried so hard to arrange for three days in that city. It has proved a larger joke than we thought when Mr. A. wrote "snowed in" opposite our names in the register. However, setting aside the detention, we have had rather a pleasant day without any cause of complaint against our hotel—the charges being about $2.50 for everything.

We are all very well and really cheerful and happy. But
the rest of the party are asleep, the fire is out, the clock
in a gloomy old church across the street has just struck
one, and as we intend making an effort to get off on a
seven o'clock train in the morning, I have but five hours
left for sleeping. So, good night."

CHAPTER VI.

NAPLES—THE MEDITERRANEAN.

" I think I wrote you last from Bologna, but I have forgotten where it was mailed, as we could not get stamps
there in the hurry of our leaving. We got on to Florence
without any hindrance from the snow. In fact we thought
if we had been in America they would have gone on until
they *found* the road blocked, instead of deciding that it
" might be," and tumbling us out so unceremoniously at
Bologna. There is very little trestleing on the road,
though any deficiency there is more than compensated
for by quite an excess of tunneling. Much of the way
the mountains were entirely wrapped in snow. It was a
cold, grand, cheerless-looking country. Peak towered over
peak, crag over crag, and it seemed to us as if eternal
silence as well as eternal snow might reign there. Toward
noon we began to get out of the tunnels, and to get glimpses
of pretty little valleys away down below us, with diminutive houses and miniature gardens, laid off and planted
with the greatest precision, up to the very brink of the
clear, pretty little stream that wound along below us. The

snow seemed melting away too. The clouds commenced rifting and the sun broke out in golden splendor, lighting up the great, black mountain sides, and making their snowy summits glitter and sparkle like diamond crowns. Entering the valley of the Arno, spring seemed to greet us everywhere, and our thermometers ran up from 48°, where they stood in Bologna, to nearly 60° as we held them out of the carriage windows.

We had not intended stopping at Florence, but there are so few trains on these Italian railways, we found ourselves compelled to lie over from the afternoon till ten at night. To add to our perplexity we could not find the right department of the endless station-house for our train to Rome. Each of the three classes of passengers here has its own offices, waiting-rooms, luggage-rooms, &c., into which no traveler of another class is permitted to enter. This, of course, requires the station-houses to be just three times the size which seems necessary to us, besides which there is a station for trains from the same points which pass through different intermediate points. After quite a walk round the depot, we found the right corner, got our satchels weighed, deposited and receipted, and immediately set off for a walk over Florence and a visit to the Uffizi and Pitti Palaces. When we were tired walking, and had despaired of getting policemen to give directions as to the way, we took a cab, showed the coachman the names of the palaces in our Cook's Guide, and were soon over the Arno, out of the cab and walking up the piazzi or open square in front of the palaces. Some other time I will tell you my impressions of what we saw, or as nearly as I can what all the splendor of the place is like. We walked and walked through the grounds, hoping every half hour would take us round, and always finding an avenue of more magnifi-

D

cence, a vista of greater beauty, a prettier lake, or a more
charming little island, till tired nature pleaded for weary
limbs, and we sought anxiously for an exit out of the wonderful place.   I do not remember to have ever seen four more
thoroughly exhausted people than we were when we got
back to the Station Hall and threw ourselves down on the
divans to await our dinner from the adjoining Buffet, as
they call the restaurant in Italy.   But beefsteaks and *cafe
au lait* soon "set us to rights," and a nice warm fire and
cheerful conversation finished up very pleasantly what had
promised to be a long, dull evening.

Once in our compartment, we settled ourselves for the
night.   A shilling in England, or a lira in Italy, dropped
into the hand of a guard ensures you the carriage for your
party unless there is an unusual number of passengers, and
this night we tried the merit of the arrangement.   Unlike
in America, there is here no conductor on the trains.
The carriages or compartments are sections of the coach
with two seats running from side to side, sufficient to ac-
commodate eight persons, who sit facing each other.   This
of course necessitates half the party to ride "backwards."
First-class compartments are furnished in about the style
of our ordinary trains at home, except that they are
scarcely lighted at night and have no heating apparatus
except for the feet—hot water in iron cases.   Second-class
is plainer.   The seats are covered with oil-cloth, there is
no foot-warmer, and occasionally there is an opening at
the ends which permits you to look, when standing, into
the compartment before you.   This is very unpleasant,
owing to the almost universal propensity of Europeans to
smoke when traveling.   But we have not found it very
comfortable on any class train at night.   Warm and pleasant as it was in Florence during the day, we really suffered

that night, though we thought we had an abundant supply of shawls, and had we been compelled to share our
compartment with others, it would have been much worse.
We made the best of it, however, shook ourselves up when
the lazy daylight dragged itself along, rubbed our sleepy
eyes, held an interesting discussion as to what we should
have for breakfast, gathered up our stray property and
held ourselves in readiness for the first glimpse of the
Eternal City. Not much of the grandeur of Rome, however, is visible on entering by our route. It takes you in, I
think at the south-eastern extremity, away from most of the
classical portion of the city, and, any way, we were irreverent
enough to defer "impressions" until after breakfast. By
half-past nine A. M. we were set down at our Hotel Al-
bergo d'Allmague; and not very long thereafter we started
for the coffee room. Refreshed and invigorated, we soon
made out our programme for the day, for instead of the *two*
days which we had certainly counted on for Rome, our
unfortunate detention now limited us to this *one*. We
took a handsome open carriage, with a span of spirited
horses and a rather intelligent Italian coachman, all for
two francs an hour, and set out bravely "to do Rome" in
part of a day. But this, too, I shall keep to tell you sometime when I feel a little more like writing than I do to-
night. We got back just in time for table d'hote, cold,
weary and hungry. Dinner over, we exchanged impressions, wrote a little and soon betook ourselves to our pil-
lows, ready for an early start next morning to Naples.

This was Saturday morning, 8th of March, and though
we had looked forward to Rome with so much interest, yet
I do not think any of us felt much regret at leaving, even
though our stay had been so hurried. Till you come to
Rome you can never have any idea of how repulsive Cath-

olicism is. There it is universal, not a nook or corner did
we see where it did not rear its head. Priests and monks,
monks and priests everywhere. And though we have now
left Rome far behind us, we have still quite a superabun-
dance of "father confessors" around us. One sits at our
table, but to do him justice he is rather innocent-looking.

Well, we left Rome about ten A. M., and had a most delightful day's travel through the prettiest valley we ever
saw. It was the first entirely bright day we had enjoyed
in Europe. In fact though, we had had sunlight a few
hours in Florence, and for a very little while in the morning at Rome, this was the first clear sky we had seen. We
very much feared we should have no opportunity at all to
see the complexion of Italian skies, but we did. The
whole ride was through a deep, green valley.

On each side the mountains piled themselves up to the
sky, with their snow-capped peaks above the clouds, while
in the valley it was but one long-continued beautifully
green garden.

Everywhere the peasants, men and women, were busy in
the fields, spading, plowing by hand, pruning, gathering
up every particle of rubbish, picking salads, pulling up
roots, riding donkeys, leading donkeys, driving donkeys,
and all stopping, straightening up and gazing at the flying
train with as much interest as we of South are accustomed
to see thrown into the same performance by a different
class of laborers. Much of this valley seemed to be
meadow land of the richest kind, and everywhere, even
amid the greenest crops, trees were regularly planted, we
supposed for the double purpose of shade from summer
heat and for trellises for the almost universal vine, which
is festooned from one to another.

We felt as if we were going South very fast, for though
it had been warm at noon in Florence, it was cold in Rome.

In fact we could not have had a worse time for our journey. Deep snows seems to have fallen all over Europe, and the severity of the cold has been much worse than the depression of the mercury would indicate, owing to the terrible east winds and the driving snow and rain which fell at the same time. In Geneva they had not had a fire in the dining-room before in twelve years. We have worn our heavy clothing all the time, and have been none too comfortable with it. But this day we rode with our compartment windows all open, and the air was as mild and balmy as in our spring.

At Paracello, fifteen miles from Naples, we got our first view of Vesuvius. It stood out in bold relief, grandly distinct from the other mountains, great, yawning chasms running down its sides deep and dark from summit to base, while a soft, white cloud hung lazily round its ragged crater. The enthusiasm of one half of the party rose to white heat with the anticipation of making the ascent and looking down into that famous old crater. The other half, however, decided that a picture gallery would be much more inviting. We ran almost round Vesuvius in going into the city, and had some beautiful views of the villages which dot its base. At our distance the houses looked like toy castles lying in the shadow of a great, grim old giant. Our first view of the bay was rather a disappointment, and the earlier part of the drive to our hotel was through a most miserable part of the city. But as we went on towards the middle of the circle which Naples makes around its magnificent bay, the view became every moment more and more beautiful, till by the time we reached the Hotel des Estrangers the most prosaic of mortals could not have resisted the enchantment of the scene. Our balconies opened out directly on the bay, and just beneath was one

of the most beautiful drives and promenades in the world.
How often have we stood out there and drank in the beauty
and harmony, the life and gayety of the scene. Across
from us, seeming to rise out of the water, stands the solemn,
smoking old mountain, forever suggesting what possibilities
may lie wrapped up in its awful caverns, while away up
and beyond us rise the heights of the city, crowned with
castle-like buildings, white and glittering in the sun-light,
and dim and shadowy in the circle of lamp-light, which
girdled the city at night. A thousand rays dance on every
wave in the bay, every shade, every tint of earth or sky
seems to linger lovingly over that quivering sheen. The
sun was just sinking below the heights when we went first
on our balcony. Not many words escaped us, except to
point to some spot which we feared the others might lose
in looking too long elsewhere, and we looked and lingered,
lingered and looked, and, for the first time since leaving
London let table d'hote wait till we were ready.

Most Americans, we suppose, patronize Des Estrangers.
At any rate, the stars were scarcely out when the organ
grinders were serenading under our balcony. Heard for a
few times, their voices seem very fine. I was struck with
the sound of the language in song. Nearly all their names
end in a vowel, and in speaking they continue these sounds
so much. In singing, everything seems to end in *ola, ina,*
or *ia.* Sabbath morning they woke us with their singing
and playing, and whenever we were on the balcony, when
they thought they had entertained us sufficiently, they
would pull off their caps, hold them up, jabber to us in
Italian, and finish up invariably with the polite French,
" *S'il vous plait.*"

We are going out now for a stroll on the streets, to look
into the shops, &c., get a week day impression of this

pretty, airy, gay-looking city. One thing we noticed yesterday was, that there was not half the business going on
that there was in Paris on Sabbath. There we saw scarcely
a closed door. Our hotel was undergoing repair and the
work went on that day just the same as on any other. Everywhere it was just the same, just as much buying and selling as on other days. Those who could afford the time
went to Mass and heard the organ and sermon, and then
amused themselves afterwards. Those who could *not* afford
the time, stayed at home and conducted themselves on the
general principle of, "Business before pleasure." Here in
Naples it is not near so much the case, but I have no idea
how it is to be explained.

The lazzaroni here, as in Rome, have beset us everywhere. Many of them are as stout and strong, and could
earn their living just as easily, as other people, but just
listen to them, just only turn your head towards them and
oh, they are the most *afflicted* beings you ever beheld.
Just put out your hand to push them out of your path and
they are so blind they cannot get out of your way, or so
lame that your touch sends them reeling headlong in the
street. They roll helplessly in the dust and declare by
their whines and groans that you have literally "knocked
them down" and are therefore in honor bound to double
the number of centimes which are certainly their due.

We never will forget a professedly lame boy who went
through this interesting performance for us yesterday
morning, nor how awfully savage he looked after us when
neither his entreaties, his being "knocked over," nor even
his tears and lamentations commanded the centimes. In
fact, independent America cannot form the least idea of
the sycophancy of Europe, the everlasting solicitation for
a "gratuity." Every public building is guarded. There

are wardens, or porters, or "housekeepers" or self-appointed guides at every door. They thrust themselves on you, and perhaps cannot speak a word you can understand except the names which you can see in the guide books, and then, oh how much "righteous indignation" flames out of their great, black eyes, if from one to four francs do not drop into their greedy palms. But we will soon be out of Europe.

We have crossed the Atlantic in safety, if not in comfort, have traversed the Continent, seen some of its wonders, enjoyed many of its beauties, and are now ready to embark on the Mediterranean. Kind Providence has kept "the everlasting arm underneath and around us," and, save our detention, at Bologna, not one unpleasant circumstance has befallen us.

March 12th.—We left "beautiful Naples" Monday, at half-past one P. M., and it was with some regret, for except the Bay and the situation of the city we felt that we had seen nothing. The day was warm and bright, and we looked back longingly at the handsome buildings, the spires and towers, and the crowded hill-tops, all glowing in the golden light. A small row boat took us out in the Bay to where our steamer was lying, and by two o'clock we were safely established in our cabin, and, for the third time, "at sea." Our steamer was the *Africa*, of the Rubatino Line, and a very quiet, comfortable boat, though I suppose I should make one exception in favor of voyagers who are not accustomed to pay "tribute to Neptune," and that is the fact of having but two meals per day—unless "black coffee" in the morning be accounted one. On the *Cuba* we had five, and became very weary of it; but here they certainly have touched the other extreme. The *cuisine* of Southern Europe is very different from our preconceived opinions. There is very much less of brandy, in all forms, and the favorite methods of flavoring are very simple. Here "vin ordinaire" is put on the table, as water is, and the meats and sauces are plain and wholesome. It seems to me quite a nice idea, too, to substitute innocent fruit and nuts, with good plain bread and butter, for the heavy, expensive and troublesome desserts now so common in the South—quite as nice as the "plain breakfast" of good, *cold* bread, butter and coffee which one finds all over Europe. At first, we saw it with some dismay, but now I would not wish anything nicer. I think, in fact, it would afford me real satisfaction to introduce a reform in the dining rooms at home, and though there might be a revolt at first, the new regime would soon become very agreeable and beneficial in a hygienic point of view.

After breakfast all who can betake themselves to the deck and while away, (as best they can) the long hours, till the musical ring of the dinner bell at four summons them to a more interesting employment. Then comes a pleasant promenade on the deck again, in the soft evening air, which is really very delightful. The two evenings "your correspondent" was so fortunate as to enjoy under these circumstances, we remained above until "the stars were out" and the moon in the sky. The first night we leaned over the side of the ship and looked long and quietly at the million of diamond sparkles in the rolling waves, our thoughts going back tenderly, in that soft evening hour to those "near and dear" in our far away American homes. Around us was a motley group. Here as everywhere else *priests* were gliding around. Indeed their repulsive black robes do seem to be ubiquitous. One sits by us at table, and looks the very picture of innocence, altogether as if there had never been a Jesuit, and never would be another Inquisition if he had his way. He and others of his "craft," under the guidance of a very Bishop of Holy Rome, are going on a pilgrimage to the Sepulchre, and everywhere they are gliding—I had almost said stealing—about the ship with their devotional books before their eyes, or else their devoutly bent heads and whispering lips proclaim the pious elevation of their thoughts to every beholder. To-day, Friday, is a fast day, and of course they are somewhat exercised about their diet—not being more inclined than others to miss the two meals afforded by the ship. The Bishop informed some of the passengers that it was permitted—*licet*—to eat as others when they were traveling, (a convenient religion, is it not?) but still they have just taken their dinners alone on soup and maccaroni, and this morning breakfast was made without meat for their consciences' sake. But contrary to what we would expect, the *Africa* with all its mixed nationalities is an extremely quiet boat. Not a loud word is spoken anywhere. The crew is the most silent set of rough, unhappy, poverty-stricken looking creatures I ever saw.

Tuesday morning at sunrise we passed through "the straits" of Messina, with "Scylla on the one hand and Charybdis on the other." It was such a morning as one sees rarely throughout even a lifetime. The Mediterranean with its changing hues, now green, now brown, was then of the deepest, clearest blue, just as was the cloudless sky overhead, while the brilliance of the early morning sun was almost overpowering. The Straits are very narrow, and seem just a little ahead of the ship to come entirely together. On each side the scenery is magnificent. I think we agreed with each other, that not even the Bay of Naples was finer. The latter seems very much alike round a great part of its semi-circular form, but at Mes-

sina the view was always changing, always new, and so
boldly, beautifully picturesque. The mountain peaks
towered grandly up everywhere, and there seemed to be
one continuous village along their slopes. Mount Etna came
into view early in the morning, and seemed to be a great
white dome on the summit of an immense cone. At four
P. M. we would pass very near and be able to secure an
excellent view, but the blinding glare of the sun, and
wind, and, above all, "the pitiless sea," drove me from the
deck, with a feeling that a dozen Etnas would not take me
back up there. Indeed, I "surrendered unconditionally,"
without any expectation of seeing either deck or table
any more till we should be ready to go ashore, but to my surprise all our party spent the last day up stairs most pleasantly. We passed near the scene of Paul's shipwreck,
looked at the precipitous cliffs of the Island of Crete, and
thought as we looked at a pretty white village away up
above the waves, of the great Apostle's reiteration of the
poet's assertion, "The Cretans are always liars."

Friday morning we knew that we were not far from our
long looked for destination, that we would see the light-
house perhaps by ten or eleven o'clock, and our thoughts
and conversation were so occupied with Egypt and our
future life and work there, that we did not feel at all like
going down to our rooms, but we were told that the entrance to the harbor was a very dangerous one, and was
attempted only in daylight, that ships always lie to and
wait for morning. So we concluded to take things quietly,
go to sleep, and wake up as fresh as possible for the first
glimpse of Alexandria. And now here we are at nine
o'clock Saturday morning lying in the harbor, the gentlemen having gone ashore to find Mr. Ewing, and the ladies
contenting themselves as best they can by finishing up their

letters before taking more than a bird's eye view of this
strange city. In an hour or two we hope to be in the
home of some of our friends, and to feel that, at least for
a time, our wanderings are over.

CHAPTER VII.

ALEXANDRIA.

" At ten o'clock last Saturday morning we found ourselves on Egyptian soil. Going on deck all sorts of strange
sights met our eyes. The city lay stretched out before us
with its mosques, domes, turrets and towers. Just to our
left was one out of the many of the Viceroy's splendid
palaces, and the whole view on the shore as well as in the harbor, had an indescribable something about it which was
different in its effect from anything we ever saw before.
Arabs were walking leisurely around the deck, while below dozens of row-boats with their swarthy rowers were
swarming around the ship and keeping the sharpest "look
out" for any simple fish which might drop into their shark-
like jaws. One of these natives was standing at the head
of the stairs when we came up laughing all over his yellow face at the idea of getting such a cargo to the wharf. On
my inquiring of the gentlemen if he were a Copt he laughed
more broadly still and answered himself in broken English,
" I your boatman." He wore a crimson turban, and a loose,
clean, white robe, I suppose I might call it in the absence
of a better name, fastened in at the waist with a crimson
girdle made of several yards of cloth twisted and bound

tightly around the person. The dress of this one was very short, reaching but little more than below the knee. The other rower was clad in the same primitive style except that his "outer garment" was dark blue. No two looked alike, in fact of all the nondescript styles of dress *for men* that ever we saw we concluded that these were either the worst or the best, the highest or the lowest. Then when we stepped ashore such a Babel!—such an Arabic Babel! How they gesticulated and screamed and literally yelled in our faces, and how angry they seemed. Yet that we found was only the Arab style of being "in earnest"— driving a bargain. Our missionary friends understand this species of humanity of course, and they pushed through them and took us directly to the Custom House, a Coptic officer of which had come from the shore to the ship in order to keep Messrs. A. and G. in sight until all our passports should be forthcoming. He kept right at our elbow until all forms were duly complied with, and we furnished with small squares of tin in order to admit us into the city. Mr. Strang took a carriage for us, got us and our luggage into it amid a torrent of deafening gutturals about the price, quietly handed the driver what he knew to be quite sufficient, though it was but one-third of his demand, and then read in his eye that it was one shilling more than he expected to receive. And now our eyes began to *dilate* more and more. One of us, at least, might have sat for a picture of Wonder, another for Amusement, and perhaps one might have passed for Disgust, while the fourth one was taking position as Philosophy.

The carriage just wound about in the narrow crooked streets with often only room to creep past the people walking, turning this way to avoid driving over a poor Arab asleep in the sun beside his basket of bread and eggs,

snoring away undisturbed by the swarm of flies which was
very energetically engaged in exploring the unknown regions of his wide open mouth; now turning that way to
keep off an old woman's feet as she cried her basket of
vegetables and shouted, "Keep off: Do you not know this
is the market?" Now we turn into a wider street, and the
driver calls into requisition all his skill to get past *a stream*
of donkeys, drays, carriages, dogs, men, women and children, all the time screaming to them, "Keep out of my
way and I'll keep out of yours!" On every side were queer
little shops, with queerer-looking shop-keepers. Perhaps
the whole "stock in trade" would be a half dozen bushels
of nuts in one, or a bushel of apples in another, a few
baskets of native beans in a third, a handful of tobacco in
a fourth, some ugly cheese in a fifth, &c., &c. All the
shops are raised two or three feet from the ground, and the
proprietor or salesman *sits* in the midst of his goods. Here
would be somebody *cooking* on the street, there a man taking his breakfast. Here was a shoemaker plying his trade.
Beside him might have been a repairer of old water bags
made of entire goat skins. Here was a dyeing establishment, with the wet goods hung in the street to dry. Here
a case of jewelry, perhaps out in the street, with the
owner sitting on the ground beside it holding an umbrella
over it or himself, or may be both. Here is a native
woman in a rose-colored silk dress. There is another in a
light blue one. Both are in *Frank** style except that they
wear a white cloth over their heads instead of a hat. But
the most marvelous of all was the peculiar native dress, or
veil rather, for the women, which is sometimes white, but
oftener black and blue. When black it is very, very dis-
mal looking, and when white it gives one the sensation of

*Egyptian term for *Foreign* as opposed to *native*.

having seen a ghost. It is called the habarah, and is, in shape, like a sheet I think. They put it over the head, bring it round in front, letting it reach to the feet all round, lap it over and push it under a belt at the waist, leaving some freedom to the arms. Of course then it gives a straight corpse-like figure which is startling when, as we did this morning, you happen to stumble suddenly upon three or four pure white habarahs gliding along the street. But, as if this costume were not yet sufficiently hideous, they fasten a piece of cloth over the face just below the eyes by means of a reed which is placed up and down the forehead, and which is ornamented with a number of gold rings. I never see one of these reeds on a woman's forehead without being forcibly reminded of the *yokes* which I used to see put on the heads of unruly animals to reduce them to submission—not that there is a resemblance in form, but it seems so uncomfortable to be bound up in that close ugly fashion. They regard it a great disgrace for the *mouth* to be exposed, particularly for profane eyes to witness such a modest, refined performance as an Arab woman taking her meals. She keeps her veil down and stealthily conveys her food bit by bit to her lips, under its thick folds. But no description can do one of these habarahs justice.

But to return to our drive to the Mission House. We reached there of course in much less time than I have taken to tell you about it, and found a warm welcome awaiting us. I am sure you can imagine our sensations better than I can describe them. I am sure I was scarcely conscious that I had never met any of the Missionaries before, and not for one moment did I feel inclined to indulge in any form of *homesickness*, that terrible malady which has always heretofore attacked me most violently on first finding myself in a new and strange situation.

It is rather a queer thought, though, that America is not to be our home any more; that here we are to live and work, and if God will, die here."

The mission to Egypt was commenced in the year 1854. In the fall of 1853, Dr. J. G. Paulding, of the Associate Reformed church mission at Damascus, visited Egypt to ascertain if a mission could be successfully established in that country. His impressions were decidedly favorable. In 1854 Rev. Thomas McCague and wife sailed for Egypt to inaugurate a mission. They were soon joined by Rev. James Barnett from the Damascus mission. In two years afterward Dr. Lansing from the same mission was located at Alexandria and was assisted by Mr. John Hogg, (now Dr. Hogg), of Scotland. Miss Sarah Dales, (now Mrs. Lansing), also of the Damascus mission, soon joined them. This was the incipiency of the mission, and nearly every year since has witnessed some increase of the working force.

In regard to this mission, Dr. Monfort, of the *Herald and Presbyter*, says: " Before I went to Egypt I had heard it as the judgment of missionaries of the American Board in Turkey, and of the Presbyterian Board in Syria, that the work of the United Presbyterian Board in Egypt was very prosperous and hopeful, and that the missionaries in charge were highly qualified and very efficient. With as much deliberation as I ever expressed an opinion, I must say that these persons, taken together, as a band of laborers, are entitled to the first rank among laborers in the foreign field." Drs. Barr and Stewart who were sent out by the U. P. Board of Missions, to inspect their missions, say in their report: " From our survey of the fields and the work, we would here testify to the faithfulness and efficiency of our missionaries, both male and female, and express the conviction that there are few, if any, more successful missions under the care of any church, than our own in Egypt." "The missionaries select great centres and operate in these, and from these. On the Sabbath they preach regularly in the churches or stations. They make use of schools, colleges and other institutions of learning. Orphanages and hospitals are established. Itinerating tours are made. Books and tracts are distributed. General visitation is done, and supervision exercised. House to house visitation or Zenana work is performed by the female missionaries."

This then was the mission into which Mrs. Giffen had entered and these her fellow-laborers in toil. The present statistics of this mission, are as follows :

Foreign missionaries, male and female,	24
Native ministers,	11
Teachers and helpers,	124
Total working force,	159
Communicants,	1149

"I know you are quite anxious to hear our impressions of Mission Work in Alexandria, and I am equally as anxious to tell you how much gratification and encouragement our first Sabbath here afforded us. The previous afternoon, just on our arrival at Mr. Ewing's, the native pastor, Aboona Buktor, called and was introduced to us. He was formerly a priest in the Coptic Church and is still so called, Aboona being the Arabic term. He greeted us in a very warm, friendly way, and seemed quite as much interested as the missionaries in our arrival. He is a tall slender man of quite brown complexion, and was altogether in native dress. You may imagine that we looked at him with peculiar interest. His presence was a most convincing argument of the success of Missions here, for had he remained in the Coptic Church he would now have been *Patriarch*. On leaving he extended us the usual good-bye —*May your evening be blessed*, and added " God be praised that you have come in peace!" Sabbath morning at eight o'clock we were off for Arabic service. On going in we found one-fourth of the church *curtained* off from the rest for the women, by means of a temporary arrangement which is easily removed when our service is over. Here we took our seats, amid, or rather in front of, those strange looking women and heard our first Arabic sermon, Mr. Strang occupying the pulpit for the day. I think I may safely say I was edified, notwithstanding I did not catch one single articulate sound from the sermon. The stillness, the perfect quiet of the audience was marked. There was not a sound other than the preacher's voice save the welcome rustle of the leaves as the men looked up every passage referred to in the sermon. The singing was really beautiful, very smooth and musical, and every way so much nicer than we heard an hour later in the English service. There were perhaps sixty or sixty-five natives present, of whom thirteen were women. After service Mrs. S. introduced me to all the latter as "Sitt Gededa"—the new lady—and they shook my hand quite cordially. The little girls first touched my hand with their lips and then raised it to their forehead, which is a form of salutation used by inferiors. The women, of course, all wore *habarahs*, either white or black, and nearly all had on quite an amount of jewelry. One of them had at least half a dozen strands of pearls in her necklace, immense sprays of them for earrings, and two or three very large rings on her fingers, also set with them. A native woman's earrings, by the way, must be seen to be appreciated. These were almost the size of the palm of your hand. The men, of course, constituted much the more intelligent part of the audience. They were very bright looking—several of them quite handsome in fact. Perhaps half of them were in Frank dress—except the tarboosh, which is never discarded. They lingered around the gate a few moments and were introduced to us. Almost all made some pleasant little remark which our friends translated for us, and one or two greeted us in very pretty English. About ten of the women are members of the church, and probably there is an equal proportion of the men, but of this I am not sure. Anyway it was a cheering sight, those native women once so ignorant, now regular attendants and members of a Protestant church, and those self-righteous Coptic men, now such careful, attentive, intelligent hearers of the Gospel of Jesus Christ!

After I learned the alphabet *and began spelling a little*, Mrs. Ewing proposed taking me with her, partly for the exercise but principally that I might accustom my ear to native accent and pronunciation. I was at first very reluctant to go. I could not overcome my repugnance to the idea of *riding a donkey*, and I dreaded the interior of native houses. I suppose I had a little wicked feeling that it would be time enough to go among them and take their famous coffee and other refreshments when I knew their language somewhat and could urge *duty* as a plea for submitting to the infliction. However, Mrs. E. continued to urge me, saying that she did not know how to explain it, but she always came back from there with such a bouyant, cheerful feeling, that she was sure it did her good to go, and that the other ladies felt the same way about it. In a desperate sort of a way I at last consented, the donkeys were ordered, and Mr. Ewing went down to see us off. The miserable little things do not look much more than twice the size of the saddle, and are very little taller than the

top of a chair. Well, yes, I suppose that is a little
exaggeration of their diminutiveness and general insignifi-
cance, but really their ears do seem to be a very large part
of them. The saddles are, like most other things here, a
peculiarly oriental institution, not like anything you ever
saw in the Western World. There is a frame of some kind
to which the stirrups are attached and the rest is cloth and
wadding. There are no "ladies' saddles" either. Native
men and women all ride alike, but for Frank women they
knot up the superfluous stirrup, and the pommel of the
saddle answers the purpose of our "horn."

My introduction to my first donkey did not greatly
prepossess me in his favor, though I suppose he was a fair
specimen of his race. If any living creature ever did look
like "patience on a monument" he did. It was decidedly
fair to say he looked all "ears, saddle and bridle," for he
wore two of the latter, though it seemed to me fine irony
to suppose that one was not more than sufficient to manage
him. To add to his ungainliness he had very recently been
both "shorn and shaven" and "his bones stood out." The
donkey boys assured us they were fine fellows, and after a time
Mr. Ewing got me into the saddle, gave me the reins and
I started. The little fellow impressed me as being very
weak in his constitution, at any rate in his back and limbs,
but they all said he would improve after we rode awhile.
We turned the corner and went about fifty yards, when
they both commenced pacing very nicely indeed. There
was a large stone building going up very near us, and many
of the fragments were lying around; just when I was
beginning to repent some of my harsh judgments about my
donkey he struck his foot on a stone, fell sprawling, tumbled
me over in the dust and wound up by rolling over on top
of me. The donkey boys pulled him up pretty soon, said

nice things to him in Arabic, and I picked myself up with the impression that I had a very badly sprained ankle. One of the workmen ran out very kindly with a cup of cold water, and Mr. Ewing very soon came to our relief. In a few minutes I found that I was only bruised a little and we got on and started again. It was a very pretty ride out, and as you pass through "the gates," by the palm grove and by large fig trees, and get out into the desert one realizes more than ever that you are in an eastern country. The glare of the sun was very trying on my eyes at first. I rode with them closed as much as I dared on my stumbling donkey, not only to shut out the light, but, what is far worse, the limestone dust, which is extremely excoriating to the eye. We stopped first at Aboona Buktor's. He lives in a large stone house—that is, like other people, he has a suite of rooms, perhaps one floor of a house ; and although the stairway looked very forbidding, yet we were shown into a nice plastered room, with high ceiling and good windows. There was a very neat set of plain parlor chairs, one or two tables and a divan, extending the whole length of the room. On this sat the Aboona *writing a sermon.* His Bible and some other books lay beside him. He and his wife received us very cordially, inquired for "our state,' etc., etc. Immediately the Sitt went out and ordered refreshments in the shape of a glass of *tam-a-ra-hind.* It is a concoction peculiar to the East, and is not quite as palatable as bad vinegar and water. It was well *sugared,* but we did not see the process of putting in that ingredient, though there were no spoons in sight. I held my breath and drank hard. The Aboona then inquired after my progress in Arabic, wished to know my particular difficulties. Mrs. Ewing told him I was past *b-a, ba, b-o, bo, etc.,* and that I was getting on respectably. He said *ty-ib,* (good) and smiled

on me approvingly. Then he had his wife to bring in their
wallad and *bint,* (boy and girl) for us to admire, and in fact
they were very good-looking children. They and their
mother were in a kind of a half Frank style, and did not
look so badly. Having made our compliments to them we
mounted our donkeys and rode on to the next house, which
was also a second story. There is always a heavy iron
knocker on the door at the foot of the stairs, and if you
want to go in, where there is no bow-wab, you strike the
knocker and call out your name. Mrs. E. gave this one a
vigorous rattle and called out, "Ana, Sitt!" which is
equivalent to "I, the lady," in English. Sitt Bista received
us very pleasantly, and escorted us through the hall into
her drawing room. I do not use this last term in any irony
either. It was a nice room, and was furnished with two
very handsome divans. In one corner was a pretty
circular table, which with a few very good chairs, completed
the furniture of the room. It sounds rather nicely, does it
not, these really good pieces of furniture in a Coptic
drawing room. It doesn't seem so very disagreeable to
crawl up on those pretty divans, loll lazily on as many
cushions as you like to have about you and look at your
full length portrait in the mirror every time you get on
your feet. Oh, but my good friends you didn't peep into
the kitchen, as we did when we went through the hall ;
you didn't see the rubbish of centuries, apparently, piled
up in there till it got *so thick* that the *cooking* seemed to
have been moved out *into the hall* from dire necessity ; you
didn't look into the open bed room door and see *bed* clothes,
wearing apparel, shoes, lamps, books, dishes, withered
vegetables, old chairs, torn mats, broken tables, oil cans
and every other such thing imaginable, mingled together as if
they might have been churned up in a whirlwind for a

week. You didn't draw your breath in easily and softly to keep from taking in an unnecessary amount of the black looking dust which has been sailing around through that house ever since it has been a house, but last, most and worst of all you didn't inhale the awful odors which breathed around that house ! How anybody *lives* in it is a marvel to me. I am sure it would give any Frank a fever in two days.

Well our hostess seated us very nicely, sat down herself and talked in a quiet, easy way for a few moments, and then went out for some glasses of tamarahind. My goblet had unmistakably the dust of a week settled on it, and there were not wanting indications that it had been used at least once before since it had been subjected to a bath. I looked at it in dismay, but I decided that delay would be fatal, and immediately I began to drink it. But I got on badly and at length gave it up with half the contents yet in the goblet. Sitt Bista saw it and concluded that Sitt Gededah hadn't learned to drink tamarahind yet, but perhaps might get on better with coffee. So off she went again and made coffee *in the hall,* the fire being in a little brasier, the coffee urn being about a half pint in size, and the cups in which the coffee was served about the size of an egg. They are of beautiful china, and instead of a saucer the cup of coffee is placed within another which has a little pedestal. The coffee is pounded very fine instead of being ground, and to it Arabs add pounded spices and not infrequently nuts also. I contrived to dispose of this decoction lest a worse should come in its place, and then the Bibles were brought out, a chapter read, and we took our leave.

The next house made no attempt at style, the divans were there, but the coverings and mattresses were all piled up in a corner and there was dust everywhere, but the Sitt was a pleasant pretty woman, just what would be called a beautiful brunette at home. She wore a neat print wrapper and her house had plenty of good fresh air about it. She is very proud of being able to read and brought in her Bible immediately. I am sure nobody in America ever heard such reading as she did. It would tear a western woman's throat to pieces to thunder out such terrible gutturals in her style. It was stunning, startling and deafening all at the same time.

At the third house there had been a whirlwind in the drawing-room as well as in the bed-room, and this without any exaggeration. The divan frames were in their place, but their furniture, the tables, chairs, rockers, baby's carriage, books and everything else were in terrible confusion. However they explained that the room had leaked the night before, and, beside, the baby, the last child of eight, was sick and its mother was shut up with it in her bed-room, where the air was truly stifling. The father is a scribe, and is a very handsome man, besides being handsomely dressed. Indeed it is a handsome family. The baby is a bright, intelligent child, and if it was treated to a moderate supply of warm water and fresh clothing, it would be hard to find a prettier one. He is *eight months* old and he is *engaged* to a double cousin across the street of about his own age. I think there are two *mothers-in-law* in both these families, and they are such looking creatures as one would run from at home, but no matter what they are doing they *always kiss us on both cheeks.* You may guess how thankful I am that they do not believe in the economical American style of doing it all at once on your lips. Even as it is, it is almost unendurable to catch their breath as they pass from one side to the other. Both houses are terrible, I never saw anything like it, and yet all these families are in good circumstances. Their houses are as good as we live in, and if they would, they might be so cozy and comfortable. Still I am sure I could soon become quite attached to these women, and after a little perhaps I shall not mind their terrible houses, their spiced coffee, the dust, the fleas, &c.

Never in my life I think did I so appreciate God's pure fresh air, as when we came down from the last house, got on our donkeys and started for home. I saw very clearly why the ladies all felt so comfortable on returning from there.

Would you like to have some additional "impressions" of Alexandria? Leaving the bazaars, the "fish market," the orange market, the fruit and vegetable markets, the native shops with their "thousand and one" venders of as many different commodities, you need walk but a very short distance to find yourself in what seems a beautiful *European* city. You "elbow" your way through a noisy, busy, chattering jam of every nationality under the sun apparently, where there is nothing scarcely that you ever saw before, where you can not throw off the feeling of being in another world almost, and you turn a corner or two, enter wide, well-paved, handsome streets, with great rows of massive stone buildings on either side, and without stretching your imagination very much, you think for a moment you are back on the Continent. It is only for a moment, however, for the yellow faces of the natives, their strange costumes, and especially the crimson *tarboosh*, which gentlemen of every nationality seem to like to wear very soon convince you that you are neither in Florence, Rome nor Naples, but in *Alexandria*, and that, at least on the square, it will not suffer in comparison with any one

of the three former cities. There is a picturesqueness, a
novel beauty about the scene on the Square here which
has no counterpart in Europe. It is especially interesting
to me to creep lazily along late in the afternoon, enjoy the
pure, fresh air, and watch these strange, black-eyed people.
The Square is enclosed by great chains fastened to iron posts,
with here and there an opening sufficient to admit pedes-
trians. All round the four sides of the long parallelogram
which it forms, runs a wide, handsome street on which open
very pretty stores, with large windows filled with ribbons,
flowers, laces, jewelry, and the whole of that catalogue.
In one window the other day I saw a *silver bedstead* dis-
played, and in another some baskets of beautiful *wax fruit
and flowers*. At the latter I stopped, looked in, made a
journey over the ocean while doing so, and walked into a
certain department in your College. It was "noon" with
you, and I venture I saw what was going on in that department very exactly. At the head of the Square is a
very handsome stone building which is colored very pale
blue, and on its front is "Egyptian Telegraph," in large
letters which gives you an idea of quite a civilized government. Just near too the United States flag floats over the
the American Consulate, but it is rather difficult to get up
much enthusiasm over it, for one rarely ever finds an
American clerk, even, in it. The Square is perhaps three
hundred yards long by one hundred in width. At each
side a double row of acacia trees form pretty avenues of
perhaps twenty feet in width, thus leaving a much wider
one in the center. In the center are two very nice kiosks
for the Viceroy's band which plays there every Friday
and Sabbath afternoon, and half-way between these kiosks
and in the center of the parallelogram is a very fine equestrian statue of Mohammed Ali, surrounded by a heavy

bronze and iron railing, outside of which are quite a number of lamp-posts of the same material, each one supporting four or five lamps. So you see the grand old despot is flooded with this glaring Egyptian sunlight all through the day, and as soon as the sun has bidden him good-night a shower of lamp light—I was going to say fell around him, but that will not do, for he is away above the lamps and they shine *up* in his face, and no doubt cause a painful glare in the old hero's eyes as he looks down on his quondam swarthy subjects. The statue stood there in its place almost a year before "public opinion" would allow it to be "unveiled." Mohammedans have a great horror of everything which bears the least approximation to anything like the worship of saints and images, and for a time they resolutely refused to see any difference between the wish to honor a national hero and benefactor by keeping him visibly in the remembrance of his country, and of making his statue an object of religious worship and thereby robbing Allah of due glory.

There is always more or less of a throng around this statue, and when the band is in the kiosks, the whole square is crowded, and the effect is almost indescribable. Half the men who are in European, or, as they say here, Frank dress, have on the crimson cap with its graceful black tassel falling from the top, and these tarbooshes moving through a crowd brighten it up in a way one never sees at home. But the entire costume of the other half of the men is something wonderful. They don *every* color, and have their suits made up in very gay style frequently. The better class have entire suits of a heavy handsome dark crimson cloth, which is very much worn. It is also much used in blue, brown and green, especially "invisible" green and a *yellow* brown. The waist is tight fitting, al-

most like the waist of an ordinary coat, though tightly
closed up in front. It is frequently "faced" with some
kind of cloth of gold, or ornamented in various ways with
gilt cord and braid. To the belt of this waist the loose
trousers are fastened. They consist of *widths and widths*
of the cloth, sewed together like the plain straight skirt
of a dress, cut long enough to reach down to the top of the
foot sometimes, but usually somewhat shorter. At the top
it is plaited into a belt, the plaits showing a depth of perhaps half an inch. At the bottom I presume it is simply
sewed together, except just enough for the foot to pass
through *at the corners.* In plain terms they are just a *bag,*
gathered in at the top, with a *foot* protruding from each of
the lower corners. The other day when I was waiting for
my Greek teacher at the Mission House, Mrs. S. went to the
study and asked the Moslem Sheikh, who is assisting Mr.
S. in the revision of the Psalms, to come to the drawing-
room and give me a lesson. He came in, gave me a
haughty glance, crawled upon the Divan and sat down on
his feet. I was as unceremonious as he, and took an in-
ventory of him before beginning. He wore an immense
turban of different colors, the tight twists of the goods going round his head ever so often. Then there was the
black, outside robe with very large flowing sleeves, and
under that was a very handsome silk one, a blue and white
stripe, which was belted in with a twist of silk goods in
various colors, green, red and yellow predominating. This
sash, by the way is an accompaniment of all the costumes
except that of the lowest class. His shoes were like slippers, made of bright yellow and scarlet leather, tapering
to a very sharp point and turning up about two inches.
The lowest class wear the gellibeyah, which is nothing
more than a coarse sack, with an opening at each of the

upper corners to admit the arms and one in the middle to admit the head. Sometimes it has short sleeves set in the openings, and simply an old white cloth will be wrapped round the head. Sometimes there will be some effort at shaping this primitive garment. It will have a little full-ness given it and a pair of long loose sleeves, and the wearer will have on a tarboosh first, and then a larger and cleaner white cloth wrapped round the outside. He may possibly wear shoes, but this class has generally no cover-ing from the knee down. Other classes frequently wear very pretty shoes. Indeed I have often admired their taste in this part of their dress, and they almost always have a finely shaped foot. The same is true of the women, too. Under a terribly ugly coarse-looking habarah you will see a beautiful foot peep out encased in a very fancy little boot of some very light delicate color, almost white. Besides the costumes already mentioned, there is another which is very striking in its effect. It is just a long white gown, in shape like the black, outside robe, only it is closed up in front, and generally has long flowing sleeves. It is almost always perfectly clean, in fact of a snowy whiteness, and is made apparently of ordinary "domestic" or "muslin." This, the tarboosh and the shoes are the only visible articles of the costume.

Now just imagine all these varieties of dress worn by people of every hue from charcoal black, through all the grades of brown and yellow up to the purest Caucasian white, see them all sauntering round the kiosks listening to and enjoying very spirited music by a band of twenty-four performers, all dressed in the military uniform, which, by the way, is a coat and loose pants of pure white with scarlet and gilt straps, braid, &c., corresponding with the tarboosh, then I think you would agree with me that there

is a charm about it which you never saw before. The trees
are not out yet, in fact they give no evidence of budding,
and perhaps will not for some weeks. But in summer the
square is said to be beautiful. So many birds sing in the
trees in the early morning, and the poor old sleepy Arabs
luxuriate in the shade, and probably never know any other
home. When we have been out late in the evening we see
many of them sleeping, apparently "taking their rest" very
comfortably on the pavements around the square, sometimes
sheltered by boxes and doorways, and sometimes not at all.
There are many "flower sellers" all round there, and I
think many of them never leave. We have frequently
seen them making up their bouquets at eleven o'clock at
night. At one extremity of the square there is a very large
head of water, like the fountains we admired so much in
Italy. It is an immense basin, where many of the natives
make their ablutions, and where the "water carriers" get
their "bottles" filled. These, by the way, are a strictly
oriental institution. Their bottles, you know, are each an
entire goat skin, and they go round with that amount of
water, in those ungainly proportions, thrown over their
shoulders, sprinkling the square and the streets out of the
mouth of the bottle, *alias* the neck of the animal, which
has this advantage over civilized bottles in that it is very
flexible, and allows the carrier to jet it in all directions, for
instance, all over you, if you don't get out of his way.

We live on the third floor here, and the "blue Mediterranean" rolls almost under my window. I often stand
there, count the sails, watch the changing hues and flying
"white caps," and sympathize to the full extent of my
"capacity" with those who "go down to the sea in ships,"
and we almost always know some missionary or traveler, in
whom we feel interested, who is either on his way to Naples

or to Beruit. There have been a great many " rough seas " on the Mediterranean since we came. At night the wind howls and moans, and the waves dash on the shore with an ever varying but ceaseless dirge. The brightest of " silver moons " shines down on it all, glittering and shimmering in a diamond shower on every wave. In the morning the glories of the night have vanished, and I look out on a restless scene. There is moaning and sobbing in the dawning light, as if an uneasy conscience were goading the genius of the sea, till a flood of golden sunlight streams over " the heaving billows " and soothes the ruffled spirit. I tell myself sometimes, when I am at my window, that I never had such an opportunity for cultivating a poetic temperament in my life, but I sadly fear it is all wasted on me. When Byron wrote,

"There is society where none intrudes by the deep sea, and music in its roar,"

he had never crossed the Atlantic in February. In fact I think it often occurs that close acquaintance is fatal to sentiment and romance. At least I frequently look out on this famous sea and think how much of both commodities have been wasted on " the waves," and how much " penny-a-line " poetry has been *manufactured* "to the tune" of the " sea-beat shore."

CHAPTER VIII.

RAMLE—SANITARIUM—FOURTH OF JULY EXCURSION.

"Perhaps you know that we are now in new quarters.

Ramle is one of the suburbs of Alexandria. It is five miles out, but is connected by rail with the city, a train coming out at the hours and returning at the half hours. Almost all the foreign business men of prominence, especially the English, have their summer residences out here ; in fact very many of them live here permanently, and avail themselves of rail connection to attend their places of business. I have no idea of the size of the place, as it is very much scattered, but it seems quite extended when we look over it from the roofs of our houses.

The Mission premises consist of four houses containing six or seven rooms each, and a chapel, which was built principally for the use of the Theological students before the Seminary was removed to Osiout. These buildings occupy two sides of a parallelogram of perhaps 150 x 100 feet. Down the middle of the figure, fronting each row of buildings, is a pretty flower garden, planted with acacia trees, young palms and any quantity of pretty geraniums, &c. Some of the geraniums at the sides of the house are six feet high. The "single fish" seems to grow more luxuriantly than any other variety. You can't imagine what a pleasure this little garden is to us, especially as most of us have always been accustomed to more or less of country life. If you go outside "to walk" you have to go so far to get out of the sand that you come back wearied instead of refreshed. Sometimes we wade through the sand in the streets and go to the palm and fig groves, of which there are a great many, and sometimes we go down to the sea, sit on the beach and watch the dash of the waves. The walk there and back is pleasant, but I do not like to listen to "old ocean's roar." First I think of all from which it separates me, of our first day "at sea," of all the sorrowful thoughts which seem to me inseparable constituents of that day. Then my mind runs on a little farther, and I imagine I am down in the "lower regions" of the old *Cuba* again. I hear a wave dash over the decks and go thumping against the wall of the berth on one side, while the next moment I seize hold of something to keep from tumbling out on the other. In plain terms, I would not have far to go to be sea-sick again, as a matter of fact and not of imagination, for I always find that I have been watching the waves coming and going until the beach on which I am sitting seems to be moving just like the ship did. Sometimes we go up on the "house-tops" and promenade up there. I enjoy that very much, for the view is really one of the prettiest I ever saw. In every direction are handsome buildings, some of them palaces, surrounded with palm groves and lovely flower gardens, in every one of which, when you are near enough, you may listen to the murmur of a fountain or the gentle flow of a little stream brought up by a windmill for the life of the flowers. Just across the street is Villa Julia, the palace to which the Maharajah Duleep Singh took his bride when he married her from the Mission schools in Cairo. Opposite my window, where I am now writing, there is a pretty fountain always flowing in the Villa garden, and the rill-like murmur loses me many a moment. It brings up the recollection of so many cool "branches" in the woods winding around great old hillsides at a dear old home, where many a happy day has been spent on the grassy banks, dabbling with idle fingers in the flowing stream. E

I think any American would be surprised at the sight if he could go with us on the house this evening and count the groves and gardens. One is so accustomed to thinking of there being no vegetation here, that it seems very wonderful to see so much floral luxuriance. Water seems to be the only requisite for growth. We are just in the Desert, and yet where there is sufficient irrigation everything grows as if in the richest soil. It does not "bake," as we say at home. Everything is planted in rows, or rather in little channels, trees, as well as flowers, and thus when the pipes are opened a nice little stream flows around everything. We will have no more rain this season, and consequently we never have to look out in the morning to see if it is clear or cloudy.

American papers have had so much to say recently about Centennials that it has excited quite a little burst of patriotism among those of your countrymen who are spending the summer in Ramle. Being entirely out "of range" of Centennials, we have fallen upon "the next best" thing which is to celebrate *the fourth of July*. As it falls on Sabbath, we are compelled, of course, to take either the fifth or the third, and as the latter is the leisure day of six or seven of us, "we, a handful of Americans," went out and took our tea in a palm grove this evening.

At three o'clock we went down to the station, met the friends from town and bravely took our way through the heat, dust and sand to the grove. We found plenty of shade and a delightfully cool breeze from the sea, but no "green carpet" of grass—nothing but sand and palms, and after a time some camels—the three distinctive features of Egypt. There was plenty of water, however, and the palms far exceeded the number which so gladdened the hearts of the weary Israelites at Elim. I think I would not exaggerate the matter if I should say there were a thousand. I counted *fifteen* in one group, *eighteen* in another, and *twenty-one* in a third, all having sprung from one root. Some of them were quite tall and very graceful, but very few of them were fruit-bearing. They were " in bloom " about six weeks ago, and now the young dates are about as large as grapes.

We selected little mounds in the sand, spread down our shawls, took our seats and congratulated each other on " the fourth," notwithstanding it was only the third. Mr. Ewing had brought out a pocket full of letters and papers, and while the rest of us were resting and enjoying the breeze, he read to us; Mr. N. constructed a pyramid of sand, somebody found a palm branch and Miss D. planted it in the pyramid and unfurled the " red, white and blue " in the shape of a red ribbon, a white handkerchief and a blue vail. Meantime the table-cloth was spread on the sand, and sandwiches, musk-melons, pies, grapes, &c., arranged upon it. Our places were assigned us, and we very gracefully took our seats upon the sand. A blessing was asked and we proceeded " to celebrate the fourth " in a very practical manner. It was very enjoyable, indeed, and I wished many times that some of you could have looked on the little scene—a dozen missionaries taking a nice, quiet tea on the white sands of Egypt, all cheerful and happy, forgetting for the time the 7,000 miles between them and those with whom they had last celebrated the American anniversary.

Just beside us stood a marble monument, about three feet high, having the top carved in the shape of an immense *turban*. The gentlemen all pronounced it the grave of a Sheik. There is a belief among Mohammedans that a Sheik always indicates the exact spot on which he wishes

to be buried, by rendering it impossible for the pall-bear-
ers to proceed further with the corpse. The body is prepared for burial, and the bearers and procession start out
in the direction indicated by the departed spirit. When
the proper place has been reached, the bearers find themselves compelled to stop, and there—no matter where it is
—the grave is dug and the monument erected. I have an
impression that it would not be difficult to tell how this Sheik
indicated his wish to take his long dreamless sleep, " under
the shadow of the palms." If it was as fatiguing to the
bearers of his corpse to wade through the sand as it was to
us, or rather if the sand was as deep then as it is now, we
suspect the shade of the Sheik was not very carefully con-
sulted.

After tea the gentlemen amused themselves playing ball
for a little while, and others of us took a promenade
through the grove. At this stage of the performance we
discovered a tin can fastened to the top of a tall palm for
the purpose of getting 'chomr—wine—from the tree.
Most of us had never seen it, and so we got a native to go
up and bring the can down. The liquid was the color of
clear water with a small quantity of milk added, and tasted
quite pleasant, something like a mild kind of beer. It
seemed a queer idea to "tap" a tree at the top, but so it
was. In India this 'chomr is intoxicating but does not
kill the tree. This one, however, had lost the whole of its
feathery tuft.

The train was coming in from Aboukir just as we came
into Ramle, and I made a mental note of it for the sake of
the little boys at home who have declaimed " The boy
stood on the burning deck." Just twelve miles from our
fourth of July tea drinking poor little Casabianca stood
and cried :

"Say, father, must I stay?
While o'er him fast through sail and shroud,
The wreathing fires made way."

The sun was just setting as we came through the town and passing one of the railway stations, we saw a moslem "praying towards Mecca." He was one of the station guards, and was performing his devotions right beside the street. He knelt first for a moment then rose to his full height for about the same time, and then prostrated himself so as to touch the ground with his forehead. This I think he did three times, looking very earnest and solemn throughout. It is of course as false a faith as that which so disgusted me in Rome, but it did not make the same impression. As we passed on the thought came into my mind that it would be a rich reward for our hard work over Arabic, our separation from home and country, if in the last great day one such moslem should make a star in our "crown of rejoicing."

CHAPTER IX.

ARABIC LANGUAGE.

"*Dear Doctor:*—I think I promised some time ago to tell you something about this wonderful old Arabic language, but it is so very difficult to find out much about it that I am afraid you will have to be content with meagre ideas for a long while, unless you get information from some one who is better acquainted with it than I am. It is not

studied as modern languages are, and though I think
this circumstance greatly increases the difficulty of acquiring it, yet it is not by any means *the* difficulty. Missionaries say the pronunciation is *the backbone* of Arabic, and
that this must be broken, if it is ever done, in the first six
months. So, for that length of time, it is considered of
comparatively little importance to give much attention to
the acquisition of words, idioms or construction. You begin, of course, with the alphabet, but you stay there a long
time after the eye is able to recognize each character, for
there is at least five of them for which European throats
have no organ at all. There are twenty-eight letters, *Alif,
Ba, Ta, Tha, Geem, 'Ha, Kha, Dal, Thal, Ra, Zay, Seen,
Sheen, S'sad, 'Dad, 'Ta, Za, Ain, Ghine, Fa, 'Kaf, Kaf,
Lam, Meem, Noon, Wow, Ha and Ya.* You see several of
them go in pairs, as in the Hebrew, and the distinctions
are very hard to make. A failure between the *'Dal* and
the *'Dad,* the *Seen* and the *Sad,* the *Ta* and the *'Ta,* often
makes terrible havoc with the meaning of a sentence. The
'Kaf is taken from the caw of the raven, the *Ghine* from the
growl of the camel. These two with the *'Ha, Kha* and the
Ain are very difficult. The *'Ha* is a terrible deep aspirate,
and must be made from the chest. The effort to pronounce
these five, and also to trill the *Ra,* is very fatiguing and
not less discouraging. You are utterly unable to make any
approximation to the sounds the teacher gives you, and as
far as you can judge yourself you see no prospect that you
ever will come any nearer to them. If your musical
" ear " is pure and acute you will get them " by and by "—
as our teacher says, " Mallish ! never mind, it will come,"
but the progressive experience of most Arabic students is
pretty severe. Not many of them ever acquire it without
having been attacked with fits of despair more or less

severe, about the only cure for which is the recollection that "what *has* been done *may* be done again." So you get up a fresh stock of courage, and in two or three lessons you get to spelling. Here you encounter fresh obstacles in combining the letters and the vowels, which, by the way, correspond to our short *a*, *oo* and *e*, and are not written except where it is necessary to show the construction. After one or two months' of drilling in these combinations the Testament is taken up as a reading book, the English translation being your dictionary. It requires a long time to become sufficiently familiar with the characters to read fluently, even when you can give the sounds. The letters are small, and they vary with the combination. If you read "with points" that greatly increases the indistinctness of the text, and if you read "without points" you have them to supply, perhaps without knowing for a long time what to supply. Our teacher had us read John's Gospel first "with points" exclusively. Now he has us read a chapter that way first, and then requires us to take the unpointed book and supply for ourselves. We have also commenced the grammar, and although there are said to be thirteen conjugations, yet I think the verb is perhaps not more difficult than in other languages, possibly it is not so much so, as there is really but one principal conjugation. The others are derived for the most part by rule, and are less complicated than they at first appear. There is but one article—al or el—which is definite and can be prefixed to either the singular, dual or plural. The adjective generally follows the noun, and the noun the verb. There are three cases, the nominative, genitive and accusative; and three tenses, the past, present and future, the two latter being just the same. The past, in the third person masculine, is the root, and is either "triliteral" or "quadriliteral."

Arabic is not what you would call a musical language, but it was not at all disagreeable to me at first as it is to some persons. It is so entirely different from anything one ever heard before that it is not easy to realize that it is language. The words are so run together, when correctly spoken, that it is difficult to tell where one ends and another begins. I have heard a good many missionaries from other countries say that, as compared with other languages, it impressed them as strong, substantial and energetic. Dr. Ellenwood, who stopped in Alexandria on his way around the Presbyterian world of missions, gave it decidedly the preference over every language with which he had come in contact. There was a force and dignity in it, he said, which he could find in no other.

Those who are familiar with it affirm that it is emphatically the language of the world *to scold in*. To uninitiated ears it is an alarming thing to hear two old Arab women berating each other in the street. You think they are upon the very point of tearing each other's eyes out, and you wonder if nobody will interfere to prevent an inevitable calamity, when they shrug their shoulders and walk off as quietly as if they had only said, "How are you?" To hear a native woman read is a most uncomfortable experience, until you have worked long enough at those hard letters yourself to envy her pronunciation. She reads as if she meant to see whether or not she could *split* her throat. She reads in that way naturally, and if a foreigner gets the pronunciation he must do so too. Our teacher says "read loud" and then your ear will become able to detect sounds, and shades of sound; and until one can do that it is impossible to imitate them. At first you feel as if you only heard a *noise*, not an articulate sound. Consequently in estimating one's probable ability to acquire Arabic it is

not sufficient that there be what is commonly known as " a
taste for languages." That is all very well, but there must
be the pure, quick ear besides. One who is not sensitive
to a discord in music will, without doubt, encounter increased difficulties in Arabic.

In preaching the minister has to judge from the appearance or character of his audience whether he is to use
" high " or " low" Arabic. If he is preaching to tolerably
educated men it *may* be high, but when he turns to the
women he *must* come down pretty low. It is a singular
fact, too, that natives will readily excuse faulty construction, but they *never* excuse incorrect pronunciation. But
our missionary friends tell us our greatest trial is over, that
the organs for the difficult letters are at least partially
formed and our ear becoming a little less obtuse, so that
we can begin to perceive differences in sounds. It will be
matter of great rejoicing to us if we can be sure *at the end
of six months* that we have all the letters.

There seems, too, to be an almost endless number of
grades in Arabic scholarship, beginning with those who
speak and read it nicely without knowing anything of the
principles of construction, up to Dr. Van Dyke, the great
master of Arabic in the East. But before you understand
the reason, it is rather discouraging when you inquire how
many years it will require to make you a scholar in the
language, to get the lofty answer—*a life time.* The Sheiks
in the Mosques are the Arabic *critics;* and Moallim Abd
'el Noor says " they spend forty years over one little question and then cannot tell whether it ought to be a *fatha* a
a *domma* or *akasra*, an *a* an *o* or an *e*.

The last time I saw Mr. Strang he inquired if I could
not tell my brother enough about the " beauties " of Arabic
to induce him to come out and try it. He went on com-

menting on the obliquities of the grammar, the origin of
the letters, the *Ghine* being taken from the growl of the
camel, the *Ain* from the bleat of the goat, the *'Ha* from
the hiss of the serpent, &c., and then suddenly changing
his tone he added "O, its the language of the Angels, of
course." A member of our class was sitting by and inquired if he meant the *fallen* Angels.

Until recently we have had the greatest difficulty in the
way of an Arabic dictionary. We had little to rely upon
except a Latin and Arabic dictionary, but this summer we
have been studying French a little and have got an excellent French and Arabic dictionary which has been invalu-
able.

You can't guess how nearly we sometimes come to *envy-
ing* our good friends in Mexico their nice *civilized* language,
particularly with reference to its *written* form. If we only
had Roman characters to deal with! But we must first
learn the names of the strange letters, then learn that almost all of them have three or more different forms according to their position in the *beginning, middle,* or *end* of
a word; then be set to write them all with a reed pen *on a
piece of paper held in your hand* and going from right to
left—which is very difficult to one at all afflicted with
nerves. You are told that the written hand is just like
print, and you go to work greatly encouraged. But after a
little you notice that you cannot read a word of ordinary letters, shop signs, advertisements, telegrams, receipts, &c.,
and when you ask the reason it is, "O that's a very different thing. That's the business hand." Then we ask why
didn't you give us copies in that hand, "O foreigners can
never learn that hand. That is our pride to be able to
write that way." And I think it is the most intricate thing
I ever knew. Letters are made above and below each

other, around and within each other and so curved and joined that it is impossible to say where one ends and another begins. All business must be done in this hand and even our college boys sometimes have difficulty to read it. *Very few* foreigners ever get all *the sounds* under a year of hard work and then there remains a great difficulty in making them in their various combinations and very, *very few ever* learn to write Arabic easily and acceptably. Thus you see there are *three* great difficulties in the language—to read, write and speak it."

In a private letter written at this time Mrs. Giffen says of this language, " It is a very steep and high mountain, and very few foreigners ever succeed in reaching the top. It is the work of a lifetime to become a scholar in this language. Although it is so terrible a language I intend to get it with the best of the men." The strenuous efforts made by her in this direction did not pass unrewarded.

Dr. Hogg, who was for several months her instructor in this language, and for four years her associate in mission labor at the same station, writes: "Her knowledge of Arabic was accurate and extensive. When she joined the mission at Asyoot, a little over two years after her arrival, she had already made such progress in the knowledge and practical use of the Arabic vernacular, that she was able at once to take charge of the advanced class in the female boarding school. All these exercises were in Arabic. To be able to teach such branches as were taught this class in an interesting and effective manner implies a knowledge of the vernacular both accurate and extensive."

" Her *pronunciation* was good. (This is rightly termed the backbone of this monstrous language.—ED.) It is a happy day for the whole mission when the latest arrival has learned to pronounce his letters correctly. Months have to pass before this report can be safely made. In many cases years have passed before the training has been sufficient to guarantee that the newly-acquired vocables shall be pronounced in all kinds of combinations with ease and accuracy. Need I add that in the majority of cases this longed-for consummation is in fact never attained."

"Your sister did attain it—or at least something very near it, but not without a protracted effort in the case of some of the letters. I have seen her more than once interrupt the exposition of a difficult point in Arabic grammar to ask or suggest the connection of the point under discussion with something that had previously been explained, or that had arrested her attention in her private reading, thus showing that her active mind had apprehended at a glance what to others required to be explained in detail."

CHAPTER X.

CAIRO, AND ITS ENVIRONS.

"You will see from the date of my letter that I am in new quarters again. There were no native influences around us in Ramle, and consequently we made slow progress in acquiring colloquial Arabic. Occasionally a native from Alexandria would make us a call and mortify us with all sorts of questions which we could not comprehend, and we naturally felt anxious to go where there would be increased facilities for acquiring the ability to make ourselves understood. Scarcely any amount of "book Arabic" would enable one to do that, still the latter must be learned before there can be any degree of usefulness in teaching.

Dr. Lansing remained here all summer, except a few days, doing all the usual mission work, and also superintending very closely the work of the new buildings. Perhaps you know that some years ago the Viceroy reigning at that time, Saeed Pasha, presented to the mission a large brick building, together with the lot on which it stood. But the present Viceroy, for purposes of public improvement, desired to have the grounds and offered to give in exchange thirty-five thousand dollars and another site for building in the very best quarters of the city. This was of course accepted and this spring the new building was begun. It is to consist, if ever completed, of a church, dwellings for two families, and rooms and halls for the boys' day school and girls' boarding school. It is hoped that the Chapel, which is designed for the large school hall, may be open for preaching in five or six months; but building here is a much more formidable undertaking than in America. In this city, as well as in Alexandria, much of the surface is old ruins or the debris of ages, which is entirely insufficient to sustain the weight of a large stone building. All this must be dug through, no matter how deep, and the foundation laid on solid ground. In this instance the lot is situated on the site of *a lake*. Ten or fifteen years ago the whole of Esbekeeyah quarter was under water, but after the Viceroy's visit to Paris he began to remodel the city. The lake was filled up by being made the receptacle for all the rubbish of Cairo, and a most beautiful public garden was laid out in it, which is the Central Park of this part of the world. The new lot fronts this garden on one side and on another the most popular hotel in the city, so that a more suitable location could not have been desired. About a month ago the walls were brought up to the surface and the corner stone is now ready to be laid. Solid ground was only reached at the depth of *seventeen* feet, and at the bottom the walls are *nine feet and ten inches* thick. This will give you some idea of the cost and labor of building before any building appears.

Opposite our window are three or four fellah huts, where live several families of fellaheen—that term meaning the poorest class of people. While we were gone to the Citadel—a space of not more than three or four hours—an old woman, perhaps the grandmother, in one of the families died *and was buried*. It was all over when we got back, but Miss T. saw the burial preparations. It was necessary, according to their ideas, to have her disposed of before sunset, and the men hurried up all the arrangements with most indecent haste, and then started off to the grave almost in a run. That is decidedly the style here. Wedding processions are ever so slow, but a funeral cortege moves rapidly. Well, when we came up from tea the "mourning" had commenced. It was very unpleasant to hear; wild, violent cries and doleful chants, so that we shut the window and put our hands over our ears in order to sleep. Next morning the men went to their work and the women took their turn. There was only one *professional* mourner. She had a long scarf which she drew back and forth in a wild way across the back of her neck, the top of her head and over her shoulders, and all of them kept up a continuous wail—an indescribable something between a moan and a scream. They all sat round in a circle, just outside the door where the death had occurred, and carried on the mourning for three or four hours. It was only "an old woman," however. Had it been a young one, or better still a man or boy, instead of the mild kind of mourning we heard, it would have been most fearful shrieking, beating the breast, tearing the hair, casting dust on the head, jerking the scarf, writhing the body, &c.; not for one time only, but every night and morning for perhaps a dozen days. I understand now what is meant when it is said in the Bible "the Egyptians mourned for Israel threescore and ten days." Then when Joseph carried the body back to Canaan and "made a mourning for his father seven days" the Canaanites said "this is a grievous mourning to the Egyptians." We could not sleep for the mourning over *one* death, and that one which was considered of small importance. Think what it must have been when God smote "all the first born in the land of Egypt, from the first born of Pharaoh who sat upon the throne to the first born of the maid servant behind the mill;" when there was "a great cry throughout all Egypt," such as never was and never shall be like it. One universal cry, one long, horrible wail, would ring out on that fearful night.

By the way, we were reading this 11th chapter of Exodus with the girls this evening, and instead of the children of Israel being directed to "borrow" jewels of gold and jewels of silver, the Arabic rendering is *yatlub* "— "speak to every man that he *ask.*" Life in the East gives a new meaning to very many things in the Bible. Every day you hear or see some fresh evidence that it was written by Orientals—by men who bear a much closer resemblance in mind, manner and appearance to those by whom we are surrounded than to ourselves. I got into such a vein of thought the other day when reading about the Abyssinian Eunuch to whom Philip preached the Gospel. My mind instantly photographed him as he went leisurely along through the Desert in a way it never did before.

Last Saturday afternoon Dr. L. insisted that I should go

out and see some of the historic ground around Cairo. So we took a carriage and drove to Heliopolis—"the City of the Sun"—and the Site of the Temple of the Sun, as well as of the Temple of Onias. Heliopolis is the On of the Old Testament, and it was in the Temple of the Sun that Joseph found his wife. The priests were at that time a highly privileged class, and Potiphera was most probably of the highest rank in this most famous of all the old Egyptian Temples.

We started about four o'clock and were almost immediately among the prickly pear and sycamore groves in the suburbs of the city. These were objects of a good deal of interest to us. The former, like all species of the cactus in this country, grows to a great size and the fruit is very much prized. The trees—I suppose I should call them such—were ten or twelve feet high, and from twelve to eighteen inches in diameter. They have a most ragged, scrawny appearance, seeming to have made desperate efforts to grow in every direction, except an upright one. But the sycamores are a beautiful sight. They were covered with fruit, which is of a pretty rose color and of the shape of a fig almost. The tree is not of a fine growth, and has very few small branches—the fruit seeming to be *stuck* on the large limbs. The latter are frequently near the ground, and, in fact, the tree is something like the prickly pear in its disinclination to grow upwards. Zaccheus of course was in all minds, and it was not hard to imagine him stepping easily up one of those twisted spreading trees to see Jesus "passing by."

After passing the groves we found ourselves quite in the Desert.

After driving perhaps two miles through the desert we entered beautiful green plantations. Lebbech or acacia trees were planted on each side of the road and their great arms met and overlapped each other in a most beautiful arch, while between them was a thick hedge of lemon trees. In the fields were orange and pomegranate trees laden with green fruit, palms, vines and mulberries; tomatoes, beans, radishes, &c., and a great deal of corn. The ground, before planting, is laid off into beds perhaps six or eight feet square, around each of which is a channel for the water. In these beds the corn is planted in rows about a foot apart—or rather I should say it is *sowed*, for the stalks seem to stand just as thick as is possible. Of course there can be but little culture, which would not matter much if the ground were really plowed before planting. It is not, however, and the corn does not grow more than five or six feet high. I have an idea, however, that it is of the kind we call "six weeks corn" at home. Six years ago these plantations were nothing but desert, pure white sand. Now the soil has been so enriched by the alluvial deposit from the water of the Nile, with which it is irrigated, that it looks as black as any land I ever saw. The road or avenue on which we were driving led to the Khedeewee's favorite palace, and perhaps three miles out we turned off from it into another, planted on each side with tamarisk and *shittim* trees—the "shittim wood" of the Bible.

Another mile or two brought us to the famous well which tradition says sprang up in the desert to quench the thirst of the "Holy Family" when they fled into Egypt. Our driver stopped under the spreading trees which now surround it, and pointed out what dragomen and many travelers consider the most interesting feature of Heliopolis—*the old sycamore tree* under which Mary sat down with the infant Saviour after they had been refreshed from the miraculous fountain. It is called the Virgin's tree—

tradition not admitting that Joseph enjoyed the comfort of
its shade.   It is an old, old tree.   The trunk is perhaps six
feet across, though not more than two the other way.   It
looks at first as if several trees had sprung up touching
each other, grown together for five or six feet, and then
separated, and yet they all seem one, though two or three
places you could see through the decayed places in the
trunk.   A neat fence inclosed it and white jessamine and
other flowers were trailing over it.   We asked the bow-wab
who erected the fence.   "Mohammed Ali," was the quick
reply.   A native always refers a great thing to Mohammed Ali, let it be ever so improbable.   The fact is that
travelers cut up the tree to such an extent as to threaten
its destruction, and so the owner, a Copt, adopted this means
of preserving it.   The bow-wab gathered us each a boquet
of roses, geraniums, &c., and I got him to go up into the
tree and get me some leaves to press.   The fence is covered with the names of travelers ambitious of letting it
be known to those who come after them that they ."have
been there."   One man, however, with an unusually skep-
tical tendency, has written, "I do not believe in this tree."

We went back to the carriage, and the first thing we
knew our driver was going at a rapid rate towards Cairo.
Miss T. stopped him and insisted that we wished to see the
ruins and the great Obelisk.   "Ma feesh! ma feesh!"—
"there is nothing, nothing at all"—he persisted, but we
carried our point and made him turn back.   It is the
month of Ramadan now, and all good Moslems taste
nothing while it lasts from half-past three in the morning
until sunset.   This driver was a "son of the prophet"
and quite impatient for his supper, and it was with rather
a bad grace that he drove us through the ruins of the
great Temple and set us down at the foot of the Obe-

lisk. The village of Mutareeyah near by is built of material from the ruins, but nothing is now visible except a line of mounds indicating the dimensions of the Temple, which are about 4,500 x 3,500 feet. It was in this temple, from its learned priests, that Moses became skilled " in all the wisdom of the Egyptians." Here Plato lived and studied thirteen years, and here Solon and Eudoxus came for the same purpose, and here too Jeremiah is supposed to have written his Lamentations. On the great altar, according to the Roman fable, the Phenix came from Arabia and placed its predecessor's bones in the nest of spices in which it had died, and then went back to live out its own five hundred years. But " the glory is departed." Only the mounds and the Obelisk remain. The latter is sixty-eight feet in height and is between six and seven feet at the base. The hieroglyphics are the same on the four sides, and extend from base to summit. It was erected by Osirtasen 2,000 years B. C., the account of which is given in the hieroglyphics. The first figure at the top is a raven. The serpent occurs twice, the hand, the ibis, other birds and two or three mathematical figures. The shaft is of solid red granite and is supposed to weigh five hundred tons. There are three or four obelisks in Rome which were taken from Egypt beside this one, the one in front of St. Peter's being of the number. Cleopatra's Needle in Alexandria was also taken from Heliopolis by one of the Cæsars and set up in front of his palace.

We walked round the Obelisk and examined it as well as we could for the crowd of young Arabs who swarmed round us for " bucksheesh." We thought of Moses and Joseph that they had stood many times just where we were, and looked up at the great shaft just as we were doing. But how different would everything else be! The

Balm of Gilead once grew around Heliopolis; now cotton is cultivated under the very shadow of the Obelisk!

By the way I have not told you anything about the famous old fortress, the Citadel. It is situated at the foot of the Mokattam Hills, on an elevation quite as commanding as any of the seven hills of Rome, and was built by the great Saladin in 1166. All the stone used in its construction was brought from the smaller Pyramids surrounding the great ones, and, in fact, the casing stones of the second Pyramid were all removed for the same purpose. It is an immense fortress, consisting of apparently endless barracks, innumerable halls of immense size, into which the government offices open, of a palace and of the Grand Mosque of Mohammed Ali.

First we looked into the immense printing department, and, among other things, we saw there an outline surface map of all Egypt up to the Second Cataract. It was on what looked like a very large billiard table, perhaps fourteen feet in length, and was a perfect imitation of the surface of the country, made in some kind of plaster. It was almost sad to look at the great reaches of desert—desert, almost nothing but desert—and then think of the millions who must live in the little bit of green country. From a front balcony we looked down on the City of the Caliphs, glittering beneath an eastern sun. It is almost bewildering to look over its wilderness of mosques, minarets, cupolas and towers from the giddy height on which we stood, for the balcony hangs almost perpendicularly a hundred or more feet over the magnificent street which winds up the hill. There were crowds of people everywhere, groups of lazy, moping camels, funeral processions, and marriage processions, too, moving through the distant streets. To the right was a moslem cemetery, to the South and North the shining river, and away in the West were, I had almost said the everlasting, Pyramids. Coming down and going through a beautiful garden full of jessamines, roses, orange, and lemon trees, we came into an open space, where knots of people and soldiers were grouped together buying and selling, eating and drinking, around what seemed to be a well. We climbed up and looked down into it. After peering into the darkness a long time we could just distinguish the sparkle of water far below. We turned into an enclosure and descending what seemed a steep earthen stair winding around the well, and having windows cut through its inside wall to admit a little light from the well. This is in two parts. The first is one hundred and sixty feet in depth, but under it, or rather to its side a little, is another one hundred and thirty feet farther down in the solid rock. This stairway on which we were is for the purpose of taking up the water from the lower well, and emptying it into the one in which we were looking. Then at the top it is drawn up from this one in the same way, having made at last an ascent of two hundred and ninety feet. It is called Joseph's well, and was dug by Saladin when he built the fortress. The depth of the well is thought to be just the height of the Citadel grounds above the bed of the river.

From the well we proceeded to the Grand Mosque. At the entrance of the great marble Court in front of the Mosque we were stopped and required to put on large cloth slippers, to prevent our profane feet from touching the sacred Turkish carpets or the consecrated marble and alabaster beneath. The building is an immense square with a great domed roof and a minaret at each of the two front corners at least two hundred and fifty feet high. The whole inside and out is encased with alabaster. There is not a picture, altar, or anything of the kind to be seen, except a most gaudy-looking pulpit, at an elevation of perhaps fifteen feet, which is occupied once or twice in the year. Mohammed Ali's tomb occupies one corner, and is surrounded by a brazen enclosure richer than anything we saw in Westminster. A square monument, ten or twelve feet high, over the vault is surrounded by the old hero's turban, or tarboosh, crowning a pedestal. Just to the left of the Mosque is the open square in which this same old despot murdered the Mamalukes. We were shown the place where one of them sprang his horse over the wall and down into the street below. There was and is a great pile of rubbish there, and the leap is supposed not to have been more than twenty-five feet. We got up on the wall, looked away down into the city, and tried to imagine the poor Mamaluke's desperation when he started on that fearful leap and the wild joy which must have filled his heart when he found himself safe.

It is in the Citadel that you get the best impression of the military power of Egypt, the absolute authority of its ruler, and his determination to spare neither care nor expense in strengthening as well as tightening his grasp on his dominions. It gives one rather a queer sensation to see American officers walking round in their uniforms among so many Turkish officials.

The great event of this week, however, has been the visit of the Prince of Wales. He came last Saturday, and Sabbath night the Viceroy had a splendid opera prepared for him. The expedition, however, is very much under the care of Sir Bartle Frere—a very pious nobleman, and besides the character of the English Nation was at stake, so the Prince declined the opera Sabbath night and went to the theatre Monday night. Tuesday Sir Bartle came over to the new buildings, saw Dr. L., and came over here to see

Mrs. L. and the boarding school, though he sent cards merely to all the other dignitaries who had called on him.

In the afternoon we went out on the street and saw the expedition pass to the station. The Prince, the Viceroy and Sir Bartle were in the first carriage. Perhaps there were a dozen other carriages, all the handsomest "elegances" with as fine horses as I ever saw. Several of the Viceroy's sons with Consuls and other dignitaries graced the escort. There were soldiers, and pages, footmen, and runners, and every other mark of respect for the distinguished guest. He was himself a very common-looking specimen of humanity, dressed in an ordinary gray suit. The Viceroy took leave of him immediately on reaching the station, and returned alone in a close carriage. As he passed us he looked out of the window and gave us a very graceful salute.

Sometime ago we went one afternoon to the Mosque of Sultan el Hasan, one of the oldest and most famous in the city. It was just sunset—the first " hour of prayer" when we went in and the Muezzin went upon the lofty Minaret— two hundred and sixty feet high—and chanted in the most sonorous and indeed harmonious tones, " God is most Great. I testify that there is no deity but God. I testify that Mohammed is God's apostle. Come to prayer. Come to security, God is most Great. There is no god but God." As soon as the "call" was finished, all those who had performed the required ablutions at a large fountain in the center of the great square came and knelt in a line, with their faces toward Mecca, and the Iman who leads in the prayer stood before them. There were twenty-five in the row, and I am sure I never saw anywhere a greater appearance of solemnity and deep feeling, without any admixture of either affectation or fanaticism. They first took position on the knees and toes, and when they bowed their heads, which they must do without moving the feet, their foreheads touched the ground. They recited in concert what seemed not very different from the " call," and after several prostrations they rose to their feet and again recited it, then knelt again, &c. Not an eye was turned towards us by the worshippers and there was something impressive in their deep, sonorous voices, echoing through such a grand old building.

As we came out little children and larger ones came trooping after us begging for bucksheesh, of course. One little one, about four years old, ran after the gentlemen, and not receiving what he asked, he did the next best thing for this country—cursed *their fathers.*

Last Saturday one of the members of the church here sent for us to go up to the citadel to see the ceremony of carrying the Kisweh or covering for Mahammed's tomb in Mecca, from the place where the parts of it are made to the Mosque of Hasseyn, to be sewed together preparatory to the setting out of the Pilgrims to Mecca. The Kisweh consisted of four pieces of black cloth, embroidered like that on the tomb of Mohammed Ali, and borne upon the shoulders of men.

The procession was headed by two battalions of infantry, containing one thousand men, each preceded by a band of fifty musicians. Then followed thousands of fellaheen, the real descendants of the prophet being distinguished from the others by a green turban. Some carried flags of all colors and designs, and others musical instruments. As the Kisweh passed many of the people ran up and rubbed their hands over it " to obtain a blessing." Just behind it was a gorgeous canopy borne on a large camel, the latter literally covered with every ornament that could be fastened to it. This camel carries the Kisweh to Mecca, &c., is therefore sacred forever afterward.

Such spectacles as these give one an idea of the strength, and power of the Moslem religion, and yet in one way its power is broken. Twenty-five years ago no Christian dared go on the streets *before a Mosque,* or be seen during one of these processions. Now there are any quantity of policemen who watch all foreigners, and take especial pains to see that no insult is offered them. When the procession was passed we were stopped and asked if anything had been said to us, or if we had any kind of complaint to make.

Fanatical devotion to Mohammedanism is rare except among the poor. But Christianity is not taking its place. There is a great spectre stalking through Egypt, and that is *infidelity.* Ashamed of Mohammedan practices, the religion of Jesus is none the less abhorred, except that foreigners who are considered its special exponents command respect for their superior intelligence and their citizenship in powerful governments."

CHAPTER XI.

OSIOUT AND ITS SCHOOLS.

" After months of waiting the Association has had a meeting and disposed of us, at least for a time. Mr. and Mrs. Nichol are stationed in Mansoora, and I am to go with them ' for the present.'

After the meeting, Dr. Hogg and others urged it on me to go up to Osiout and see the work there before going to my own field. The distance I think is two hundred and thirty miles, and as we traveled second-class it was in many respects an uncomfortable day. The country was beautiful. The inundation had subsided, and the wheat was everywhere of the richest green. Much of the way we were in sight of the river, and only now and then did the valley widen out so much that you could not see the limits on both sides. Indeed it is only a narrow strip of green between the two ranges of mountains, and the more you look at it the more the wonder increases that so many millions live upon its products. It is true, however, that the support many of them receive is of the scantiest kind, In fact it is the boast of the Viceroy that his fellaheen need but a few metres of cloth and a few bushels of the seed of sorghum to live upon a whole year. For this miserable pittance they toil all the year, live in a mud hut, sow, reap and gather in their abundant harvests only to give it all up to a merciless oppressor. If there is "a large Nile" and good crops, the rich are made richer, but to the poor fellah it is all one. A most careful calculation is made of just how little he can live on, and every farthing above that is violently taken from him. What other nation would labor on in this way, year after year, patiently, industriously, and still not grow low and groveling in their minds? Perhaps most people think of these poor fellaheen as heathen, as coarse in their dress, manner and appearance. But they are not heathen. They are intensely religious, and they are innately polite, so much so that Franks often impress them as very rude. Nowhere in the world is there a keener sense of propriety or a more rigid adherence to the forms of etiquette, albeit the points on which they lay most emphasis are not always the same as with us. They are quick and shrewd, and need but small opportunities to develop most respectable mental characteristics. Travelers are flooding the Western world with glowing accounts of the magnificent developments of the Viceroy of Egypt, that he is restoring the country to its original place among the nations, that he is educating and enlightening his people, and that he is one of the most able sovereigns of modern times. And he is—if the most intense selfishness the world ever saw is greatness. It is true that he is making Cairo like Paris, true that there are large government schools in it and in a few other cities, true that there are magnificent palaces all through the land, true that there are parks and gardens and nurseries which cost millions of dollars, true that there are aqueducts, canals, bridges, factories, museums and libraries; but they are all for the rich. From the poor all is taken. Dozens and dozens of boys were hard at work in the fields along the railroad as we went up, without one particle of clothing. True, the last of November is not just the same here as in America, nevertheless we, inside the cars, were dressed about as warmly as we would have been at home. How often we thought of the Egyptian bondage of other days, the brick that must be made without straw, and of the cry that went up to heaven.

Osiout made me think often of Due West, not of course that the people of the two places resemble each other, or that this mud city of 30,000 inhabitants is anything like our little town. But it is an educational centre. There is the College, the Girls' Seminary and the Theological Seminary. Almost all with whom we came in contact were either teachers or students, and it was a pleasant sight to see.

The first morning I awoke at early dawn with the sound of voices reading aloud near me. I soon found that it was the college boys preparing their morning lessons out in a palm grove just beside the house. By the time we had taken breakfast they had assembled in the church for roll call and general chapel exercises. Our former teacher, Moallim Abd el Noor, officiated, and woe to the boy who for a second deferred answering to his name. There was not a whisper in the whole house, and only two out of the one one hundred were absent. Most of the boys are of a yellow complexion. Some of them are a good deal darker, but you don't have any of the feeling that they are dull Africans. They have almost universally fine sparkling eyes and bright, intelligent countenances. Many of them are very handsome, but, as in other parts of the world, a few of them are unfortunate enough to be, according to Southern idiom, very ugly. I don't think there was one of them in Frank dress, and only two or three are able to afford the red tarboosh. All the rest wear caps of the same shape made of coarse white cloth. The outside garment in most cases was a long blue gown, to which those who could afford it added a shawl of some kind, worn cornerwise, like a woman would do at home. The college is just near the church, and we walked over with the teacher. He showed us through the dormitories, kitchen, &c.

The beds were simply reed mats on the stone floors. On each three boys sleep and have one or two blankets to cover them. A slate hanging on the wall showed how many boys belonged to one room. In one room twenty-one were marked, in another twenty-five. The two sick boys were lying on their mats, and, oh, how little comfort they seemed to have, and yet we knew it was far more than they were accustomed to at home. Not long ago one of them was delirious one night and ran round like a madman over his sleeping room-mates. We next went through the recitation rooms, four in number, Mr. Strang using the church as a class room for his department. These in summer would not appear uncomfortable, but in winter, the stone floors, brick walls, and thin clothing of the students, give one a very unpleasant sensation of shivering. We took seats in each of the rooms and listened to the recitations. Three of the native teachers are graduates of the Beruit College, and they know well both how to teach and to govern. I never saw better order or closer attention in my life. Indeed there was a docility in the appearance of the students which I never saw before ; an eager, anxious desire to profit by every advantage which would gladden the hearts of college professors at home, and more than repay fathers and mothers for the sacrifices they make in sending their sons off to school. These boys know what they are in Osiout for, and by the time they have finished their course, any institution might be proud of them.

The third morning we went out with Miss Lockart to her day school. All the pupils are little girls, who are taught what is required for admission into the boarding-school. While we were there a woman come in and invited us to her house, though Miss L. had never seen her. She ran off ahead of us and had the court swept, mats and rugs spread out for us, and brought in her sister-in-law to see us. Coffee was served on a silver salver, and she brought out a beautiful lot of gold embroidery for us to see. She said her husband read the Bible to her at night, but would not allow her to go to church. She listened very attentively to all the ladies said and seemed so pleased with the visit. From her house we went to the "Congregational Academy," that is, the school supported by the Osiout congregation. We found three teachers and seventy-seven little boys in a room about fifteen by twenty feet. The boys were packed in rows three deep all around the room, which left a little space for teachers and classes in the centre. Two little boys read for us in the Gospel who were four and a-half and four years old. What do you think of that? The little creatures were sitting flat on the cold stones, and we could but wonder how their little heads got as much in them as they did under such untoward circumstances. Oh, how it does make you long for money to see such things, and yet if we could have been in Osiout ten years ago we might have wondered what to do with money if we had had it.

Osiout is a *mud* city. We were told that you might dig down most of the houses with a mattock, the brick being only dried in the sun. A very few of them are plastered and whitewashed, and quite as nice to live in as the stone houses of Cairo and Alexandria. One evening we went up to the mountain just back of the mission house, and got from the summit what Dean Stanley pronounces "the finest view in all Egypt." The mountain is, perhaps, six or seven hundred feet high, and enables you to sweep the narrow valley with its green fields, mud villages and winding river for perhaps twenty-five miles in each direction. We counted twenty-six minarets in the city, their white spires towering up among the brown mud houses and glittering like burnished steel in the bright sunshine. Murray's Guide book says there are twenty thousand inhabitants, but it looked like a little village only, and from the mountain there was no appearance of a street anywhere. This mountain is a famous place. Its sides are completely "honey-combed" with chapels and niches for mummies. One of the chapels is three hundred feet long, and once had its sides and roof covered with idolatrous paintings. But after the introduction of Christianity into the country, these chapels became the dwellings of Christian monks, who covered the painted walls with a cement which still remains. It is pretty well established that Jeremiah lived for a time in one of these rock-hewn cells, and in another lived for a long while the celebrated Monk John, to whom the Emperor Theodosius sent to inquire the result of a war into which he was entering. Everywhere were human bones, pieces of mummy cloth and fragments of mummy cases. We sat down at the summit to rest and to look over the moslem cemetery at the base, and while we sat there one of our donkey boys, who had seen us picking up bones, &c., ran off to a cell and came out with what looked in the distance exactly like *a little baby mummy.* Dr. Hogg was with us and had just buried little Artie. The sight cut us all to the heart. The boy had stuck a stick into the cloth bandages and was carrying it away up in the air. While we looked the bandage gave way, and it fell with a thud which made us shudder. However, when he came nearer he threw it down among us, and it happened to be the upper half of a woman's body—evidently an old one. The pressure of the bandages had been so great that the breast was lapped and the shoulders seemed not more than nine inches across, though the forearm was nearly as long as mine. The tongue looked like a piece of black leather, and the mouth above the tongue was filled with mummy cloth. When the boy—a Moslem—threw it down, he said, with an expression of contempt, "Cupteya"—Copt. Dr. Hogg said, "La Wothaneeya"—an idolater. We could pick the dried flesh to pieces with our fingers. It came off like the *grain* of decayed wood, and looked very much like that. When we were sitting round it, not much imagination was required to bring up the time when the soul had left this dry, broken body. We wondered where its abode was now, and the hope rose in our hearts that curious hands might never so handle our bones."

On the last day of our stay we took breakfast, bade good-bye, and left the house just at dawn. Dark as it still was, however, the college boys were all out *sitting on the cold ground* in an open place in front of the house *studying with all their might.* Poor boys! and yet how rich and fortunate they are compared with their fathers. With no beds, with little but coarse bread to eat, with the scantiest clothing, with no fire but the sun heat, with no lamp except the moonlight, they will yet attain a point of which many a favored student in America will fall short.

We left Osiout with the feeling that Dr. Hogg might well look round over his work for these ten years and say, "What has God wrought;" and also with the conviction that what had been accomplished in that city would, before the end of the century, be repeated to the very sources of the Nile. God grant that it may be so, and if it is his will, that our eyes may see it."

CHAPTER XII.

DORE'S GALLERY—"DESCENT OF CHRIST FROM THE
PRÆTORIUM."

I think that which most Americans look forward to in
the tour of Europe with the keenest anticipation, is the
painting and statuary of the Old World. No volume of
journeyings, no series of newspaper articles is complete
without some ecstatics on " the subject of the old masters."

Of course we got the infection, and we meant to see all
the galleries on our route, but somehow or other in London
we never could find the National Gallery open. We still
hoped to succeed till the last afternoon, and failing then
we decided to go to the private gallery of Gustave Doré—
a Frenchman, to see his new picture of " the Descent from
the Prætorium."

In the ante-room were numerous woodland and mountain scenes of great beauty, but the special attraction was
"The Dream of Pilate's Wife." It was 8 x 12 feet, I
think, and represented her as having risen hastily from her
couch with her mind full of distressing thoughts. She is
hurrying out from her bedroom with her hand on her brow
as if she *felt* she was dreaming when she *knew* she was
awake. But what is so mysterious to her is plain to you.
An Angel is following her and speaking in her ear. Perhaps
the painter's solution of the cause of the dream may not
be a very orthodox one, but it seemed a beautiful thought,
when we were looking at the picture.

But the crowd was pressing into the next room and we
went with them. Here was such a collection as one sees
once in a lifetime. There were three very fine illustrations
of the Inferno, The Slaughter of the Innocents, The

F

Coliseum by Moonlight, with the dead gladiators lying on the sands and the lions and tigers walking round their victims. There was also a very large picture of St. Augustine and his brother monks, and a scene in the Alps, so like nature itself that I several times afterwards, imagined that we passed through the identical gorge. But it was some time after we entered the room before we knew that these pictures were there. Another one shut these all out and swallowed up every thought and feeling. If the centuries had been rolled back for us and we had stood in the streets of Jerusalem itself on that fearful day, when Pilate delivered Jesus to be crucified, if we had really heard the shouts of "crucify him, crucify him!" and had really seen the malice and wicked satisfaction which looked out of the eyes of the chief priests and rulers as they saw "that deceiver" descend the steps of the Prætorium. I am sure it would not have been so real to us. Had we seen the actual remorse written on the real face of repentant Peter, the great agony of our Saviour's mother and the tender care of the beloved disciple manifested toward her in that fearful trial we could not have understood and appreciated it half so well.

The picture is 25 x 30 feet, and just fills up one end of the gallery. Crimson velvet curtains variously arranged throw light and shade in the most artistic manner, and the moment you enter the door your eyes rivet themselves on this picture. Away back in the blue, hazy distance are the domes and towers of the holy city, while just in front are two large buildings, from one of which Jesus is descending. He is about half way down a flight of thirty steps, is clothed in a long white robe ; the crown of thorns is on his head, his hair touches his shoulders, and the blood is trickling through it and falling on the white robe. No gory drops ever seemed more natural. It is just as if you *saw* them rolling down his temples and dropping from the ends of the hair. But he does not seem to feel it. There is perfect calmness on his face, a far away look in the solemn eyes, and an utter ignoring of his terrible surroundings, but there is no contempt in his glance. It is rather as if not long before he had been saying, " O Jerusalem, Jerusalem, how often would I have gathered thy children, &c.," while the sorrowful heartstrings yet vibrated, though the thought itself had passed away, as he was fixing his soul upon his Father for strength to sustain him when he should be made an offering for the sin of the world. Just behind him stand Annas and Caiaphas on the stairs, and you feel as if you *heard* them gloating over their triumph. Just below, on one side, stands Peter, a great sorrow on his face and wonder in his eyes, that He who walked on the sea, He who could foretell his denial and convince him with a look when the cock had crowed thrice, should allow Himself to be led away to death. " Can He be the Christ?" speaks in every line of his face. Below all is another sorrowful group. Mary stands with her hand on her breast. There are no tears in her eyes, and her lips are still, but her whole brow quivers. It is an unspeakable agony, and you are sure that " a sword is piercing through her soul also." The beloved disciple is leaning forward and speaking to her with the deepest sympathy and affection, while two great rough Roman soldiers stand gazing at her as if spell-bound by the sight of such great agony. Another woman, perhaps " the other Mary," is standing by, ringing her hands and weeping bitterly.

These are the only countenances in those surging thousands where there is one trace of sorrow, one hint of compassion. On the railings of the stairs, in every window, on

every house top, in every balcony, the infuriated multitudes
are pressing for a sight of the despised Nazarine. On every
hand the soldiers are thrusting them back, and, like the
wild beasts which they seem, they are trampling each other
down.   Here is a woman tumbling from a balcony, but not
more than two persons seem to see it.   Yonder is a man
crushed against a wall and crying fearfully for help, but
no ear hears him.   Everywhere the great black eyes glare
on one object, and malice and envy and hate and every
evil passion stream out as if the rays might scorch.   The
muscles in their bared arms are rigid, and the veins in
their foreheads stand out under the pressure of fearful excitement.   Their lips writhe, and their chests heave, and
you are sure you hear the terrible cry over and over again,
" Crucify him !" "Away with such a fellow from the earth!"
" His blood be on us and our children."

For a long time we could not speak.   In perhaps half an
hour we exchanged thoughts in a whisper, and later we
took a Testament and read the four accounts of the cruci-
fixion.   Then we tried to examine the other pictures, but
we *would turn* back to this one.   And when we left we had
not the heart to go anywhere else as we might have done,
but went quietly to our hotel and waited for the time to
leave London.

In Rome we saw Michael Angelo's " Great Judgment,"
and other pictures by the old masters, but they made no
impression on us.   They are all *Catholic* paintings, and
Catholicism wears a hateful aspect in Rome.   Doré is a
Protestant painter, and our thoughts always went back to
his gallery when we saw so many painted Popes, Virgins,
Saints and crucifixes.   The cross in Doré's picture lies at
the foot of the stairs, two soldiers are raising it to lay it on
the Saviour's shoulders, and the shadow it casts on the

steps looks so real that it seems it must be there. You feel, too, that it is no *crucifix*, but the veritable cross.

Nothing that I saw in Europe so lingers in my mind as this magnificent picture. It is soon to be engraved, and then perhaps our friends at home may get a sight of it sometime. Doré is a great painter, and has opened a new school in his art. On this one picture he spent *five years* of thought and labor."

This was, I presume, the first picture gallery, worthy the name, into which Mrs. Giffen had ever entered. Certainly before this she had seen isolated specimens of the art, and read much of "the old masters" and their great creations, yet we may truly say that this was her first introduction to the art. But we question much if the annals of art criticism can show anything more vivid and powerful than this wonderful description of a still more wonderful painting. The picture here described, and which made so profound an impression on Mrs. Giffen, has with every succeeding year become more and more admired and celebrated. The civilized world is to-day flooded with copies of it—fully justifying all that is here said.

Mrs. Giffen wrote with great facility, and at "railway speed." What was once written "was written." She revised little which flowed from her ready pen, for the double reason that she was very averse to such labor, and often had not the time to spare for this purpose. Many of her published letters, covering page after page, were not only written very hurriedly, but never even read over by her, the manuscript showing not a single erasure or substitution. The thought that her friends in America, knowing little of the unfavorable circumstances under which her letters were written, might think they were the best she could write, troubled her. Her manuscript of the letter just read, although one of the few which she revised, perhaps showed not a single correction. It was written in less than an hour's time, and six months after seeing the painting, without a single note or help of any kind to refresh her memory. When she saw it first, she had as she expressed it, "put her memory on its honor and it was faithful to the trust." But lest her impressions might in some particular be incorrect, she submitted this letter to one of her traveling companions, who stood with her before the marvelous picture, and he pronounced it very " clearly reproduced."

CHAPTER XIII.

LIFE AT MANSOORA—STUDYING AND TEACHING—GLIMPSES OF NATIVE CUSTOMS.

It will be remembered that Mrs. Giffen was, by the association, assigned for the year to Mansoora. Hence she writes:

"I left Cairo for Mansoora on the 9th and came down alone. This is a rather more formidable matter than at home, especially when you can speak no language that will be understood. I was greatly surprised at the number of trees through the country. The roads are always along the banks of canals, and these trees are a most delightful institution for the poor fellaheen. They are often set out when the trunks are a foot or more in diameter and the rapidity of their growth is simply amazing. I passed through the " Land of Goshen " but I had no one to tell

me where it began or how far it extended, so I cannot describe it now.   The fields were full of laborers, part gathering the cotton stalks, binding them nicely in great bundles, lading them upon donkeys and camels and sending
them away to the markets *for fuel;* and the rest plowing
up the soil where the cotton had grown.   There are no
single plows there.   Generally you see *a cow* and *a camel*
harnessed together.

Mansoora, as perhaps you know, is situated on the Da-
mietta branch of the Nile.   It is the centre of the largest
and richest cotton district in Egypt.   It contains forty
thousand inhabitants.

Our house is right on the river.   The foundations touch
the water and the masts of the cotton boats sometimes
strike the porch.   We have the second story, and the
porch extends out over the water.   The house is very comfortable except that it is very cold.   The river is exactly
on the northern side, and now when we need it so much
we do not get a ray of sunshine in our living rooms.
However, Mr. Nichol yesterday received the present of a
stove about the size of a "half bushel" measure, from a
hardware firm in Alexandria, and when we get that up we
will not shiver so much.   I never prized sunshine so much
before, and oh ! what I would give for just a little fire in
my room.   How glad we will be when summer comes
again."

Although the Association did not require it and Mrs.
Giffen had only studied Arabic eight months, yet on her
arrival in Mansoora she at once opened school under what
difficulties we can readily imagine.   She says:

"The next Monday after I came Moallim Tadrus announced to the boys that they were to bring their sisters
Tuesday morning and there would be a school for them in

the church. I went next morning and found *eleven* girls.
Seven of the girls had the same name and when I called
that name the whole seven either screamed, "Nahm!"—
here I am, or came running in wooden sandals like a small
avalanche. I was so tried and frightened that I couldn't
command the little colloquial I knew and they talked so
rapidly and used so many contractions that I could
scarcely understand one word in ten. However we read
in the Testament, spelled and read in the primer, and had
Arabic and English alphabet on the blackboard. I had
read most in Matthew, and so I began there in school, hoping that by asking simple questions I would learn to talk.
But the three large girls knew it from memory almost ver-
batim, so that when I got a question only started they
would run on and repeat perhaps three or four verses. So
I decided that would not do, and I would put them in Revelation *with the hope* that they didn't know so much about
it. Next day I had seventeen girls, and I had the satisfaction of finding Revelation quite a success. Thursday
another large girl came from Jaffa with two others from the
city; but, oh, what long, hard days those were! The girls,
as well as the women, have such fearful voices. None of
them have the faintest idea that quiet can be a desirable
thing, or that it is not proper for every member of a class
to scream at the top of her voice to any girl in the room
who was not giving general satisfaction. Each one was
sure that she, and only she, understood what I was trying
to say, and that only herself could set the others straight.
Often I was almost in despair, but *Saturday*, that boon of
even a missionary's heart, came at last. Sabbath came
also, and found *eight* of my little wild Egyptians in
church, nicely dressed for them, and about half of them,
with their hearts set on having me go home with them

from church; but I said " La." This week I have about
twenty-five on the roll. I am getting a little order into last
week's chaos, and now and then I make the wild little
things exceedingly happy by understanding all they have
said and giving them a suitable answer. I have found out,
too, a most delightful way of completely defeating them
when I find I can't understand. I put on a bold face and
talk English to them just as fast as they talk Arabic.
They cannot stand two sentences. It would amuse you
to see them run, literally *run* from it. My success with
the girls delighted me so much that I concluded to try it
on my teacher, and it had precisely the same effect only
that he turns round in his chair instead of running. However, he always has more patience with me after I admin-
ister a dose of English.

It was at noon as I came home from school. The street
was crowded with a little of almost everything under
heaven. The mosques were full of men praying—it is the
Moslem Sabbath—and there were great crowds still rush-
ing to them. My elbow was jostled at almost every step,
for the long trains of laden camels and wagons give pedes-
trians but narrow limits. A donkey almost ran over me,
and as I was getting out of the way the driver said most
briskly, " Oo-ah, riglik, ya uchtee!" Take care of your
feet, my sister. In escaping from one evil, however, I ran
into another. When I looked up a camel boy was shout-
ing to me, "Shemahlee!"—to the left—while the animal's mouth was almost touching my head. Sometimes I
climbed over the ends of cotton bags, and sometimes I
stood and waited for room to slip by a wagon wheel.
Sometimes I " tip-toed " through the mud to get past an
old woman's "market"—bread and eggs on a plank in
the street, and sometimes I stepped into a corner and let

the cotton rollers get their bales past me. I got home "safe and sound," however, and feeling that with all its trials, I would not exchange the life on which I am entering for any other. I will think of home as it looked last Christmas, of the little town as it was then, of all my friends as they looked then, of "the students" base-balling or riding, and of "the girls" as they looked when I saw them last in the College Chapel .About the time we sit down to dinner to-morrow I will send to them "on the wings of the breeze" a happy greeting—a "Merry Christmas"—for each one a warm, loving thought from a missionary's heart. May it be said to each of them, "Inasmuch as ye have done it unto one of the least of these, ye have done it unto me."

Some time ago I was passing through a narrow street lined on each side with mud huts and swarming with women. Five or six were sitting on the ground round a door, and I asked if they could read. They said no, and made a place for me beside them on the ground. I read them the conversation of the Saviour with Nicodemus about the "new birth." I soon discovered that they had never heard of a Saviour, and must therefore be Moslems. They listened and seemed highly pleased. One woman put her arms around me and patted me in a very affectionate way. When I got up to leave the street was blocked up, and three men were standing just behind me. Of course it was soon "noised abroad" that I had sat down in the streets and read to Moslems, and the Protestants thought it not very safe. I didn't know if it was or not, but a day or two before Dr. Watson was down one of the women came behind me as I was going to school, put her arms around me, and seemed troubled that I hadn't gone back. Dr. W. told me there was no impropriety in it and I in-

tend to go every day.   But I will try to get into the houses.
The girl who took hold of me in the street says " her heart
just opened and Mariam went into it."   They had asked
me my name.   I think they know that I am a Protestant,
but they do not seem offended at it.   Every new one, however, asks if there is anything about Mohammed in my
book, but when one asked if there were any Muslemeen
among the English, the rest said, "Shame on you!"   Of
course their kindness is only because they are pleased to
have "a Sitt" come into their poor little houses and furnish them something new and nice to gossip about.   Every
time they pass behind me, unless I am reading, they kiss
me and pat me and call down every blessing on me.
There is, of course, much to repel one, and not much to
encourage the hope that one can ever communicate the
truth to such determined Moslems, but when I see how
pleased they are when I go, and how empty their lives
are, I think I ought not to regret the time it requires.   It
will give me an opportunity to learn something about
Moslems, besides helping me in talking.   They have commenced teaching me the proper answers to polite expressions, and they almost "eat me up" when I do it correctly.   It is perhaps in my favor that I cannot talk
much, and I do not intend to let them know that I understand a good deal more than I can say.   I can find
out their animus in this way.

Each side of the river here is almost lined with
boats, and hundreds of people seem to live in them.   In
fact the Nile is the great centre.   No wonder idolatrous
Egypt worshiped it, calling it a God.   It comes up over
the land, bringing food and gladness with it.   It is the
Arabs great highway of travel and commerce, the generous fountain from which he quenches his thirst, and the

plentiful bath in which he cleanses his not over fastidious
person, and especially is it the great *sewer* for every city
on its banks. Any time you may look out you may see
the women going down with their water jars and clothes
to be washed. The latter are flapped over and over in the
water and then rolled up into a lump and beaten on the
bank, then put into the water again. When finished the
woman gives her feet and limbs a bath, and without moving out of her tracks in the edge of the water, fills her jar
with water and goes home and drinks it. But when our
water man wishes to be very nice he takes a boat and goes
into the middle of the stream, which is perhaps four hundred yards wide here, and fills a goat skin there. The
popular belief here is that the water of the Nile is *purified*
from *anything* in running *a foot.* But since I went to
Osiout and saw all the washing and bathing done in the
river and canals, and since I have been here on the very
bank of the stream, I don't enjoy the water as much as I
did when I was in Alexandria.

I have just returned from a house of death, a house of
Egyptian mourning, and if you had seen what we did, you
would thank God for a Christian country and for Christian
burial when life is over, as perhaps you never did before.
The boy was in his seventeenth year, and had been
pretty well educated in our boy's school, could speak English quite fluently and wrote it beautifully. In fact his
father had almost consented for him to go with the Consul
to the Centennial, as his interpreter. He was a promising
boy and his father's " first-born "—which has a wonderful
amount of meaning here. So of course it was a terrible
blow. When I went to the house I found about sixty or
seventy men, the father among them, seated in perfect silence on each side of the street in front of the house ;

though long before I reached there I could hear the wailing of the women up stairs. I went up and found the body lying on the mattress of a divan in the centre of the drawing-room, an ordinary lady's shawl being spread corner-wise all over it. About fifty women were crowded into the rather small room and were all sitting on the floor just as near the body as it was possible for them to get. The step-mother sat at his left side. Everyone had a small fancy silk handkerchief in her hands, which she moved in such a way as to keep perfect time with the chant and wailing. The body is swayed to and fro continually, and the little shawl is grasped, an end in each hand in a loose, graceful way, and the time is kept by dropping both hands on the lap and then throwing them up again. Sometimes, too, to indicate stronger feeling, the shawl is taken nearer the corners and thrown round and round until it twists and then is suddenly jerked out as I have often seen children twirl a button on a string. Every new-comer stood up as near as she could get to the corpse and did this leaning over it. Then sometimes they would lay down the shawls and placing both hands together strike their faces with the palms, all in perfect time with the chant. When I went in they gave me a seat on a divan where I could see all that was going on. The step-mother's sister sat at the feet and was screaming at the top of her voice, "Ya habeebee! Ya Azeezee!" O my beloved one, O my precious one! Then perhaps in the next breath she would literally yell at some servant or some one who wasn't pleasing her, or get up, give them a shove or a jerk in the right direction and come back to her wailing. The mother was more quiet, but as night approached they all became more violent. Sometimes the whole fifty would shriek in concert, a peculiar scream which cannot be described and which can never be mistaken for any other cry. Sometimes part would chant and part wail, and sometimes only one would chant and at certain points all the rest wail in a wild, fearful chorus. In the chant itself there was something very beautiful. But I could not catch the words. The last refrain however sounded exactly like "O thou holy one!" in English, but of course it wasn't.

Up to the time the coffin came I had seen little evidence of *real* feeling or sorrow. And it seemed to me if Satan had designed to invent the custom which would most effectually choke reflection and right feeling, he could not have devised a more fitting expedient than oriental mourning.

After the procession was gone I went and sat down by the mother. She was chanting a soft and most touchingly pathetic lament over her son. "Ya Ibnee, Ya Ibnee!"—O my son, my son! O my beloved one, my lamented one! Gone this night, my boy, O my boy! Would to God you could come to me, my precious one, my light-giving one!" I never heard anything like it, but I thought instantly of David in his great sorrow, "O Absalom! my son, my son!" though that always impressed me as the expression of *passionate* grief. This, however, was a regular chant, in a soft, touching, minor, an improvisation to the accompaniment of the voice, the gentle swaying of the body and the motion of the handkerchief—such a "lament" as poets describe and yet never hear. It rings still in my ears and I know will mingle itself with my dreams.

Another soul gone to stand before its Judge! We hope it may have been washed in the cleansing blood, clothed in the precious robe, but there is *only a hope.* May we all be the better for the terrible scene through which we have passed this day, and with strengthened faith and deepened

love exclaim from the fullness of grateful hearts, "Thanks
be unto God for his unspeakable Gift!"

Yesterday one of my little girls insisted that I should
go home with her at noon.

I found two families in the house, and as I went in the
little blind brother of the girl called out, "Welcome, welcome!" on hearing my voice. I had my Testament in my
hand, and after a little "small talk," they ask me to read,
but my eyes were still so hot I didn't dare to use them, so
the two women took advantage of the opportunity to find
out something more about me, as, for instance, where I
lived, who was in the house with me, if I were a Copt or a
Moslem, if I had any friends, if my father and mother
were alive. When I answered the last question in the af-
firmative they seemed greatly surprised, and asked if they
loved me. No native here can understand how we can
leave a father and mother to go to a foreign land. Even
the members of our churches do not find it easy to comprehend. They regard it as deserting those to whom we
are bound by indissoluble ties, and it is sometimes rather
hard for us to listen patiently to their assertions that we
are destitute of natural affection. They always ask me if
I have any brothers, but they feel no interest in knowing
that I have sisters too. When I say I have brothers they
ask instantly if they are married, and when I tell them
one is, their curiosity is at white heat to know if he has
any little ones. Yes, I answer, two boys. "May they be
blessed," they exclaim. If I should say, "Yes, two nice
little girls," their countenances would fall instantly, and
they would say in most pitying tones, "Meakeen, meakeen!"
"Poor things, poor things!" It is wonderful the meaning
they can throw into these two words, "Bint bess,"—*only a
girl.*

I read the 6th chapter of Matthew, and we talked about it a little. But of course it is yet very difficult for me to make very much explanation, especially to those who know nothing of the Gospel. The blind boy came and sat by me while I read, and occasionally made some remark. When I finished, he said, "That is Matthew." I said it was, and asked him how he knew, when he told me he knew all the Gospels, because he went to a Coptic school. I then told the women that Dr. Watson was coming to-morrow, and would preach Sabbath, and they both said they would come to church. The boy said, "O that I could hear him!"

"You might 'put yourself in our place' with a good deal of accuracy, if you would imagine yourself and Mrs. B. [This letter was written to Dr. Bonner, editor Presbyterian.—ED.], engaged in work among the freedmen of the South, in a city where there was just one family working with you, but whom you rarely had time to visit, and whom you therefore did not often see except to meet at church twice on Sabbath. There would be the difference, however, that Arabs have more mind than our freedmen, and that some of them have wealth, but we do not have much to do with the rich ones, as a rule, and even if we did, very, *very* few of them have habits which would make it really *pleasant* to associate with them as we do with our friends at home. And I think there is probably no missionary who does not feel more or less repugnance at first. I have heard different members of our Mission speak of this, and some have confessed to a degree of it which I never felt, though I think it would naturally be expected that I should have felt it most. You soon see that the people have mind and are capable of being taught, and the consideration that it is " for Christ's sake" reconciles you to much that would otherwise be very repulsive.

Before I left home, I read a letter from this Mission describing the things that Missionaries were expected to eat which very much shocked and discouraged me, but now that I have had the experience I count all such things as one of my very small trials. It is often not at all pleasant at the time, but when I come out into the pure air, come into our own clean, comfortable room, and sit down to a nice, clean dinner, the contrast only makes it the more enjoyable. So do not think that considerations of this sort should frighten any one from undertaking mission life."

The year spent in Mansoora was to Mrs. Giffen a most trying one. In her private letters she said : "I would not live over that first year again for a great deal. Opening school in eight months after coming to the country, with such a limited knowledge of the language, with no grammar or dictionary, or adequate help of any kind—it was the hardest thing I ever undertook, and with all the other attending perplexities it almost killed me."

At the end of the year she was entirely prostrated by anxiety and overwork, and in addition was seized with jungle fever. Throughout Mrs. Giffen's entire mission life she labored too hard for her good, endeavoring to do more than her strength warranted, thus making herself more liable to the attack of disease. Had she been compelled to labor on in the same way and under similar circumstances, another year would have cut short her mission career and laid her to rest in the cemetery at Alexandria. But fortunately her marriage rescued her from this peril.

Yet during this same year she writes : "I am happy here and think I always will be. Nothing troubles me but my anxiety to get the language." "I am perfectly satisfied with the lot I have chosen, and know no other in the world for which I would willingly exchange it."

So thoroughly was her soul enlisted in her work, that during this year when the missionaries and more devoted converts began to agitate the question of establishing a mission in Abyssinia, twelve hundred miles further south, she wrote her friends in America to this effect, " In a year or two—just as soon as a lady can go, I will consent to go and work among the seventy-five millions of Abyssinia, who have never so much as heard of a Saviour."

CHAPTER XIV.

THE PYRAMIDS.

"Before I left home a great many of my friends gave me special injunctions about different things which I was to look at for their special benefit. Prominent among these was " *The Pyramids.*" But it was not until just as I was leaving Cairo that I visited them. I had heard so much about the difficulty of the ascent, the weary, worn-out, eighty-years-old feeling of the first three or four days succeeding such an excursion, and also of the overpowering sensation of terror which seizes almost every one who goes inside the great monument, that I must confess I was not very enthusiastic about making the visit. However, as much from a sense of duty as otherwise, I decided to go. Mr. A. and Misses J. and T. accompanied me. It is a drive of about ten miles from the city, and we took a carriage and started after early breakfast.

Formerly it was rather an undertaking to get over these ten miles, but on the ocaasion of the Empress Eugenie's visit to Egypt the Viceroy had a beautiful carriage way constructed the entire distance.   Trees, perhaps a foot in diameter were set out closely on each side, and now their thick branches overlap each other in beautiful arches and form the largest and prettiest avenue I ever saw.   Scarcely a ray of sunlight can pierce the thick foliage, and even when the day is quite warm you need a liberal supply of wraps to make the drive to the Pyramids a comfortable one.

Perhaps you know that there are about thirty-eight or forty of the pryamids of Ancient Egypt still standing. They extend over about a degree of latitude, and are situated on the western side of the river, just on the edge of the Libyan Hills.   They, therefore, overlook the sandy wastes of the desert on one side and the green valley of the Nile on the other; and during the inundation the water of the river comes up very near to the base of the great pyramid.   When we went most of it had disappeared, and the people were busy sowing grain on the mud.   Two or three miles before we reached the place Arab boys began to troop after us, regarding us as legitimate objects of booty.   They take it for granted that all travelers have plenty of money, and if you have not some skill in dismissing them you will have the identical dozen at your elbow from the time you step out of the carriage until you enter it again.   One boy had a kooleie of water—the native mud bottle—and he assured us we shouldn't be thirsty all day.   Another one, who could speak a little broken English, would see that we were understood and attended to, &c.   Our driver whipped his horses most unmercifully in the effort to escape the boys, but let him go as fast as he would there they were beside the wheels and there they stayed.   There was no sensible

ascent in the drive until about an eighth of a mile from
the base. There the hills begin rather suddenly, and
there the patience and long-suffering of our horses quite
failed them, and not a step further would they go until we
all got out and walked on before them. Then, by dint of
a very liberal allowance of the whip, they consented to
take our lunch up to the top of the hill.

As you approach the pyramids, you are surprised that
they do not seem to grow larger. You have heard so
much of their magnitude that you feel disappointed until
you get almost up the hill, then you make a great effort to
get control of all your emotions in the presence of such a
monster as the great one is when you come up to its base
and run your eye up its ragged sides away to the flagstaff
on the lofty summit. If you accept the commonly received opinion that this vast pile of stone was built for the
sole purpose of affording a distinguished place of interment for a haughty heathen monarch, you will look at
the immense stones of which it is built, and think with a
sigh of the *ten thousand* poor suffering Egyptians who
toiled here for *thirty years*, in summer's heat and winter's
cold, to gratify the pride and ambition of one single man.
But if you are a believer in the more recent theory that
the Great Pyramid is a pre-historic monument of an eminently grand and pure conception, which though in Egypt
is yet not of Egypt, and whose true and full explanation is
yet to come, then you will run your eye over the long rows
of stones in the lengthy sides, you will let it travel slowly
up the dizzy height from base to summit, and from summit to base again, until the one grand whole fixes itself
in your brain forever. Then you will long to know what
the great purpose of its construction was, and where in all
its vast interior is the hidden chamber which holds its
hoary secret.

But, if you wish to moralize or philosophize to any considerable extent, you will have to do it somewhere else than on the pyramid hill. It always *swarms* with what are known the world over as *Pyramid Arabs.* That is, it is considered the legitimate calling and occupation of the inhabitants of the village of Geezeh to assist travelers or visitors to the top of the pyramid, and in the meantime to extract from them buksheesh on every possible pretext which Arab ingenuity can invent. Mark Twain says they clamored buksheesh for allowing him to get out of his carriage, buksheesh for handing him his overcoat, buksheesh for permitting him to put on his gloves, buksheesh for allowing him to take a drink of water, buksheesh for eating his lunch, and buksheesh for getting into his carriage. And the story is perhaps not greatly exaggerated. These Arabs have wonderful memories, and rarely forget a face they have once seen. They said I was the only one of the party who had never been there, which was true. Mr. A. had made the ascent in the spring and they remembered him, though thousands of travelers from all over the world go there every winter. They recognized Miss Johnson as a resident of Cairo and a member of the American Mission, and consequently they conducted themselves very properly.

I must confess I felt rather appalled at the idea of climbing to the top of such a ragged mass of stones, but I had come for that purpose, and was determined not to let my heart fail me. Only Miss J. and myself were to go up. So we got into the carriage and took a nice lunch in the way of fortifying ourselves for the undertaking. Meantime Mr. A. selected three Arabs for each of us, made a bargain with the sheik that we were to pay one dollar for the ascent and two francs for the interior, and nobody was to even whisper buksheesh. They agreed, and we went round to the entrance, and went up fifteen or twenty feet of rubbish. When we came to the stones, one of the Arabs gathered up our dresses and made them into a mysterious knot behind, so that we should be in no danger of stepping on them. Two precede you, and you give each a hand, and one follows and partly lifts you where the layers are very high. Sometimes from one step to another is five feet, and that, of course, is difficult climbing, but much of the way the stones are so worn and broken that you can stick your foot into crevices and climb with comparatively ease without much assistance from the third man. At short distances we stopped, rested, and enjoyed the beautiful views spread out around us. Much of the drive from Cairo could be traced by the trees, and the city with its mosques and minarets stood out boldly against the Arabian hills in the back ground. The river, canals, and many small lakes yet remaining from the inundation, broke the monotony of the great level plain, and looked as blue as the blue sky above us. It was desert air we were breathing, and this, or something else, infused into my whole being such a feeling of exhilaration and keen enjoyment as I never knew before. I felt no fatigue nor any sense of fear, and I could have walked all round any one of the layers without the least approach of giddiness.

We were at the summit before I had thought of our having accomplished more than two-thirds of the distance, and instantly one of my Arabs almost convulsed me with a comic bow, and a still more comic salutation of "*how do you feel now?*" in broken English. It wasn't comically meant; he merely wished to inquire with an imitation of French gallantry if I was weary, but his slow-labored enunciation sounded so like the questions which are often

addressed to "sick people," that the contrast between a
sick bed and my own feelings at the moment was almost
too much for me.

The level space on which we found ourselves at the top
is about thirty feet square, that is, that much of the apex
of the pyramid was torn down when the casing stones were
removed by the Caliphs. Some of the loose stones yet remain and serve for seats. Their sides and the whole surface of the platform are covered with the autographs of
ambitious travelers, and prominent among them is that of
the Prince of Wales. However, I do not suppose he put
his name there himself. We didn't leave ours, under the
impression that future visitors would be able to survive
the omission. We simply walked round and looked down
all the sides. Oh! what an immense pile it seemed. Only
think of *thirteen acres* of stones towering up to a point at
the distance of four hundred and seventy feet and yourself standing away up on that point. If you never felt
humble before, you certainly will now, and if you should
never feel insignificant again, you will get an experience
here which a lifetime will scarcely efface. I can imagine
the awe which Niagara inspires, the wonderful impression
of *force, power* and *motion* which might almost overpower
one when looking upon its leaping waters and listening to
its deafening roar. But the great pyramid is something
different in the impression it leaves from anything I ever
saw before. There it has stood since before the time of
Abraham, and there it is likely to stand until the end of
time. It seems a magnificent monument of *silent endur-
ance.* The Coliseum is vast and impressive, but it is a *ruin,*
and the light of day shines through every rent and chasm.
All is known, the people who built it and those who enjoyed it. But on the pyramid hill there is a silence like

that of death, a stillness like that of the "everlasting hills," an incomprehensible, undefinable something, which makes you feel like subduing the laugh on your lips. You do not feel that you are in the presence of simple matter, matter which will some day return to its original dust. I, at least, felt myself in the presence of *mind*, of mind in sympathy and communion with God, of mind which knew the secrets of the world.

But I will stop, lest you write me down a heretic. If you are not acquainted with the new theories about the great pyramid, you will not sympathize very deeply in the sensations I experienced. Next week, perhaps, I will give you some account of the Piazzi Smyth doctrines, and you can then judge for yourself if it is probable that this immense structure was designed simply for the grave of one man.

We were almost ready to begin the descent before it occurred to me that there was a *Sphinx* down in the sand beneath us. I am afraid Prof. K. is horror-stricken ; but it is a fact, and when I did look it was principally for his sake. From our lofty position it seemed almost nothing, and when we came down and went to it, there was positively nothing to excite enthusiasm. It is *a big head* simply, with a face and expression just like many of the purely native Egyptians. There was just one other point of interest—that the huge mouth wore a pleasant expression. It is of later times than the Great Pyramid—Bruchs Bey and his new hieroglyphical stone, which is to be at the Centennial, to the contrary—and moreover it belongs to the old idolatrous religion. Nothing except the top of the lion back is visible now, so that there is really nothing but the complacent old face, always smiling on those drifting sands to impress one.

We all went inside the pyramid, had the chambers and passages illuminated with magnesium wire, and saw pretty well all that was to be seen. But I will tell you about that again. We came out, took another lunch, paid off our Arabs, and drove into the city just at sunset. It was a very, very pleasant day, and I came back less fatigued than I have often felt from a long walk."

CHAPTER XV.

PYRAMIDS—CONTINUED.

" About forty years ago an Englishman by the name of Taylor became interested in the subject of the Great Pyramid and began the close study of all the scientific measurements made upon it. He arrived at some rather startling conclusions, but died without ever seeing the pyramid. His views however were taken up and adopted by several distinguished men. Prominent among them is the Astronomer Royal of Scotland, Piazzi Smyth, who came and lived for months on the pyramid hill in order to have every opportunity for testing the great problem.

The commonly received opinion that this pyramid was designed as a magnificent monument and burial place for the king who built it, is supposed to have grown out of the fact that a stone coffer of about the usual size for receiving a mummy case was found in the interior when the Caliph Al Mamoon forced an entrance into it, coupled with the fact that all the other thirty-seven or thirty-eight were *known* to have been constructed for sepulchral purposes.

They all abound in the pictorial and hieroglyphical repre-
sentations which were part and parcel of the ancient religion of Egypt, and therefore proclaim themselves the
products of heathen builders.   But in the Great Pyramid
there is not a vestige of heathenism, nor the most distant
allusion to the worship of the sun, moon, or any of the
starry host of heaven.   Manetho and Herodotus affirm
that it was built by a power which was " an abomination
to the Egyptians," but which they implicitly obeyed, working however under such compulsion and constraint as compelled them to refrain from putting any of their accustomed decorations on the finished building, or in any way
identifying it with their impure and hieratic form of worship.   And when the power was relaxed, though they hated
its name so as to forbear even mentioning it, yet with in-
voluntary bending to superior intelligence they began im-
itating, as well as they could, its more ordinary mechanical
features.

Taylor decided in his own mind that what was hateful to
the Egyptians could not have been in itself bad, must on
the contrary have been good, or at all events that the
builders were of *a different religious faith.*   Combining this
with certain historical facts, and with the numerous and
peculiar symbolizations of both exterior and interior, he
declared his belief that its builders were of *the chosen race,*
in the line of, but preceding, Abraham, and that he had
discovered in the arrangements and measurements of the
Great Pyramid scientific results in the shape of numerical
knowledge of grand cosmical phenomena, both of earth
and heavens, far above the scientific attainments of any
ancient Gentile nation, and essentially above even that of
our own time.

By removing all the debris from the northern face of
the pyramid an almost exact measurement of its original

base was obtained. There, too, were found *two* of the original casing stones, five feet high, eight feet wide and twelve feet long, yet in position, with their edges beveled and joined in a cemented seam of no greater thickness than *tissue* paper. These enabled Colonel Vyse and his engineers to contrast angular with linear measure, and thus to arrive at the exact original height. Consequently they were able to verify Taylor's first proposition, *that the height of the Great Pyramid is to twice the breadth of its base as the diameter to the circumference of a circle;* or that the area of a right section is to the area of the base as one to 3.141594; or stating it differently, that the vertical height of the Great Pyramid is the radius of a theoretical circle the curved length of whose circumference is equal to the sum of the lengths of the four straight sides of the actual base.

This of course is the celebrated practical problem of mediæval and modern Europe—"the squaring of the circle" and its solution in this great building must have been the result either of marvellous accident or of deep wisdom thousands of years in advance of its own time—wisdom however which did not address itself to its contemporaries, but left it for distant posterity.

Second, Taylor claimed that owing to the complicated fractions arising from assuming the British foot or the Egyptian cubit of 20.7 inches as the standard of linear measure used in constructing the pyramid, that some other unit must have been used. Accordingly after various tests he found that the base lengths of each side—which is about seven hundred and sixty-three feet—when divided by the one ten-millionth of the earth's semi-axis of rotation, *gives the length of our solar year*, or conversely if the semi-axis be divided by the number expressing the solar year, the result is the one ten-millionth of the semi-axis, or close upon twenty-five British inches. This measure Taylor, Smyth, and others call the "sacred cubit," or the cubit of the Bible, in contradistinction to that of the Egyptians and Babylonians. The unit of this measure, one inch, is the one ten-thousandth part, or half a hair's breadth less than the British inch, and the whole measure with its multiple of five is a dominant number all through the building. The French metre you know was obtained by taking the one ten-millionth of *a quadrant of the earth's surface;* but late progress in Geodesy has shown that the earth's equator is not a circle but an irregular, curvilinear figure of as many different lengths as there are meridians of longitude. Consequently after Taylor made known his theory of the origin of the sacred cubit, Sir John Herschel said: "So long as the human mind continues human, and retains a power of geometry, so long will the *diameter* be thought of more importance than the *circumference* of a circle." Here, then, according to pyramid theorists, is a standard of linear measure for the whole world infinitely superior to the French metre with its false basis and its adoption by a nation which declared there was no God, and which even counted its Sabbaths in decimals.

I have said above that the circle typified by the base of the great pyramid was claimed to symbolize the solar year, or the annual revolution of the earth around the sun, and the radius of that circle the ancient height of the pyramid, would then represent the semi-diameter of the earth's orbit, or the radius of the earth's mean orbit. Consequently, if these assumptions can be proved, it will be no difficult matter to arrive at the solution of the great problem which so stirred the scientific world last year on the occasion of the " transit of Venus"—the question of the distance of the sun from the earth. During the last half century this has been held to be 95,000,000 miles ; and our theorists felt sure that this number would result from a calculation based on the 5,813 pyramid inches of the pyramid's height; but when the computation was completed, to their amazement, it turned out 91,840,000 instead of 95,000,000. But in a year or two this latter quantity was strongly called in question by even the best astronomers of the day, one group affirming it to be from ninety-one to ninety-one and a-half million miles, and another that it was from ninety-two to ninety-two and a-half million miles. So Smyth and his disciples took heart again and concluded that theirs was the true mean— the golden medium, and are waiting with great anxiety to hear the summing up from the observations of last year on the "transit of Venus." *

When Napoleon's Parisian savants were in Egypt they made many measurements and observations on the Pyramid. The result which surprised them most was that its sides were *oriented*, that is, it is placed with its sides facing astronomically due north, south, east and west—lacking only about one minute—a proof as they supposed " that the azimuthal direction of the earth's axis had not sensibly altered relatively to the great Pyramid's base during probably 4,000 years." These savants also used the apex of the pyramid as the *zero meridian* of longitude for all Egypt, and this they did from regard to its peculiar position. Afterwards Henry Mitchell, of the United States Coast Survey, in reporting upon the Suez canal in 1868, was greatly struck with the regularity of curvature along the whole of Egypt's northern coast. It seemed to him

---

*The distance from the earth to sun is now estimated at 92,500,-000 miles.

to have been developed in successive curves, all struck one after another from a central point of physical organization; and then after long and careful search he thought he found this center in the great pyramid, and decided in his own mind that "this monument stands in a more important position than any other building yet erected by man." It stands on the very cliff of the Geezeh Hill, so close that the edges might have broken off under the immense pressure had not the builders banked up there the immense mounds of rubbish which came from their work, and which Strabo searched so carefully for, without finding them, 1,800 years ago. The pyramid thus occupies the position of the handle of a fan—the delta being the fan, or, to express it differently, the pyramid is the apex of a triangle whose base is the northern coast of Egypt. Besides, if you proceed along the globe due north and south from the great pyramid there will be found to be more earth and less sea in that meridian than in any other all the world round, causing it to be essentially marked by nature as a prime meridian for all nations. And the same is true of the pyramid's parallel of 30°. It contains more land surface than any other. Finally summing up all the dry land habitable by man, the wide world over, the center of the whole falls within the great pyramid's territory of Lower Egypt.

These, then, according to Taylor and others, are the symbolizations of the exterior of this wonderful structure:

First, That it gives the long sought quantity, so necessary in all mechanics known to mathematicians by the Greek character p.

Second, That it furnishes a standard of linear measure from the unit of which the British inch was without much doubt originally taken, and which has many claims to superiority over the French standard.

Third, that it furnishes the true diameter and circumference of the earth's orbit, and also the true distance from the sun.

Fourth, That the azimuth of the earth's axis has not sensibly altered in 4,000 years.

Fifth, That it gives the best meridian of longitude for the whole world.

And sixth, That it stands in the center of the land surface of the earth.

Perhaps you may not feel inclined to accept any of these deductions, but I think you must allow that they are at least remarkable, and some of them very interesting. At any rate, after having heard them once fully stated, I think one must be either very credulous or very incredulous, if he can hold on to the old theory that the wonderful mechanical skill, and the many and strong evidences of design everywhere manifest in this vast structure, were only intended to furnish a safe place of burial for a body which never came into it.

But the theory is mainly built upon the interior, of which I will write you again.   There is another point, too, which perhaps I should mention.   It is that these mathematical quantities and symbolizations are not found in any other of the thirty-eight or forty pyramids of Lower Egypt, which have been measured and tested.   Every one of them errs in angle, size and position, being all little else than crumbling monuments of idolatry.

The ancients knew nothing of the interior of the Great Pyramid, except that like all the others it contained a descending narrow passage with a chamber at the bottom, and a tradition that somewhere within it there was a vast store of hidden treasure.   Externally it was complete in its casing sheet of beveled limestone, and when in 820 Al

Mamoun determined to penetrate the secret, if secret there was, tradition could only dimly direct him to the northern face, and as the builders must have foreseen, he began in the center. But it was hard work quarrying into stone almost as solid as the hill on which it was founded. The workmen gave up in despair, declaring the thing impossible, but the Caliph affirmed that it should certainly be done. So after months of toilsome exertion they had penetrated one hundred feet from the entrance, and one day they were rewarded by hearing a stone fall in some hollow place, within a few feet of them. They pushed on then in the direction of the noise, hammers, fire and vinegar being used until they broke into the hollow passage way, through which the Romans of old had penetrated to the subterranean chamber. But now another secret was exposed. A large angular fitting stone, that had made for ages a portion of the ceiling of the narrow passage, had dropped on the floor, revealing that there was another passage clearly ascending towards the south, out of this descending one, the entrance to which had perhaps been known to the Romans. The ascending passage was however still closed by a series of granite plugs, slided down from above. To remove these was impossible with the rude tools of that day, and so the Moslem crew dug round and above it in the softer limestone, and opened the way from above. They found the passage ascending at an angle of twenty-six degrees for one hundred and ten feet, but only forty-seven inches in height and forty-one in breadth. Suddenly they emerged into a long tall gallery, seven times the height of the passage, and one hundred and fifty feet long. Just on the right hand of the entrance was the mouth of a dark well, one hundred and forty feet in depth, leading into the descending passage near the subterranean chamber. This grand gallery, nowhere more than six feet wide and contracted towards the top, was also of polished marble-like stone throughout. At the top of the slippery plane they found another narrow passage, very like the one which had admitted them into the grand gallery, and creeping through this they found themselves at once in the grand chamber which forms the conclusion of the Great Pyramid's interior. This apartment is thirty-four feet long, seventeen broad and nineteen high, and is of polished red granite, floor, walls and ceiling, in squared blocks so skillfully put together that the seams are barely discernible.

But where was the treasure? Al Mamoon was amazed. Not a single dirham was there anywhere, *only an empty stone chest without a lid.*

Ages went by, and finally Europeans began to visit the pyramids and to wonder what could have been the purpose of that stone chest. Gradually the notion grew that it might have been a sarcophagus, that it *was* a sarcophagus, then that it was intended for the Pharaoh of Red Sea fame, who had not the opportunity of being deposited in his own tomb. But it came to light finally that the pyramid was not only built, but had been sealed up long before even the birth of Pharaoh. Then some one wrote that it was King Cheops, or Chemmis or Shufo, who was buried there, but his body was removed. But this theory also falling to the ground, the world settled down into the belief that *somebody* must have been buried there. Strange to say, however, in 1837 Colonel Vyse discovered "air channels" leading through the solid masonry to the outside air, evidently intending that it should be ventilated in the most admirable manner. There is also another unfinished chamber, also ventilated in the same way, except that there was

G

a small crust of stone to be broken through to open them—
Dr. Grant, the mission physician in Cairo, making the dis-
covery only two years ago.

Finally the Englishman Taylor came out with his theory,
" that the coffer in the King's chamber was intended to be
a standard measure of capacity and weight for all nations,
and that certain nations did originally receive their weights
and measures from thence." For instance, the British
farmer measures his wheat in *quarters*, but quarters of
what? He does not know; he simply calls it a quarter.
So, in pity for his ignorance, Taylor comes to his help and
tells him *it is quarters* of the contents of the stone coffer in
the King's chamber. Accordingly, Vyse and Smith made
the most accurate measurements of the cubical contents of
the coffer and found the agreement between the British
quarters and a fourth part of the contents of the coffer as
17,746 : 17,801.

Great emphasis, too, is laid, as I said, on the dominance
of the number five. The casing stones were five feet thick,
there is a marked division into five of the ceiling of the
ante-chamber under which you must bow your head before
entering the last narrow passage into the King's chamber,
and the ceiling stones of this chamber are in five and a
half. They are of all lengths, but exactly of the same
height, and five of them reach from the bottom to the top.
Yet for some mysterious reason the lower row extends just
five inches below the surface of the floor. The whole number of stones in the entire chamber is just one hundred.
Also the courses of masonry of which the pyramid is composed are not of the same height, but whatever height or
thickness of stones any one course is begun with, it is kept
on at that thickness *precisely*, right through the whole extent of the course, although the area may there amount to

acres. And on reaching in this manner the fiftieth course of stones, you have the level of the floor of the King's chamber, on which rests the stone coffer, a vessel with commensurable capacity proportions between its interior and exterior, and between the walls and floor in a room with five courses, composed of one hundred stones, and with a capacity proportion of *fifty to the fifth of these courses.* Says Smith, "the dullest person in existence could hardly fail to see that this chamber should have been called the chamber of the standard of fifty." So let me whisper that he who does not see it in this light lays himself liable to an imputation.

This chamber furthermore is claimed to be the most suitable place in the known world for making those experiments which determine the density of the earth—one of the most puzzling of astronomical problems. Air tight rooms closed in with glass have been used in England where the experimenter had to remain outside. In Pulkova, near St. Petersburg, these experiments are performed in subterranean chambers, and in Paris the most perfect pendulum in the world is kept going in a subterranean chamber known as "the caves," ninety-five feet below the surface, in order to secure such a uniformity of temperature as shall prevent any variation in the apparatus. But still perfection has never yet been reached. It would be, however, Smith affirms, if scientists would only come to the great meteorological center of the world—the King's Chamber of the Great Pyramid, which is everywhere shielded from summer's heat and winter's cold by one hundred and eighty feet of solid masonry! He declares there never has been, and most probably never will be, a scientific observing room erected by any nation to be at all compared in its very leading requisite with this remarkable chamber.

But to go back to the *descending passage*. The entrance to this was, of course, found and opened after Al Mamoon had forced his way into it within the pyramid. It is twenty-four feet to the west of the center of the northern face, and is forty-nine feet above the level of the base. The passage is of the same dimensions with the narrow ascending one, and also descends at the angle of twenty-six degrees. It extends to the center of the pyramid, and is, of course, almost four hundred feet long—the chamber into which it leads being situated in the solid rock *one hundred feet below the line of the pyramid's base.* Just before entering this subterranean chamber you pass under the mouth of the dark well which I mentioned as leading down from the northern extremity of the grand gallery.

From the bottom of this descending passage the light of day shining in at the entrance is just as if you saw a star through a long telescope; and this, aside, of course from furnishing an entrance, is supposed to be the design of this passage—to furnish a telescope *with a fixed degree of elevation,* bearing upon any star which should be, *at the time of the pyramid's erection,* three degrees twenty-four minutes from the Polar point. Sir John Herschel declared that within the last five thousand years only one notable star had been at the required distance, namely, *a* (alpha) of the constellation Draconis; and that it was in such a position 2170 B. C. Hence the deduction from this and other astronomical data and arguments too complicated to be introduced here, that the pyramid was built at this date—2170 B. C., and is therefore four thousand and forty-six years old.

Pyramid theorists also find great resemblance between the Ark and the Tabernacle of the wilderness and the Pyramid and its stone coffer. The cubical contents of the

Ark, Smyth affirms, to be almost identically those of the
coffer as near as the measure of the former can be approx-
imated. It was also a lidless box of the same shape as the
coffer. Great prominence was also given in the tabernacle to weights and measures, and everywhere it was the
sacred cubit of twenty-five inches. He also remarks that
the Pentateuch contains five books, that Pentecost occurs
fifty days after the Passover, and that the year of Jubilee
was every fiftieth one. The number five, says Sir Gard-
ner Wilkinson, "was an abomination to the ancient Egyptians," and is "the evil number" of the modern ones, and
is represented by a cypher. Particularly galling, therefore, it must have been to the Egyptians when they saw
the Israelites go up out of Egypt in ranks of five, for so
Smyth says the word "harnessed" should be translated.

But last of all the passages, gallery and chambers of the
Great Pyramid are held to symbolize *the Christian religion.*
The *descending* passage is a type of human depravity, ever
gravitating toward that final abode at the extremity of the
descent. But from this ruined condition, this *facilis descensus Averni* there was one Exodus, but only for a few,
typified by the *ascending passage* showing Hebraism ending its original prophetic destination—Christianity. But
another escape is possible before reaching that fearful
abyss, namely, by "the straight and narrow way," typified by the dark and narrow well leading from the lower
part of the "*descensus*" into the grand gallery. Giving
an inch for a year, and measuring backwards from the
north beginning of the gallery, the exodus is found either
at 1483 or 1542 B. C., and the Dispersion at 2528 B. C.,
up at the beginning of the entrance passage. Then going
back to the northern entrance of the grand gallery, typi-
cal of the birth of Christ, thirty-three inches bring you

opposite *the mouth of the well*, the type of his death and resurrection.

Some time after all these measures and conjectures were published, Smyth was reminded that he and Herschel had fixed the date of the building, or completion at 2170 B. C., that he claimed for the builder divine inspiration, that if that were the case the builder surely knew and would have marked the years which would elapse from the date of the Pyramid until the birth of Christ. And he was asked to find some mark of this fact in the passages leading backward from the northern entrance of the grand gallery. If the completion of the building really occurred in 2170 B. C., this date would fall three or four hundred inches only from the mouth of the entrance. Smyth was then—1873—in Scotland, and accordingly he wrote to Dr. Grant and Wymar Dixon to make a careful examination. They did so and at the very spot found a very peculiar line ruled into the stone on each side of the passage. They made the examination without knowing for what purpose it was intended, only they were desired to be very exact. Herewith the cavilers expressed themselves entirely satisfied, and the Astronomer Royal, of Scotland, went on his way rejoicing.

The entrance to the pyramid is some distance from the outside or northern face. All the stones around it are of immense size, and above it they are put in in the form of an arch. It is rather a forbidding prospect to go creeping down that narrow passage, so steep that you have the greatest difficulty to keep from sliding down in a manner neither dignified nor comfortable.

The grand gallery was a wild, beautiful sight, when illuminated by the magnesium wire, only it was such a difficult matter to find a sure enough footing to enable you to

look at it in any comfort. In the king's chamber the
Arabs struck the coffer with their hands and it rang like
the finest bell metal. Then one of them shouted. And,
oh, such a wonderful echo! There was such an amazing
volume of sound, and it seemed to roll and roll and roll,
winding upward in constantly decreasing spiral curves
until we could imagine it was issuing from the very apex
of the pyramid. The ventilating passages, however, are
choked up or stopped up by the Arabs, and we did not
care to remain very long in Smyth's royal apartment.
There were none of us frightened, as we had a good supply of candles, but none of us felt any regret when we
looked up the long "telescope" on our return and saw
the star-like glimmer of the day."

Of all sciences Mrs. Giffen most loved mathematics and
was never more happy than when engaged in the solution
of some difficult problem. It is said that "when a little
girl she was known to work three days on one sum in
addition in Davies' Algebra, rather than pass it over or to
take the say of the teacher, without a perfect understanding of why it was so."

CHAPTER XVI.

ROME—COLISEUM—VATICAN—ST. PETER'S.

"Most travelers I think indulge in a great deal of enthusiasm over their first day in Rome, not perhaps because they really *feel* a great deal but because they *thought* they would when they left home, and because they knew their friends expect at least a small outburst from them. They usually jump up early the first morning, write a letter home and date it from "the Eternal City," the contents consisting largely of very sage reflections on " seven hilled Rome,"—"Niobe of nations," etc., etc. But we were not just travelers—with one exception—we were on our way to a new and trying life, and we thought much more frequently of what awaited us there than of the sights and scenes through which we were passing. When you travel as far as Egypt I think most persons become conscious of considerable indifference to even "the wonders of the world." There is so much to disgust one, particularly an American. His credulity is appealed to so incessantly that he falls into a kind of mental desperation and feels like affirming that he doesn't believe anything. Even in Westminster Abbey at the very outset of our sight-seeing our appreciation of the grand old building and its innumerable treasures of art was very considerably lessened by the absolute reverence which the keepers and guides manifested for the mere relics of kings and queens who had only cursed the world while they were alive.

If you could see all the famous places in peace and quiet and examine them at your leisure, the effect would be different; but to one just passing through it seems that Europe literally lives upon the credulity of travelers. There is *always* somebody at your elbow to tell you in the most triumphant tones that you are just on the very spot where some wonderful saint performed some most wonderful miracle, and that he only asks you a franc for the valuable information. It would undoubtedly have left a gap in your life not to have heard of it and you give him the franc to get rid of him. By the time you reach Rome you are so surfeited with priests and nuns, with endless pictures of the Virgin Mary, with St. Peter's keys and mitre that you almost forget, or wish to forget, that the one *was our Lord's* mother, or that the other was a great apostle and martyr, and that both are now before the "great white throne."

I think there was but one place among the many which we saw in Rome that we really enjoyed in itself. This was the Coliseum, of which everybody has read and heard so much. But for those who forget figures and dimensions, I may say it was an oval structure consisting of three stories of arches and each story composed of eighty arches. Those of the first tier are marked with Roman numbers, as they formed so many entrances, through which by internal stair-cases the upper stories were reached. These are on the plan of open galleries, each succeeding one receding like the seats in a circus. The first one is necessarily quite wide, affording space for a very wide hall in rear of the gallery and stair-cases, the second tier of arches forming its windows. In this first gallery was *the Podium*, the place occupied by the Emperors, their families, the magistrates, the senators, priests and vestals. On the second floor is another gallery and a narrow hall, and on the third floor merely a gallery.

It is impossible to conceive anything better adapted to the purpose for which it was designed than this great

structure. The eighty entrances, the absence of a roof, and
the great wide halls must have made it a delightful place of
resort for those who found their highest enjoyment in wit-
nessing blood and slaughter. It is about five hundred and
eighty-five yards in circumference, and perhaps fifty-five
in height, and was capable of seating one hundred thousand
persons. It was built by the Emperor Vespasian on the
ground formerly occupied by the stagnum of the garden
of Nero, and served for the purpose of gladiatorial com-
bats until the year 523. During the six hundred succeeding years it was used as a stronghold by some noble families, and in 1332 a magnificent tournament was given
there.

Pius VII., Leo X., Gregory XVI., and finally Pius IX.
all made important repairs and restorations. The latter
has restored the upper tier for about one third of the circumference to its primitive condition, so that one may now
form a tolerably accurate idea of the original, while "the
magnificence of the ruin" is but the more enhanced. Our
one regret was that we could not see it by moonlight,
though if we had I think our thoughts would not have
glided into that old worn channel which most travelers fall
into, a practical lament over "the ruins of time."

To enjoy "the imposing spectacle which this monument
presents," as the guide books would say, we ascended the
highest part, and sat down on the stones where so many
old Romans had been before us. Perhaps they were poor
plebeians, crowded up to the higher seats by the haughty
patricians below, or perhaps they were gay boys and girls
who enjoyed getting up above their patres familias, and
who gave few thoughts to the martyrs on the sands below.
The same bright sun looked down upon us as upon them,
but how different was all else. The whole arena is strewn

with great broken columns, appropriate emblems of the power which once was so triumphant here, the lovely little flowers were springing everywhere in the crevices which once were worn and dry from the trampling of a thousand feet. Busy workmen were carefully excavating the cells and dens in which lions and tigers were pampered to render them fit combatants for him who dared to "believe in Jesus." Behind us lay the great city, not as then *pagan*, persecuting Rome, but *Christian*, persecuting Rome ; just as merciless, just as blood-thirsty as when the perfect Coliseum rang with the applause of a hundred thousand hard-hearted pagans.

The abutment which receives the third tier of arches projects about a yard, and from the hall you can step through the open arches upon this projection. If I remember correctly the wall was here at least five or six feet in thickness, so you may form some idea of the thickness at the base, and the immense amount of material required to construct it. I walked out on the projection, gathered some flowers, and intended to walk all round that side but the gentlemen looked such strong objections that I gave it up and contented myself with the view of "the Seven Hills" which, from the height of the Coliseum, is one of the most beautiful scenes in the world, at least as far as my experience goes. Just to the right is the Palatine Hill with the ruins of "the Palace of the Cæsars," where the great Apostle stood in chains before cruel Nero. Persecutor and persecuted, both now are dust, as to the mortal part ; the gilded palace too has crumbled away, and the saints which were "of Cæsar's household" all are gone. Most of them no doubt passed away from earth by violent hands. But what a monument is this Coliseum of them "of whom the the world was not worthy!" May it stand just as it does

to-day, *a magnificent ruin* to the end of time! a mementor
of the broken power which poured out on these white
sands the blood of thousands of martyrs.   May it stand as
it does now a silent witness of the advancement of that
kingdom which will one day fill the whole earth, which is
stronger than Roman legions and mightier than many
Cæsars.

There is a quiet and silence about the place not found
in other quarters of Rome.   After paying the entrance fee
no one disturbed us and we walked leisurely around enjoying our own reflections.   As we passed around one of the
long halls, and with our hearts touched and softened at
thought of the agony on which those dumb walls had so
often looked down, I said to Mr. G. : " How amazing that
thousands of people once thronged these great galleries to
make a pastime of death!"   And he answered softly :
"They were *pagans*.   ' By *grace* you are what you are ! ' "

In Byron's " Manfred " there occurs a beautiful description of the Coliseum by moonlight.   There is now in possession of Dr. Phillips a copy of this poem, and on the
margin opposite this description, an entry in the handwriting of Mrs. Giffen, in these words : " I would give twenty
of the best years of my life to stand where he stood on
that night."   This sentence was penned twelve years before
this letter was written.   Such a change does the grace of
God work in the heart.

The lines which called forth this longing desire to view
this beautiful ruin were these :

> " Upon such a night
> I stood within the Coliseum's wall,
> Midst the chief relics of almighty Rome:
> The trees which grew along its broken arches
> Waved dark in the blue midnight, and the star
> Shone through the rents of ruin : from afar

The watch-dog bayed beyond the Tiber ; and
More near from out the Cæsar's palace came
The owl's long cry, and interruptedly
Of distant sentinels the fitful song
Begun and died upon the gentle wind."

In regard to her visit to the Vatican and St. Peter she says:

"Sometimes when I have leisure to think of something else than my immediate surroundings I recall the time when I used to "devour" books of travel and provoke a smile from incredulous friends by affirming that I intended some day to stand "beneath the dome of St. Peter's." But when we drew aside the massive curtain which shuts out the profane light of day from Rome's most venerated Basilica, how the romance had fled! It was not the old dream nor I the same person. I was in "Sunny Italy," I knew, but it was not now the ultimatum of my ambition. The "land of the caliphs" and the sons of the desert were of far more interest, and I walked down that magnificent Nave with feelings as widely different from what I had dreamed I would experience, as was the means which gratified my school-girl wish from my original expectations.

The Vatican, you know, was the palace of Charlemagne when he was crowned by Leo, but it has been indefinitely adorned and extended by the Popes who have resided in it. It is of three stories, and contains a perfect labyrinth of halls, galleries, chapels, corridors, libraries, museums, and court-yards. Of course we ascended one of the eight grand stair-cases—there are two hundred inferior ones—but I have forgotten the length of it. I think, however, it cannot be under three hundred feet. It is a magnificent ascending marble hall, richly ornamented like every other part of these great buildings, but the only statue I remember is an equestrian figure of "Saul the Persecutor" when "suddenly there shined round about him a light from heaven." The splendid horse is rearing in silent terror, but it is only amazement which speaks in the rider's face. He has not yet "fallen to the ground." He still "breathes out threatenings and slaughter." It is the lion heart still unsubdued, the eagle eye gazing, undimmed as yet, into the very rays of the streaming light. But the days of his rebellion are numbered. After this day he will persecute no more, and "Saul the Jew" will be henceforth "Paul the Apostle." It was the only thing about St. Peter's which seemed pure and true and which it seems pleasant to remember.

At the head of the stair-case we found some galleries containing modern paintings, but I could detect little excellence except in richness of coloring. Popes and Cardinals in scarlet robes figuring largely in all of them. We passed on to the *Sistine Chapel* with every expectation of being overwhelmed with the world's masterpiece of painting—Michael Angelo's "Last judgment." It is in fresco and covers *one end* of the hall, but—sorry I am to confess it—we could not detect the "magnificence" of the painting. Like everything else, it is distinctively a *Catholic* picture, and is badly injured by damp and *candle smoke*. Afterwards we went through hall after hall with their walls covered with the works of "the great masters" but without time to study them. Inexperienced eyes I think will always come away disappointed.

The Nave is vaulted and richly decorated with gilding. The pavement is of various marbles, inlaid in beautiful mosaic designs, and indeed such a wealth of marble can surely not exist anywhere else in the world. Many of the statues of popes and saints were literally enveloped in *marble lace.* Such grace in the drapery and such exquisite carving I could not have believed possible. "But the pity of it"—all thrown away on mitred popes!

On the left of the Nave were many confessionals—little rooms scattered up and down the long aisle, with a priest in each and the language he spoke printed above the door, but there was but one penitent in them all. It was a woman, and we waited to see her face when she came out. She had soft, dreamy eyes and a sweet, sad face; and as she passed out we wondered what secret she had poured into the ear of that hardened-looking priest.

But I am sure you want to know how we were impressed by "the grand whole." Well, I must admit it again that we were *grievously disappointed.* And I think this is the experience of everyone who sees St. Peter's only once. It is like "the great masters"—must be studied. There is such a vast amount of statuary and ornament of every kind, such vast rows of arches, vaults and columns that one loses all idea of proportion, and really forgets that it is a large building. It is said to be so perfect in its proportions that one feature does not call attention to another by any contrast, and it is not until one has seen it several times that the impression of its great size begins to be formed in the mind. Unfortunately we could not get access to the dome, and were compelled to be content with almost dislocating our necks to look up its great height.

Now shall I make a confession. You will smile and others will perhaps feel inclined to criticise my taste, but I must say that nowhere in Europe did I see any building which pleased me so much as the exterior of the Capitol at Washington. I think I will never forget that beautiful facade literally glittering in the evening sunlight as you

stopped to let me take a last look at it.   Nothing I saw in
London and Paris, nothing in the bewildering Palace Gardens in Florence, nothing even in Rome can at all com-
pare with the *native* magnificence of our Capitol grounds.
I think of the Capitol, and Notre Dame seems like some
great gloomy old prison.   The Florentine palaces externally, might pass for an old fortress with its barracks, and
when I come to the Grand Piazza of St. Peter's with its
magnificent colonnade, how tame and spiritless it seems
compared with the grass and the trees, the great winding
walks and carriage drives of our Republican grounds."

After Mrs. Giffen had graduated, the chiefest desire of
her heart was to visit Europe.   The glowing descriptions
of the wonders of the old world, with which the books of .
travel were filled, had excited in her an irrepressible desire to see for herself these beauties of nature and miracles of art, which had so captivated other beholders.   To
stand beneath the dome of St. Peter's, on "the banks of
the yellow Tiber," the "Coliseum's ruined wall;" to float
some calm, starry night on the beautiful bay of Naples; to
see the blue skies of "sunny Italy;" to be privileged to commune face to face with the great creations of "the old masters" in painting and sculpture—the
"Last Supper" of Michael Angelo, the "Apollo Belvi-
dere"—to gratify this all-pervading desire was the ultimatum of her earthly hopes.   But now when she does
stand in the presence of these mighty creations of art and
genius, what a change has "come over the spirit of her
dream."   The Coliseum is the same magnificent ruin,
and St. Peter's the same bewildering pile of marble—why
does she now look upon them with different eyes?   The actu-
ating motive of her life is not the same.   The dazzling
dream of her girlhood has vanished, and she now stood

the strong, self-reliant woman, purified and emancipated by the almighty grace of God, "*a new creature*," whose one purpose and inspiration was to see, not Rome, but that "city whose foundations are eternal and whose builder and maker is God" to stand, not upon "the seven hills of Rome," but upon "the everlasting hills;" not upon the banks of the Tiber, but upon the shores of "the river of life;" to see, not St. Peter's—the temple of God "made with hands," but to wonder and worship in that "temple not made with hands, eternal in the heavens."

CHAPTER XVII.

MRS. GIFFEN'S MARRIAGE.

In a little more than a year after Mrs. Giffen's arrival in Egypt she was united in marriage to Rev. John Giffen, of the same mission, and one of her fellow-travelers on the voyage out from America. He was born near St. Clairsville, Ohio, where his family now reside, and entered the mission at the same time that Mrs. Giffen did. But the particulars in regard to this most interesting event are best given in her own words. She says in a letter to Dr. Bonner: "Do you remember that after you had taken leave of me on board the *Cuba* the day we sailed from New York you met Mr. Giffen just outside the cabin door, and that you put me in his special care? Well, he most faithfully fulfilled the promise he made you, of performing a brother's part to me, not only on the long journey, but during all our stay here. You put me into his care as a sister,

but now, as you will have heard, I have given myself into
his care in another relation. My name is changed somewhat, but I am " M. E. G." still—*your missionary* just all
the same. My work may not be altogether in the same
shape, more of it may be in the house, among the mothers,
but it will be quite as effective so, and more encouraging.
Be that as it may, however, you will not find that a change
of name has changed anything else. I am *yours* just as
before and hope to be able to communicate with you just
as often as before.

We were married at Dr. Lansing's on the 5th of June,
and though neither of us had any claim of relationship,
we were made to feel just as pleasant, just as much at home
as if our wedding guests had assembled in a certain parlor
in Due West. The Consul-General, Hon. Mr. Farman,
was present, with the Vice Consul, Mr. Hay and family,
Judge and Mrs. Batchelor, of the Internal Court, Mr. Rem-
ington, of New York, and all the missionaries now in the
field, except Mr. Ewing, who was detained by illness in
his family. You know that Mrs. Lansing's early missionary letters are the first things I ever remember to have
read, and that they had quite an influence in turning my
thoughts and inclinations towards mission life. And the
last time she was in America she made an appeal to the
theological students of Xenia which had more weight with
Mr. Giffen than anything else of the kind brought to bear
on his mind in deciding the question of his coming to
Egypt. It was, therefore, a very pleasant coincidence that
we were married in her house. Her marriage with Dr.
Lansing was the only precedent one we had in the mission,
and Dr. L. pronounced our ceremony."

This union proved to both " a marriage made in heaven."
There entered into it none of the selfish and mercenary

motives which too often lead to marriage and misery. Those feelings which God and nature has ordained shall constitute the true basis of marriage, alone operated in this case. With her hand she gave her heart—not partially but wholly. A more loyal, faithful, loving wife never lived. All the affections of her nature, and they were intense and powerful, went out to her husband and children. She literally lived in and for those whom she loved. From the hour of her marriage self had few of her thoughts.

In a letter to her mother she says: "I have as good and kind a husband as ever blessed any woman. Nothing that thoughtful love and care can bring to me will ever be wanting. I think my sleepless nights, and the nervous anxiety which has almost killed me the last months, are things which will never come back to me. Mr. Giffen is a very pious man, one whom I can trust to the last degree—deeply affectionate, and a man to command and retain regard. We are as happy as we can be. The world wears a different aspect from what it did, before we knew that each cared for the other. So do not be troubled about me any more. O! that God would make me worthy of the blessing He is giving me, and that it may be the better for the world that we have lived together in it. I hope we will be as useful as we are happy, for I am sure our facilities for usefulness are greatly increased."

At first the Church feared that Mrs. Giffen's usefulness and efficiency as a missionary would be impaired by her marriage, but this fear proved groundless. In this new relation her zeal suffered no abatement, and in earnest labors to prepare herself for the full work of a missionary, her hand slacked not. Just the reverse proved true.

In the east there are more, and effectual doors of usefulness opened to the married than the unmarried missionary, so that she truly says "our facilities for usefulness are greatly increased." Of this period of her life Dr. Hogg writes: "Not only did she forget herself in the ardor of her zeal, but sometimes she seemed to forget those who were dearer to her than self. Loving her children with a doting affection, yet the cases were very rare—unless compelled to leave Asyoot—in which she allowed the sickness of a child to interfere with her daily work."

Perhaps in some there might have been the sentiment that it would be romantic to toil on and alone to the end of life as "Miss Galloway." But in that dark and distant land, there is little of romance and poetic sentiment in the life a lonely and cheerless woman.

After their marriage Mr. Giffen was sent to Alexandria. Of the first night they spent in that city she says: "It was with very solemn feelings that we knelt for evening prayers the first time here. We felt that our coming had not been of our own seeking, that we were in effect charged with the responsibility of opening almost a new mission in this great wicked city. Had Jesus come in with us, and would he make his abode with us? Or had we left him without still knocking at the door? How fearfully empty the large bare rooms seemed with the possibility that He might not be in them! and how beautifully furnished, how greatly adorned with the hope that he not only was in them with us, but that he himself had brought us and would in his own good time "fill this house with his glory."

CHAPTER XVIII.

VISIT TO A TURKISH HAREM—BANNER GIRL.

"Just at the end of our terrace we can look down into a beautiful garden owned by a Turkish Bey. There is a very large, handsome dwelling back in the grounds, and near the gate a large building containing a large parlor furnished in Frank style, a ball and billiard room. We had often looked in and wished we could see the people who lived inside, but the gate was always so carefully guarded by jet black harem servants that it always seemed rather a forbidding prospect. However, we ventured to send our Moslem gardener to inquire if a visit would be acceptable. A very polite message was returned and we went over. The servants at the gate "rose up" to meet us just as the Bible represents inferiors as doing to those they wished to honor, and the brother of the Bey passed us in the grounds and very politely invited us to enter. The women were sitting in a beautiful front gallery which is entirely closed in with glass, some of it richly "stained." They seated us and then gave us a regular scanning. I had a thin blue veil on, and the woman who seemed freest to talk told me to put up my veil. I hesitated and she insisted very positively, using the word " Iftahee " which means to open like a door. They then inquired all about us, where we all lived, what we did, what we came here for, if we had no friends who loved us at home, and finally, of course, if we were married. But before anyone could answer they said they had seen me in the street with a Chowagah. Who was he? Miss J. told her and then she said, " Well, I like him, and I am coming to live with you." They were greatly surprised that none of the

other four were married and inquired very earnestly if
they didn't want to be. The spokesman of the party answered for herself that she didn't, but told them to inquire
of the others themselves. They began and put the question very nicely to each one, "If the man was *very* nice, if
everything was nice wouldn't they take him?" To their
amusement and gratification one of the ladies said "Yom-
kin"—perhaps—and they dropped the subject, feeling that
she was a sensible woman, whom hard fate had condemned
to a miserable existence. They brought us sherbet on a
very handsome silver waiter, and then showed us through
the house. The woman who talked was a widow. The
wife of the Bey was dressed in dark print, made with a
basque and *very* long trail and she wore beautiful white
satin, high-heeled French slippers over red and white
striped stockings. The wife of the Bey's brother came
next in dignity. She wore a trail, too, but shorter than
the other. In fact you could tell the position in the house
by the length of the trail. There were a good many inferior wives who did not sit with the others, but either stood
or sat humbly on the carpet. The house was on the Turkish style, all the doors being furnished with heavy damask
curtains. After we had passed through several rooms
back from the front, one of the women told us we were
then in the harem.

In the garden they talked more freely than in the house,
perhaps because we had them singly, said they were prisoners in the house, could not get out because the Bey's
mother had died a year before, that they could not read or
write, and had nothing to amuse themselves with. The
brother's wife said she was married in Stamboul (Constantinople) sixteen years ago, and she had never been back,
had never heard a word from her mother, and did not know if

she were dead or alive. We were walking, when she said
this, through the most beautiful grounds, under immensely
long grape arbors just laden with great luscious clusters
that almost make one think of "the grapes of Eschol."
There was their magnificent house behind us which would
have seemed a palace to us, and there were any number of
slaves to perform every service, and yet how discontented
and unhappy they seemed, how they longed to get out into
the world as we did! They seemed wholly unable to understand how it could be that we heard from our mothers
every week. We passed through a delightful little grotto
at length and came out upon a little lake. Here they
stopped us, gave us chairs, and had coffee brought. After
taking this we went up an artificial hill in the corner of
the garden and from the top of which the wall was not
more than a yard high. You could look down perhaps
twenty feet into a little narrow street through which we
always pass on our way to the sea, and now we knew how
it was that they knew me and had seen my Chowagah. It
is from that hill that they see the world, and we imagined
we could rather understand their feelings when they stood
up there and looked down at us going to the sea with the
gentlemen.

When we came down they took us into the parlor and
opened a very nice piano. I played some for them, and
sang to my own accompaniment, which seemed to interest
them immensely. They brought a very fine rose while I
was playing and stuck it in the candle-holder—a fixture of
all European pianos—right before me in special compli-
ment. I think they have a Greek governess for the children of the establishment, but we did not feel free to ask
how many of these there were or how many wives there
were.

On the whole we quite enjoyed the adventure, and I
have no doubt it gave a great deal of pleasure to the poor
"prisoners," as they called themselves. Some evening
when we have a little leisure we propose calling again,
taking some music with us, and finding out a little more of
our Turkish neighbors.

It will be remembered that, at the instance of Mrs. Giffen, the various Sabbath-schools of the church forwarded
contributions for the support of some needy and deserving
girl, to be called the "Banner Girl." In regard to this
girl she writes:

"I have delayed writing you in reference to the Banner
Girl, until I could give you definite information about
her. The little girl's name is Saloma. She is about eight
or nine years old. Her father is a poor weaver in a town
eight miles from Sinnoris. He is the leading Protestant
in his village, and always walks to Sinnoris to church, being generally the first person there. Then he walks back
home, collects his friends and neighbors in the afternoon
and conducts a service himself. Mr. Harvey regards him
as a man of great worth, and one who has studied the
Bible with unusual care. As I have said, he is very poor,
poor even for Egypt. But he has agreed to pay fifteen
dollars per annum on his daughter's expenses. Mrs. Harvey says that is a great sum for him to get together, and she
thinks him deserving of much credit, since this child for
whom he is willing to make such sacrifices is "only a girl."
He says Saloma shall be educated "if he has to sell his
cow," and I guess few people in America know how great
that sacrifice would be. It is considered very important
that people here so learn the value of an education as to
be willing to exert themselves to obtain it, and also *in the
case of girls* it is regarded as almost indispensable that

mission beneficiaries belong to respectable families. Otherwise it is very improbable that they will be taken in marriage by the class of young men whom we wish to see our girls marry. In that case, should they not be fitted for successful teachers they become great burdens on the mission. For this reason it is considered undesirable to support and educate many orphans. It is true few other girls can be so completely brought under the influence of missionaries, but as soon as they are through with school they unhesitatingly claim that it is *the duty* of the mission either to find them husbands or salaried positions. This difficulty of course is obviated in the case of girls who have parents living. Should Saloma prove a daughter worthy of her father and of the care she will receive in the Cairo Boarding School she ought to be a great light in her native village."

Again she writes : " Miss Johnson says that the ' Little Banner Girl ' surprised them very much by the style in which she returned to school—*so neat and clean*—and that she was studying well and trying very hard to please them. You may not understand just how much it means for a girl to return to school *clean*. Neither parents nor girls know much of that virtue before the latter are taught it in school, and many of them regard it there simply because they know *they must*. When they go home some of them relapse into former habits and when vacation is over the teachers often find that no real progress has been made. Clothes are soiled and out of order, bath tubs have been ignored, and their heads—well, I will spare you that. But Saloma showed that she had not thrown away her four month's training, and Miss J. hopes she may continue to do as well as she has begun."

To a letter written by Rev. E. P. McClintock, asking

for photographs of the Banner girl, Mrs. Giffen replied: "Perhaps you know that it is a rare thing for Egyptians to have pictures made, and the few girls in our schools whose pictures have been sent to societies in America, have been so spoiled by it, that we thought best not to give Saloma ground for supposing she was a remarkable girl. It would be hard for you to appreciate the difference between her home life, and her present life in school, although we try so much to keep down expense. But when a wretchedly poor girl is taken from her home and placed in a school it is nearly impossible to keep her from thinking that it is because she is better than others. I have not heard any special complaint of this kind in reference to Saloma, but I do not think it would be wise to take her to an artist.

We sometimes meet with great disappointments in the people we assist here. All of us have girls or boys whom we support ourselves in the schools, and after years of effort and expense they sometimes prove so proud, unthankful and useless, that one has need of all his faith to begin with another. It is esteemed a distinction to be aided by us. But we are making strenuous efforts to convince beneficiaries that such aid is *charity*. It would amuse you to hear the tone in which they affirm that it is *aid* and not charity."

Saloma's education is still incomplete, lacking one year. She is now at home, in Rhoda, where she is going out, twice a week, among the women reading to them in their homes, from the Bible. She will probably become a useful Bible woman.

"Last week a fellaha woman who is a church member in a town fifteen or twenty miles from here, brought her little girl and begged to have her taken, although she could not even furnish her clothes. She is well spoken of by the men in the church there, and has to bear the reproach of having *five daughters* and no sons. Her husband is a Copt, and very poor, and though he does not oppose her in wishing to educate her daughters, yet he laughs at her and says, " Do you think you can make *boys* out of them ? " The little girl seemed so bright and full of curiosity that we thought we might make something out of her, so I have taken her and will support her out of the tenth of my salary. She seems to think she has lighted upon Paradise, and, as the native teacher said, is in a chronic state of wonder ! Her name is Mayan—Mary ; and Miss McK. calls her my little witch.

Some years ago a Scotch gentleman brought his little invalid daughter to Egypt with the hope that a Nile voyage might prolong her life. But the little flower drooped and died. Meantime the parents became interested in the mission, and as their little girl held some property in her own right they made an arrangement to furnish forty pounds—two hundred dollars—annually from her property to educate orphan girls. The little girl of a very useful " Bible Woman " and a blind girl are at present supported by this fund, in the boarding school. And two weeks ago Dr. Lansing received from this same gentleman a check for one thousand two hundred and fifty dollars "to assist in completing the girls' department in the new building." It was a most generous gift in a time of sore need, as work would soon have had to stop for want of money to pay the workmen."

CHAPTER XIX.

ASYOOT SCHOOLS—COMMENCEMENT.

" I wrote you sometime since of our then approaching examination. It took place as we expected, and in its results has been all that we could have asked. When we began Thursday morning there was no one there from the town, but very soon they began dropping in. Last year our Protestant business men and the teachers in the government school had surprised everybody with their presence. But this year we scarcely expected many Moslems, as some of them had taken great offense at a speech made in the church by one of the theologues a month before. However before the morning was half over, one Moslem dignitary after another walked in. Sometimes they came in little companies, and every time Dr. Hogg would get up and salute them. It would never have done to let them sit quietly down, no matter if it did cause confusion. And then immediately the servants would come with coffee and sherbet. At every such batch of new comers—Moslem officials I mean—you should have seen the faces of Miss McKown and Dr. and Mrs. Hogg. Fourteen years ago the former spent the heat of her first summer here teaching some days *two*, and some days *three* little girls of five or six years of age, and was hissed at, reviled and stoned in the streets, so that she did not dare to go out without a man to protect her. Now, there was a small sea of heads before her, made up of Protestants, Copts and Moslems, men of every degree and rank in the city—Copts who have hated and opposed our work for years, *and every Moslem official of high position in the city except the Governor.* These Moslems make a most delightful audience. They sit quietly, listen

patiently, ask questions and sometimes give the right answer when a student is incorrect. Copts, on the contrary,
are most objectionable and undesirable. In their churches
they never sit down, *nobody listens,* every one talks and
every one tries to get a better place than his neighbor.
However we felt at first that *everybody was welcome,* and the
examination went well. Mrs. Hogg and I examined our
own classes. To me it was a great trial and the dread of
it for days before was most oppressive. No lady had ever
done it in Osiout until this year and then it was frightful
to think of talking Arabic to the assembled learning of the
whole city. *None* of us used a book in any department
except in English. I had not intended to do it, but I saw
that I must talk faster and louder than the men around
me if I held my ground and I did not open the book in
Arabic.

On Friday the crowd was immense, and it became impossible for one twentieth part to hear or even see what
was going on.

But the great event of the day was the exhibition of the
girl's work. Miss McKown had a quantity of black cloth
which was sent her for the school from Scotland. This
was tacked over the walls of our largest school room and
fancy work pinned on it. Then there were little tables in
the corners and a long one in the centre of the room all
nicely filled with many kinds of work. In a side room
we put all the sewing consisting of bed covers, underwear
and many dresses. But we did not dare to let everybody
come up at once; so before the invitation was given we
had guards stationed at the foot of the stairs and at every
door, and only admitted about thirty-five or forty at a
time. It was almost amusing to see the amazement of the
Moslems that our girls could do so much nice work, and

one of the dignitaries asked for a little fancy tobacco pouch after it had been exhibited. We went round with them and explained everything and when they were satisfied we took them through the sleeping rooms. These were the greatest wonder of all. The first-class boarders who pay pretty well, sleep in the room with the Syrian teacher and their beds have white covers on them. One of the men stopped in this room and exclaimed, " Is everybody here, in such a place as this, and our daughters staying at home ! " The second-class girls sleep down stairs and have only a comfort on their beds—all the bedsteads being a gift from Miss Wolfe, of New York—but the rooms are as clean and neat as the others and as such are wonders to most Egyptians. From this part of the house the men were passed out of the back door into the street and here we had to have guards again to keep others from coming in there. Sometimes the guards would be almost overpowered and once they sent to say they were worn out contending against the people for after " the big men " had passed up the people lost all sense of decency and every man fought his way to the front and was literally pushed up the stairs. Almost every one who wore a turban—rolls and rolls of twisted cloth over a tarboosh—came into the first room adjusting his head gear and panting as if he had been running a foot race.

After candle lighting there was an exhibition of orations, dialogues, &c., and at the close two wealthy men presented prize books to boys and girls to the value of forty dollars. The name of each student was called and he was required to come forward and receive his book. The big Moslems were all sitting, and the person who was distributing the books hindered them from seeing the girls as they came for their books. So they took hold of the man and pulled him to the other side, so that they could see, and during the whole examination Dr. Hogg said that there was quite a marked preference for hearing the girls.

At the close of the exhibition the French teacher invited the audience to wait in an open space outside to witness the sending up of another balloon. While they were making ready, Dr. Hogg stood with us, and, looking out from his study window on the hundreds below— amounting to a thousand or more—said that he had *never seen* such an assembly in Osiout. Next year the gentlemen say they will issue invitations to individuals *by name* and not admit three times the number of people who can sit down in the church. But oh, the change from the days when the touch of a Protestant was contamination! Then it was "the Nicodemuses" who came to the mission, and now, as Arabs say, "all the world" came to see our schools.

Dr. Hogg thinks the girls quite enjoyed the *freedom and novelty* of the thing, for indeed it was a most unheard of performance in this part of the world, and I doubt exceedingly if any other hundred "college boys" ever did gaze at a set of school girls with so much surprise and satisfaction before. Once when I was traveling, a physician told me a story of a boy who had been shut up until he was seventeen years old by a misanthropical father to save him from the snare in which he had been caught and ruined. At seventeen, however, the boy escaped his prison bounds, and innocently encountered a pretty school girl. He ran immediately to his father, described the wonderful sight in extravagant terms and demanded what it could be. In great alarm his father informed him that *it was a bird.* Whereupon the boy clapped his hands and cried with great enthusiasm, "Buy me one, papa!" So these boys know our unveiled girls are not birds, but anybody's sisters except their own are almost as novel a sight as this boy's bird.

In mission work the importance of schools can hardly be overestimated. It is by their influence that missionaries best succeed in breaking down the entrenched, and nearly impregnable customs of the East—customs of 3,000 years standing—and of imparting Western and Christian ideas of progress and morality. Intense conservatism, a complete stagnation in everything which constitutes true progress, either in the moral or mental world, is a distinguishing feature of the masses in Egypt.

In these schools the character of every pupil is more or less modeled after the Christian idea, and they go forth, each a missionary, propagating these opinions. With such agencies at work, the undermining and gradual but complete overthrow of the old superstitions and tyrannies of such countries as Egypt, is but a question of time. Give a man a Christian education, and you destroy forever in his mind the old Eastern idea of woman's subjection and inferiority. Educate his wife and you have a Christian family—a miniature church. It is of prime necessity then, that the customs in regard to the seclusion and inferiority of females be broken down. Before Egypt can become a nation in the true sense of the term, there must be the existence and influence of the *family,* as constituted upon the *Christian* idea—one husband and one wife—and the recognized equality of both.

The training in these mission schools is one of the most successful means of instilling these desired ideas, hence the time and labor devoted to make them effective and influential."

Since the above was written, the following letter, illustrative of much there said, has been received :

"*Dear Mrs. Balph:*—As you and other friends have requested me to give you a letter for your Society, it has occurred to me that perhaps I could not better interest you than by giving you some account of the efforts of our church members here in supporting and carrying on primary schools independently of the mission.

This work was begun about three years ago by two of our wealthiest members. They each took a school, rented a house, supplied water, &c., and agreed to pay the salaries of as many teachers as the congregation might judge to be necessary. Not long after a third school was organized to be supported by a wealthy Copt who believes many of our Protestant doctrines but is not in connection with the Church. This was a school for boys and it was located in a quarter where there are many Moslems in the hope that it might be the entering wedge to work among many of these unapproachable people. Then about nine months ago a *girls' school* was organized in the same quarter, to be supported by one of the younger and less wealthy members of the congregation. This school was placed in two small rooms above the boys' school, and one of the advanced girls from the boarding school was procured for a teacher, at a salary of two hundred dollars per month. She was, however, very happy to secure the position, as there was no other means open to her of earning so much. She opened school with six or eight little girls, from six to ten years of age. None of them had ever been in a school room, and none of them knew the alphabet. So she worked along with them during the hot weather, in the primer, while we were away in Ramle, but when we returned and the heat had subsided enough for me to go out in the afternoons I went over to see how she was progressing.

I had to enter through the boys' school, which is on the

ground in an open square or court. On three sides the
square is roofed over and rooms built above, forming thus
three sheltered places below for the boys, from the heat of
the sun—the whole amounting to perhaps twenty-five or
thirty feet square. Here I found ninety boys and four
teachers, each having a class.

The head of the school is a *blind man*, who teaches
Arabic, reading and grammar and gives religious instruction. I suppose he knows almost every chapter and verse
in the Bible, and after the boys have learned the alphabet
he gives them a Testament and starts them to spelling the
words. Then by the time they have spelled through four
or five chapters, they are required to go back and read
them, and it is surprising what rapid progress they often
make. Sometimes when I go in a boy will move out of his
place to get a better look at me, but in an instant the
Areef—which is a name common to educated blind men—
will point to him and require him to sit down immediately,
frequently calling him by name. No other teacher keeps
as good order in his class as he, and none of them can keep
the school so quiet.

A narrow, dark, mud stair-case leads up to the girls'
school, and here the first time I went I found Fardoos
(Paradise), the teacher, well employed with about thirty
girls. They were crowded into one room about ten feet
square, sitting on high benches, packed in as closely as they
could sit, with only room to pass from the door in front of
the table and down by the ends of the seats to a little dark
room used for storing away shawls, and little bundles of
coarse dinner. There was no place for them to play, or
walk about except on the little roof. This would be comfortable in winter, but unendurable under a summer sun.
About ten of the girls had learned enough to spell and

pronounce pretty well, but none had yet been required to read. I also found that the teacher had followed the native custom of hearing each of the thirty *separately* and that it took the whole forenoon to give them all one lesson. So I had to grade them in classes, and this worked quite an improvement. Then I procured thread and knitting needles, and cut and basted patch-work for them and allowed them to spend half the afternoon in this work, which pleased them very much. By the close of the year the first class had read twelve chapters in John, and reviewed two or three times, and had committed beautifully two-thirds of Brown's Catechism.

Towards the last of January of this year it was arranged to have an examination of the two schools together, and as it would not be proper for the teacher of the girls to open her lips or show her face in the presence of the men, I agreed to examine the girls, though it was no small ordeal before an Osiout audience. To our surprise all the wealthy influential Copts, and Protestants, and many Moslems attended. The whole place and its surroundings was packed, a space of only a few feet square being left in the center for the classes to stand.

I wish you could have heard the Areef's examination of his advanced class of little boys in the Testament. He began by asking in what language, to whom, and when each part of it was written; how many miracles the Saviour performed, where they were wrought, and what were the attending circumstances ; how many times and to whom Christ appeared after the resurrection, &c., &c. Then he *examined* them by calling on them to read the account—for instance—of the raising of Lazarus, the conversation with " the woman of Samaria," the turning of water into wine, &c., the boys being required themselves to find the chapter and verse. Mr. Giffen said that it quite reminded him of a theological examination at home. But you cannot imagine how much interest was added to it all by the person of the Areef himself. He was dressed in a long loose gown, the sleeves of which were nearly a yard wide. As he stood before his class very erect, and with his sightless eyes always seeming to look up to heaven, he was a most interesting-looking character.

The girls and boys alternated, and although the classes were all primary, yet everybody gave the most patient attention, and those who could asked questions. But what most surprised me was the notice taken of *the girls*. You know women are here universally regarded as inferiors, as having little mind, and as having no right to compete with men in anything. But the audience at this examination manifested the most decided partiality for the girls— favored them in every way and showed the same tenderness for the little frightened things that we are accustomed to see at home.

When all was over it was past *three o'clock*, and though we had been there since *nine o'clock* no movement was made to go home. In a little while speeches were called for from the native gentlemen, and after three or four had been made, in which honorable mention was made of the two supporters of the two schools, Dr. Hogg arose and gave a graphic account of the opening of the first Protestant school in Egypt away in Alexandria twenty-two years ago, *with eight pupils*. He recalled the opposition, the trials, the persecutions which had been endured, ending with the statement that there were now more than thirty Protestant schools in the Province of Osiout alone, most of them supported and conducted by natives of the country. He called upon them as patriots, to see to it that not only their own children, but those of their neighbors were educated, and closed by assuring them that the prosperity of their country did not depend on Rivers Wilson from whom they were expecting so much, *but upon the schools of Egypt.*"

CHAPTER XX.

EASTERN CUSTOMS, AS ILLUSTRATIVE OF THE BIBLE.

" When I was a little girl I used to wonder if Ephron the Hittite was not a very hypocritical man in offering Abraham the Cave of Machpelah for nothing—distinctly taking the "sons of his people" to witness that it was a free gift, and afterwards when Abraham had insisted upon buying it, asking what was no doubt an exorbitant price, covered over with " What is that betwixt me and thee?" But here it is the custom of the seller to say, "Take it, take it! never mind the money; that is nothing." And once or twice Mr. Giffen has apparently accepted the offer, picked up the article and started off with it. Then you could have heard some pleading to get him to come back. A price is then set upon it, and usually this is about *twice* what they will take. In that case, if you know the value of the article, you need not say anything at all; just walk off, and nine cases out of ten the shopman will run after you and inquire *what you will give.* If Abraham had not been in affliction, I feel almost sure he might have bought the Cave for two hundred instead of the four hundred shekels of silver.

One morning last week the Bible lesson in the chapel included the request which a man made to Jesus: "Suffer

me first to go and bury my father." The explanation
usually given of this in commentaries was never very satisfactory to me. But Moallim Moosa put a new phase on
it for me. He asked the boys if they supposed the man's
father was really dead. They said, No, they supposed not.
He then said, No, he wasn't. It merely meant his father
was an old man. He might have been infirm; his death
might have seemed probable, or he might live some years.
In any case the greatest respect the son could pay his
father would be to be there when he died and give him
honorable burial. But in this instance it seemed evident
that the man made this custom a cloak or pretense for ne-
glecting a *present* duty. The boys seemed to see no difficulty
in the matter at all. It was all in strict keeping with their
own styles of speech. They have a proverb that "the
way to *honor* the dead is to bury them." During the
meeting in Osiout, just as Presbytery had taken a vote to
admit one of the students to the theological class, a messenger came for the young man to go home, saying his
father was very sick and wished him. All knew that was
the Arab style of saying the father was dead. It was but
two hours' ride to the village, and Dr. Watson started
with the boy immediately, but when they arrived *the man
had been buried some time.*

Perhaps you may remember a letter of Dr. Lansing's
published in the *Instructor*, a year or two ago, giving an
account of a man who had been a soldier, but being dis-
abled had been compelled to cut stone in the mountains,
and who had in a wonderful way been brought to accept
the truth. He works all day in the quarries, and frequently comes to Dr. Lansing's after night. While I was
there he came in great distress. His son was with him—a
slight boy of fourteen. The family lived in Upper Egypt

and the boy had run away from home to keep the officers from seizing him for the army. His father could not find him support or employment, and he brought him to Dr. Lansing. After the case was disposed of, the usual religious conversation began, ending with prayer. At such times the man generally brought some other person with him from the quarries, and both would sleep there and leave before day for their work ; and even when the religious talk and prayers had been extended, Mrs. Lansing said the light in their room would still be burning when she would retire, and she could hear the murmur of his voice as he read and explained some part of the Bible to his companion. The night he came with his son Mrs. L. took Mr. A. and myself in the study to see them as they would never come to the table, and *there were both father and son wearing raiment of camels' hair, with leathern girdles around their waists.* We made a remark about it, and Dr. L. said, " Yes, that one coarse garment was their only clothing, and that the similarity in raiment was not the only resemblance to John the Baptist." No doubt this man and others like him, often think of the poverty of John, of the disciples, and of their Master and find comfort in it. How much better they can understand some things in the Bible than many of our Western Christians who wear " purple and fine linen and fare sumptuously every day "—who, when they read the description of John's raiment, naturally conclude that he was a hermit and denied himself better clothing voluntarily. People in America are not accustomed to find acuteness of mind associated with poverty so great as to admit of only one coarse hair garment, but here we often see it and have therefore little difficulty in imagining John the Baptist as much such a man as our poor friend in the quarries.

I think there are very few customs described in the
Bible which are not pretty well understood by the people
here. When told of some of these perhaps they might
say, "O that's an old fashion," but still they know of it,
while many are current still, exactly as they were then.
There must therefore be a meaning, an internal evidence
in the Bible to these people, which Western Christians
never perceive.

The more we see of the people here the more evident
does it become that the Bible was written by and for Orientals, and the more perfectly do they seem to illustrate
those old characters. In consequence many of our impressions of Bible worthies have been considerably modi-
fied.

I have often heard great emphasis laid on the salutation of Boaz to his reapers, and their equally pious reply,
as indicating a very happy state of society. But the fact
is there is not a particle of religion in the matter. Boaz
simply meant to say "Good morning" to his laborers—a
thing never neglected here—and they only answered in
the prescribed form. The mass of the people *do not know*
that their salutations, exclamations, good wishes, &c., have
or admit of any other meaning than the sense in which
they use them. When I went to Mansoora I was shocked
to hear one of our members say to another "Yallah,"
when he wished to start after a call. I asked my teacher
what it meant. He said, "Let us go." I affirmed that
the man said "O God." "O no," he replied, "it don't
mean that when we use it." The same teacher would
always exclaim "Ullah!" if surprised, as in case of meeting any one suddenly, and he and others like him being
often in the house, a little mission child, which was just
beginning to talk, got that among its first words, and if

any one came in unexpectedly would exclaim "Ullah" with the most perfect imitation of the native tone and manner.

Orientals are *exceedingly* polite, but to be so they *must* refer everything to God, must connect His name and attributes with it in some way. No matter how careless, improvident, unreligious or even openly wicked a man may be, he has an unfailing resource in *any* calamity. "Ullah kareem"—"God is liberal or generous"—meaning He will provide for us. One who only understood the language without knowing anything of Eastern character, would be almost sure to exclaim, "What perfect resignation to God's will!" The most pious ejaculations, or what would seem such to us, are showered on everybody by everybody.

New missionaries are usually very much shocked by these customs. What seems very pious in the Bible seems very profane when constantly tossed from lip to lip in every day life, and they set themselves against it, but by the time they get a moderate use of the language they see that the customs which have stood for thousands of years are likely to stand a while longer, and insensibly they glide into the habit of saying some of the same things. Such things are *the language* of the people and nothing else is intelligible.

If Orientals are not angry they are very scrupulous in bestowing honorable titles on each other. I have heard ministers refer to the language of the sons of Heth when Abraham wished to purchase the Cave of Machpelah from them as evidence of the high esteem in which the Patriarch was held. No doubt he was highly regarded, but the language is not certain proof of it. Every man here is, or may be, addressed as "Ya Seedi"—my Lord. It is merely a polite address much used by superiors to inferiors and much more so by equals. Every woman so addresses her husband. Sarah called Abraham "My Lord," honoring him of course, for no woman here would think of imagining herself as good as her husband, but I doubt if Sarah ever heard a husband addressed in any other way. Abraham would call her "Ya bintee"—my girl—or at least all Arab husbands do, provided they are in a pleasant humor. If not the wife, like the rest of the female servants, is just screamed at as "Ya bint," when anything is in requisition. The *ee* termination is a little like our y and indicates the first person, and if added to a noun means "my," and also has in some instances something of an affectionate tone.

Extravagant in the use of polite terms when pleased, Orientals when angry with each other, surpass the world in ability to heap up abusive epithets. The acme of their wrath, the very culmination of hate and contempt is to call a man *a hog*—"Ya chanzeer,"—he may be *a dog*, or *the son of a dog*, but there can be nothing left unsaid when he has been called *chanzeer*. Swine's flesh is not very abundant here, and most Americans often long for it and would have it were it not so expensive, but I do not feel comfortable to have natives see us eat it, and will I think soon come to dislike it. All eastern people regard it as unclean, and I have to keep my thoughts busy about something else to eat it in comfort. You have no idea how it sounds to hear the cook talk about *lahm chanzeer*, when he means pork.

Reviling is one of the greatest sins of the east. It is an Oriental's sweetest revenge. It does his whole soul good to curse your father and your father's father, but you he never curses. I have seen men stand and scream "You son of a dog, son of a dog" till their breath was gone.

Then they would call on the Lord to curse your father. These two expressions indeed are in every child's mouth and are heard at every corner.

As I said before an Arab does not speak to his wife as if she was his equal, nor does she take his name as we do. If you inquire for her where she is not known by her given name you may distinguish her as "the wife of" such an one. But her real name, her womanly title, she gets *from the name of her child.* Should the first one be a girl it is *a great misfortune,* and deeply lamented, but still the woman takes the name of its mother, until the birth of a boy. Then there is a great feast, the most extravagant joy is both felt and expressed, and ever after the mother is known by the name of her son. Two years ago when I used to go with Mrs. Ewing to Carmoose there was a little woman there learning to read, who had a babe name Rufka or Rebecca. She was always spoken of as "Om Rufka"— Mother of Rebecca. Last fall when I went back there alone I found I had forgotten the location of her house, and went into some others to inquire—the families being related, I asked for "Om Rufka's" house. Not one of them seemed to know anything about such a person, and as I did not know the name of her husband I was about giving it up in despair. However I concluded to make another effort, and made the description so plain that they were obliged to understand—which I am confident they had done from the first. The woman's mother-in-law then growled out in no gracious tone "You want " *Om Ibraheem.*" Instantly I was enlightened. A boy had been added to the family since I had been there, Om Rufka's "reproach had been taken away," and her relatives could not help resenting my ignorance.

It is *a very rare* thing here to see a man and his wife go anywhere *together.* Even when both are at church the husband will either go off with a company of men or linger behind to talk to some one, leaving his wife both to come and go alone and also to carry the baby herself. Then she does not sit down to eat with him. Very, *very* few natives have any table except a little thing a foot high on which the one dish is placed. This is placed on a mat and *the husband and sons* gather round it sitting on the floor and dipping their bread into the dish, *always with the right hand.* The wife and daughters stand around and serve—that is replenishing the supply of bread and water and make coffee and bring the pipes and tobacco after the meal. When all that is over and the men and boys have gone to sleep or to their business, the women and girls eat *what is left.* But I suppose of course if there isn't enough of that they can have the privilege of cooking more.

A few minutes ago I opened my door, and hearing a voice I went through the next room to the hall door to find what it was. I soon discovered it was the Moslem bowwab* praying. He is quite young and excruciatingly deferential, always takes off his shoes before coming towards us, walks backwards when leaving our presence, and rises the moment we come to the hall door, though it is fifty feet from his seat, *except when he is praying.* Then he doesn't notice us in any way. He keeps his rug beside him, and at the regular hours puts it on the floor, turns his face to Mecca and *prays aloud* with amazing energy and earnestness. Sometimes he seems to speak, at other times one word is repeated with great rapidity just as long as he can without breathing and at other times it is a kind of an organ. Before beginning he always leaves the door open, so that he need not stop to open it for any one wishing to enter as he would then be required by the Koran to go back to the first and repeat all he had said. If we have

* Doorkeeper.

sent him out, or he is employed in his work at the "house
of prayer" he will omit them then and repeat them all at
night. And then you should hear the echoes he wakes
up out there with the grand roll of *allahu il alee, allahu il
azeem.*

It seems wonderful to us how the Mohammedam faith is
instilled into children, with what *intensity* they believe in
it and how entirely they are strangers to anything like
shame in being seen worshiping. They do not shrink
from any observation. This servant knows that we have
no faith in his religion, that we consider it the essence of all
that is bad, and in everything else he shows us the most
unquestioning deference, but when it comes to the matter
of his prayers we are absolutely nothing in his estimation.

Moslems pray anywhere. One day our teacher passed
one praying and was excited to stop and listen. And here
was his petition : "O God, destroy my enemies, pluck out
their eyes, cut off their hands, break their feet and crush
their heads." All this he had arranged in rhyme and was
just going over and over it. The words of the regular
prayers are prescribed by the Koran, but after they are
said, anything else may be added.

One day while the servants were packing our furniture
in a car Mr. Giffen heard quite an outcry round him and
soon saw that he was giving great offense somehow. On
looking down he noticed that he was standing on one of a
series of stones laid in a row from a water faucet to a
small platform on which the Moslimen railroad servants performed their devotions. Before every prayer they must
perform a thorough ablution *in running water*, and then
must not touch the ground, stepping immediately from the
bath with dripping feet into their shoes, or else on a
"prayer carpet." These men however dispense with the

carpet and have a wooden platform, used in common, which was reached from the faucet by the stones on which Mr. Giffen had inadvertently set his irreverent feet. He got off immediately, and to the indignation of the rest one of them said apologetically, "He doesn't know," and immediately they ran and brought water and gave the polluted stone a thorough scrubbing."

CHAPTER XXI.

LETTER TO THE LADIES' BENEVOLENT SOCIETY IN NEW-BERRY, S. C.

"It gave me great pleasure to hear through your kind pastor, of the prosperity of your Society, and of the very happy reflexive influences which you are exerting. It is a peculiar treasure if in doing good to others we are blessed in our own souls also. Many a munificent charity has been made to redound to the glory of God, and the good of fellow-mortals, which yet sent back no blessing into the hand which gave it. May this not be your lot. When you meet to work and consult together about the best means to be adopted for advancing the pecuniary interests of the cause in which you are engaged, may each one of you feel that you have come together for a far more glorious purpose than simply to raise so much money. May you realize that you are in the immediate service of the Great King to whom all nations belong.

All your missionary meetings are witnesses for Jesus. They affirm before men and angels that you believe in the final triumph of His kingdom over all the world, that He is a Master whose service is a joy to your own hearts, and that you work and pray that other sin-sick souls may be brought to the Great Healer.

And when "the fire burns" in your own hearts, when you are rejoicing in belonging to so great a Master, when you realize how glorious and all-powerful He is—then my friends pray for missionaries, *pray for your own mission-aries*, for I hope you now feel that you have *two* here. You cannot form any idea of how much we need the prayers of the people of God. You think of us as leaving home and all we love behind us, and perhaps you feel that only a superior faith could enable one to do that, and therefore that what we most need is material support, assurance of Christian sympathy, and the preserving care of God over us in the long journey. I think it is true that it requires *genuine* faith to enable one to come forth alone into such an unknown world almost; but it by no means follows that it is faith which does not need to be strengthened every day. The great struggle which one must make in giving up all, and yet keep natural emotions in subjection, does not always sensibly advance a missionary's divine life. In many cases after the great tension has subsided I have no doubt that heart and soul both seem dead. I myself felt smitten with a paralysis of all feeling, and when we landed in Egypt everything was in "an unknown tongue." Even the family prayers were in Arabic. How hard under such circumstances for the deadened shriveled soul to get back its life and freshness again.

There is no Sabbath in the streets. There is just as much business on that day as on any other. The shop windows are just as gay with ribbons, laces and flowers, as if

God claimed no part of the day for himself. All occupations go on just the same, as if the "buying and selling and getting gain," were the one purpose for which the world was created.

Then, too, on Sabbath, for a long time after we came, we knew nothing of what the minister was saying, and even yet our closest attention is necessary to make a running translation. When one has been drilled a year and a half on pronunciation, idioms and general construction, there is such a temptation to criticize the preacher, to notice every sound which he failed to make distinct and to wonder "why he used such and such a word in such a way." Perhaps it is a very profitable lesson in Arabic, but it is a very small portion of food which the soul has received.

I hope then you can realize now something of the difficulties which missionaries encounter in their first years— how very much they have to deaden and dwarf their spiritual life. Of all people we seem to need the fullest measure of the Holy Spirit. We need it before we are able to work and we need it after we can work. We need it to save us from despondency in our first efforts to use a new and exceedingly difficult language, and then when you become able to deal with the natives you so much need it to enable you to combat the false doctrines which *centuries* have implanted in them, and to be able to meet and defeat the cunning, deceit and falsehood which are parts of the religion of the East, and for which I suppose there is no parallel anywhere else in the world—without becoming yourself like them.

If heaven blesses our labors to the good of others we are in great danger of missing the blessing ourselves. Then pray much for us. We endeavor to consecrate ourselves anew every day we live, to feel that we have no part or lot in this world's trade, commerce, or emoluments, but only to work that souls may be brought into the kingdom of our Master. But we have much to hinder us.

Our mission has passed the *persecuting* stage among the Copts, and as yet we can do little among the Moslems. When the truth is new and men eagerly embrace it in the face of great trials—even at the risk of death itself, it begets an enthusiasm in the whole church which swallows up self, lightens labor and increases faith. "Times of refreshing" like this were enjoyed here when Dr. Hogg first came to Asyoot, or rather a few years afterward, but now we have the far more up-hill, prosaic work of *educating* the church—just such work as grieved the hearts of the Apostles when they found their converts turning away from the truth. In this way the present year has been a marked one in our mission, but the brethren hope that the results will not be as serious as they had reason to fear at first. You see then how *greatly* we need your continual remembrance of us at the throne of grace. We regard our mission as one of the most important in the world, and yet we have so much to discourage us. You cannot guess how much we need the "wisdom of the serpent with the harmlessness of the dove," or how much we want the faith which is able to remove mountains and cast them into the sea. You cannot form an idea of what it is to live in a country where there is *no Sabbath,* and where the name of God is more lightly used than any one in the dictionary ; nor can you appreciate what it is to spend years here before you can fully enter into the meaning of, and enjoy the services of religion. All of us suffer in this way, and some missionaries feel that they *never can* fully recover from the injury.

So do not forget to pray for us. Without the spirit of God we can do nothing, and when we look over our mission

stations here, it makes us feel as I have often felt at
home when looking upon a field of corn, parching up in a
summer drought—" O ! for the rain."

In writing to these friends of her childhood all barriers
of reserve and restraint are broken down, and we here see
Mrs. Giffen's character as it really was. They were tried
friends and to them she writes in all the unreserved confidence
and sincerity of friendship. We have here a glimpse of her
character not seen in any of her *public* letters. The curtain of modesty and privacy is drawn aside, and we have
a most distinct impression of the strong yet dependent
faith which actuated and sustained her under her sore trials in
that remote land. All noble natures shrink from display-
ing to the world the inner and most sacred feelings of
their souls, and especially their communings with their
Maker. In no people is this shrinking modesty and delicacy more manifest than in the refined, educated women
of the South.

CHAPTER XXII.

AHMED'S CONVERSION.

" We have all been greatly interested recently in
news from Cairo of the apparently genuine conversion
of Miss Smith's Arabic teacher—*a young Moslem of good
social position.*

A missionary's lessons are largely in the Bible, and this
gave Miss Smith the opportunity to preach the gospel to
him—which she seems to have done well. The most abom-

inable of all our doctrines to a Moslem is the idea *that God can have a Son.* It is not safe among them to use the expression " Son of God," if you are not known to them or have not some guarantee of security. So last summer Moallim Ahmed asked Miss S. if this doctrine were taught in the Old Testament, and how the Jews knew to expect a Saviour. She referred him to Isaiah and Daniel, helped him in every way, borrowed books for him, &c., but did know until recently how well she had succeeded.

Moallim Ahmed's father is a "head scribe" in one of the government offices in Cairo, and is a Moslem of the most rigid type. He, however, appreciates education, and therefore sent his sons to the mission school. One rule of the school of course was that every pupil must study the Bible. So to secure the secular advantages of the school, and at the same time counteract the religious influence, he engaged a famous sheik to come *every evening* and go over the Bible lesson with the older son and point out to him everything which went against the teachings of Islam. Dr. Watson then, as now, gave a general Bible lesson to the whole school as a part of chapel exercises, and he says this older boy often just seemed to gnash his teeth at being compelled to listen to these Scripture explanations. Moallim Ahmed was the younger and does not seem to have been guarded as was Mohammed, or ever to have shown such bitterness. When we were in Cairo two years ago he seemed about twenty years old, and had probably been a couple of years out of school, during which time he was dragoman or interpreter to a Doctor Warren of Virginia, who was in the Viceroy's service. In the family of Doctor W. he seems to have imbibed a great liking for Frank customs, and his first admission of a change of belief was in the matter of the Moslem treatment of women. We were, however, much surprised when perhaps a month ago he gave Miss Smith a written confession of his faith in Christ, stating clearly the process of inquiry through which he had passed, ending in what seems to be a deep, warm, affectionate reception of the truth of the gospel. He stated in an affecting way his trials at home, his efforts to avoid compliance with Moslem rites and his sorrow when compelled to do so. His father required his children to follow his example of praying five times a day, and poor Ahmed must have had a hard time evading it. He said he knew well that his father would either kill him instantly or poison him, and he therefore felt that he must leave Cairo.

Secret death from his nearest relative is what every Moslem knows he must experience if he becomes a Christian and leaves himself in the power of his family. So at first it was thought best to send Ahmed up here, but afterwards Dr. Lansing persuaded him to come to his house when he would leave his home and he would protect him, and then they hoped they might reap good fruit from the discussion which was sure to follow. So Ahmed left letters for his father and brothers, and I suppose quietly left the house. Almost immediately two brothers followed him and begged him to go home with them and " keep his religion in his heart," adding that they had not told their father. Ahmed knew that this was a falsehood to get him into his father's power. The next day the brothers brought sheiks with them to argue the matter. Drs. Lansing and Watson were greatly pleased with the manner in which Ahmed sustained his part of the question. This plan failing, they then tried to induce him to go to the great mosque of Azhar and meet the Ulema of Islam, but Dr. Lansing told them even he would not trust himself in the Azhar without a guard of soldiers, much less Ahmed. Sometimes his mother came and wept over him, beseeching him to go home. Other times just one brother would come and talk to him, and again all the family would come together *except the father and a little brother.*

Our fear was that, all other methods failing, the father would demand him from Dr. L. on a charge of theft. In that case the Consul said he would have to be given up, and would then be at the mercy of his enemies. But the last letters say he has been let alone for four days. His father lodged information against him with the Viceroy, and also sent word to Sheik el Islam in Constantinople. The former answered by a very expressive idiom in universal use: "*Just as he likes. There is freedom of religion in Egypt.*" But the sheik replied: "*He deserves to be burnt.*" The Viceroy's deliverance will have the effect of preventing any legal proceedings now, and perhaps the anger of the father will subside after a little.

Altogether this is a wonderful event in Egypt. Of course Ahmed *may* be deceived in himself, but so far the opinion of all the Cairo missionaries is strongly in his favor.

December 1st.—I wrote you a few weeks ago an account of Moallim Ahmed's conversion. He was baptized about the time I wrote, and has since informally joined the Second Theological class, which is studying this winter in Cairo. He is still at Dr. Lansing's, and still gives very satisfactory evidence that he has really been brought to the knowledge of the truth. The trial of leaving his family was at first very great, but they say he is now quite cheerful. Many of his Moslem friends call to see him and he takes every opportunity to preach the gospel to them. One of his brothers he thinks is coming to the light. His father has never had but the one wife, and they seem to have been an unusually affectionate family. One daughter is one of *four wives*, her husband being one of the Judges in the International Court of First Instance in Alexandria, but Ahmed thinks she is the favorite wife. His mother seems quite a nice woman, and bore herself with dignity when she came to Dr. Lansing's. Her other sons had told her Ahmed was *magnoun*—crazy—but when she came and heard him talk she said to them to let him alone, he wasn't magnoun. The first time his brothers all came together to see him they staid almost all day and made it very hard for Ahmed, yet when the left they each *kissed* him. He did not come to tea, and when Dr. W. went to his room to see what was the matter he was *lying on the divan crying*. The first night he left home they sent for the "mourning women" and mourned all night as for the dead. They do not tease him so much now, but he knows very well that they will not give over yet. He says himself that his father cannot do otherwise than persecute him, as he would else_ be suspected and held to account as an infidel to the faith. Ahmed has studied more or less for some years under the great sheiks in the Azhar, and the first thing his father did on hearing the news of his defection was to send and accuse these sheiks of having taught his son false doctrine, or at least to have failed in fortifying him in the faith, but I suppose everybody would understand that this was merely a strong way of asserting that the false doctrine had not been imbibed at home.

Our church members in Cairo were very slow to give Ahmed the hand of friendship, and up here those of whom we expected more boldly affirmed that it wasn't genuine. "Moslems were *all bad*. There wasn't a good one among them." It seems just the old story of the Jews and Gentiles.

Ahmed had never attended our church until he went to
Dr. Lansing's. It was all very wonderful to him, and he
seemed greatly troubled that he could not sing. He told
some of the mission that it certainly was "a new life" on
which he had entered. They say he gets on wonderfully
well in adapting himself to our ways and seems to enjoy
his food very much, though it is so different from what he
has been accustomed to all his life. Dr. Lansing in one of
his letters to some one here remarked that he was "an exceedingly agreeable person to have in the house." I think
that is more than he could say for any Copt or Syrian that
I know in the mission. Should the power of Islam be
broken in this war I think we might reasonably hope that
it would open the door to work among the Moslems. That
would be a happy consummation for our mission. As it is
now, our gentlemen can *preach*, but Moslems cannot *hear*.
When they can listen in safety then we may look for a new
era in the East.

December 27th.—At the date of my last letter the excitement seemed to be subsiding, but last week we were
startled with the news that he was missing. He was not in
his room and no one had seen him. Inquiry was made immediately, and getting no clue the missionaries went at
once to the Consuls and from there to Shareef Pasha—the
Minister of State. Next day it came out that three men,
who were said to be the spies of the government, were
standing together under a window at which Mrs. Lansing
was sitting, and that when Ahmed came up alone he was
seized by the back of the neck, a hand placed over his
mouth and himself thrust into a close carriage. The sus-
pense and anxiety felt by the missionaries was of course
very great, and that night special prayer was made in the
Mission Chapel—the church members seeming to take

much interest in the matter. The first information received was that " Ahmed was in his father's house, and that
being such, his father had the right to keep him a few days,
but that he was safe from violence." We here do not
know how the information came, or whether the missionaries endeavored to communicate with Ahmed personally,
but we are certain they have done everything which seemed
possible. For some days we wondered at the indefiniteness
of their letters, but at last Mrs. Lansing said we must excuse *initials* and mere allusions, that they could not be ex-
plicit, as " everything was closely watched." She said Drs.
Watson and Lansing were much worn, and that there was
but one subject of interest and conversation. A day or
two later Dr. W. wrote, " No further news of Ahmed, except that he appears to be standing firm." But two days
ago Miss Johnston wrote that they were in an almost indescribable state of anxiety, as " the Viceroy had told our
Consul that Ahmed was at liberty, that he had signed his
recantation, and that in two days there would be an opportunity for him to testify to it publicly at the Zabteeya—
police court—in presence of the chief of police and the
Consul." Miss J. added, " we do not believe that Ahmed
is denying his Master, and are very doubtful if any such
thing occurs at the Zabteeya." Of course we here are very
anxious to hear the result, but even if Ahmed is forced
through the form of a recantation we do not despair of
him. It is true he may have been himself deceived, but
it seems strange that if he were not one of Christ's chosen
ones that he would make not one false step in the month
during which he was in Dr. L.'s house, and was subject to
the closest scrutiny from every member of the Cairo Station. Probably no human being in Egypt ever stood in
such a place as he has occupied—alone, against the whole

might of Islam, *in Cairo, its greatest stronghold.* What a
subject of praise and thanksgiving it would be to us to
know that he was dead, for then we would know that he
had gone to receive a martyr's crown. We feel sure that
he must recant or die, unless it should please God to send
him special deliverance, and if he die, we are not likely
ever to know it.

We have almost no doubt that the Viceroy is deceiving
the Consuls in this, as he does in other matters. He probably does not care himself what Ahmed's faith is, but when
the heads of the Moslem sects come to him and say that
this matter must stop, nobody doubts what he will say.
Ahmed's family stand high, and *the shame* of his defection
will be felt in a way and to a degree that we cannot comprehend. Any crime, the sum of all crimes, indeed, they
would lightly esteem in comparison with this. Should he
remain faithful, years may pass before he is secure from
their deep laid plots, but the probability is that his days will
be few.

January 4th.—Misses Johnston and Smith have come
up from Cairo and have given us full particulars of Moallim Ahmed's case, and very sad they are. The day before
they left the Consul sent for Drs. L. and W. They went
to the Consulate and met there Ahmed, his father and
three brothers. They said Ahmed had recanted and they
wished his books from Dr. L.'s house. The latter said to
A., "Is this true? Have you returned to Islam?"
"Yes," he replied, but did not speak again. Dr. L. thought
him much changed, his face worn, thin and pale. On
leaving Mr. L. inquired of the father if Ahmed would
come back to his work in the school. "Not just yet," he
said, as he wished him to go to Minyeh to his plantations.
The father used to live in Minyeh, which is three stations

from here on the railroad, and these plantations were given to him by the Viceroy. Mohammed, the oldest brother of Ahmed, has charge of a very large Government school there, and was sent for immediately after A. came to Dr. L.'s. On coming to Cairo he spent almost a whole day in hot argument with Ahmed, being much harsher with him than the others, and telling them all when he left that he would return next day to Minyeh. Various lies were told Ahmed to convince all concerned that Mohammed really had returned to his school and the afternoon that Ahmed was kidnapped a younger brother brought a list of books *and left it with Mrs. Lansing,* as Ahmed was at the school, saying Mohammed wished Ahmed to select them for him and send them on to Minyeh. All this was to prevent any suspicion of Mohammed's presence, though at that very time he was sitting in the carriage below Mrs. L.'s window.

When the missionaries found Ahmed had been captured by government officials, they supposed he would be either instantly killed or sent directly to the White Nile; and when after a day or two no tidings of him came, Miss Smith resolved at least to attempt calling on his mother. She had always seemed so fond of Ahmed, and the latter had frequently expressed the hope that Miss S. might some day be able to visit at the house and induce his mother to learn to read. The young ladies thought it probable that the mother was in ignorance of Ahmed's whereabouts, and Miss S. thought she might be able to touch her heart if she went to talk to her about her son. So she called up an old Moslem bow-wab and told him to bring a donkey, and that she wished him to go with her to Moallim Ahmed's house. *He refused to go* most positively and would not bring the donkey. " Why ! " he said, " they will kill you

and me both long before we get to the house." Miss S.
told him that she was going and asked him if he called
himself a man and was afraid to go with her through a
street of Cairo among people of his own religion. He
said: "All the same, I can't go." After a little two of
the teachers in the boys' school rode up. Miss Smith
asked for their donkey. They told her she could take the
donkey, but how on earth could she venture into such a
place! *They would certainly kill her.* The house they
said, was in one of the densest of Moslem quarters, the
streets were very narrow, and no Frank ever went there,
that a Frank woman would attract everybody's notice, and
that if she went she would never return. She asked the
others to pray for her, got on the donkey and told the old
bow-wab to come along. One of the teachers who objected
most, is rather a rough sort of a man, and, they always
supposed, destitute of any very tender feeling. But they
sat down to wait to see if Miss Smith would come back or
not. The others tried to talk and this man would answer
questions, but every few minutes he would say, "She's in
the Mooskey by this time." Then again, "Now she's at
such and such a place, but they'll kill her, they'll kill her."
Then again, "Now she's there, and if they *do* strike her
she's got no body and they would kill her at the first blow."
(Miss Smith is very small and delicate looking.) As Moallim Farag had said, she got to the place in due time, winding through all sorts of dark, narrow streets, with thousands of black holes along the way into which "a dog of a
Christian *might* have been thrown to die, but without any
such calamity befalling her." No one seemed to notice
her or wonder about her. She remembered the address on
the letters Moallim Ahmed had sent to his family while at
Dr. L.'s, and told the servant to stop at the right door.

He insisted that wasn't the one, and after wandering
up and down the street two or three times, declared he had
forgotten the house. She then got off the donkey, went to
the door and ordered him to rap the knocker. He refused
and she went up and did it herself. A slave woman came
and peeped out of a crack of the door but refused to open
it. Miss S. pushed it open by exerting all her strength in
a quiet way. She told the woman she wished to see the
Sitt. "Well, she isn't here." "Yes, she is," Miss S. replied, "and I must see her." "No, she isn't here, and you
must get out of here immediately. We killed a man right
here where you are standing, right down there. Don't you
see the blood?" Miss S. said she didn't and must see the
Sitt. "Go away! I say! Don't I tell you we killed a
man here." When Miss S. wouldn't go, the maid had reluctantly to go in to see what was to be done, but over and
over she warned her not to stir one step from where she
was. In a minute or two a male servant came in closing
the door behind him. Miss S. approached him and offered
salutations, but he wouldn't salute and ordered her out.
She begged again to see the Sitt. But he only said, "Go
out, *please* get out;" and when she didn't move he took
her by the arm and *put her out.* In a few days the Viceroy told the Consul where Ahmed was, *and that he must go
to the Consulate and recant.* The day before they took him
there Mohammed took him out walking and brought him
past Dr. Lansing's house, Mohammed holding him by the
arm and another Moslem walking on the other side. Then
two days after they were at the Consulate the bow-wab
saw them on the street, Mohammed holding Ahmed's
hand. The bow-wab went immediately towards them to
speak, and A. turned towards him. "Come along! You
must not," said Mohammed. "But I will," Ahmed re-

plied, and saluted. Then the old servant with great tact
began to inform him about Miss Smith's visit to the house,
asking, "Was it proper to turn her out of doors when she
went to visit your mother?" Ahmed said he didn't know
she had been there, and said to beg her not to be angry.
We have no doubt this was the first piece of pleasant news
the poor fellow had had, and are sure it would greatly encourage him. The next day one of the Cairo church mem-
mers got a Moslem and a great infidel philosopher to take
him to the house. When he asked to go with them, they
said, "You go there? Why, they'll kill you!" But he
went, and Ahmed was permitted to come down. After a
little the philosopher stepped out, and the Moslem not understanding English, Ahmed and the member could speak.
He said "his heart was on fire," that he was with us still,
that he was so persecuted and *must* do something to save
himself from them. But the word he used for saved was
in Arabic, and may mean either to save or escape from.
Afterwards this same Copt was in a government office and
heard one Moslem inquiring of another about Ahmed,
what he was doing, etc. The answer was that "he was a
stubborn fellow, and was just sitting in the house, sometimes crying and sometimes rejoicing."

When the books were sent home all the mission circle
wrote notes to him and put them in different books.

We are hoping and praying that it may all be overruled
yet for Ahmed's and the church's good. ˑ Certainly, as far
as we can see, there is no comparison between this case and
that of Peter, and yet the latter became a great Apostle,
and finally a glorious martyr for the Saviour he was so
swift to deny.

January 17th.—My last to you in reference to our Moslem friend was closed when we felt very anxious about

him. I think I mentioned that he came to Dr. Lansing's while the young ladies were up here. Afterwards he called on a shopman who is one of our elders, declaring himself firm, and once or twice more he came to Dr. L.'s. These visits to Dr. L.'s were kept secret from our members even, though of course Ahmed might have been seen entering the house. Last Saturday when he was there he talked a great deal and encouraged them very much. Then to everyone's great surprise he came to our *English service.* There had been a little vacation in the boys' school which was just closing, so it was decided for the gentlemen to write to A.'s father and ask permission for him to resume his work as a teacher in the school. The letter was sent Monday night last, and I suppose led to a hot discussion.. The father promptly refused, insisting that Ahmed should take work in the Government schools, or in the Government office, in which he himself is employed. Ahmed as promptly refused, insisting that he would retain his own position, and telling his father that he had "*forced* him to do what he had done." A part of this *forcing* consisted in the father writing a recantation and compelling Ahmed to transcribe it. This was the paper the Viceroy told our Consul Ahmed had written of " his own free will."

Next morning after the father and brothers had gone to their offices, Ahmed's mother told him *he had better leave, that he was in danger.* So he is a second time at Dr. Lansing's. It would appear that the mother had not given information of his whereabouts, as it was the second day before they came to inquire if he were at Dr. L.'s. Miss Johnston writes that Ahmed is very nervous, and that they all feel that there is no safety for him in Egypt. Our Consul went to Shareef Pasha and asked to be allowed to

take Ahmed there to tell his story himself, but Shareef declined the interview.   You will remember he is the Minister of State.   He said " a separation would be necessary,
as even should his own family permit him to live as a
Christian in his father's house, other Moslems would not."
He said he would give orders that Ahmed should not be
molested, " but could not promise that harm would not
come to him."

Dr. Watson wrote us last night that there was " a bad
prospect for calm in Cairo now."   They say their every
movement is closely watched, and are afraid to mention
names to us, or give us any but general information.

You cannot imagine how interesting the case is to us all.
It is Islam against Christianity.   Ahmed had more than
usual worldly inducements to remain in the faith of his
fathers.   In declaring himself a Christian he knew that
he must leave his home and all his friends, that he lost his
legal rights of inheritance, and, as he said himself, " all the
probabilities were that he would lose his life in the end."
If the mission were able to get him out of the country, it
would not seem desirable, as the next case would require
the same ground to be gone over.   So we cannot see what
the end will be.   We would hope for great things if
Ahmed could become the evangelist of his own people;
but he will not dare now to show himself without protec-
tion.   We suppose that there must be much excitement
among the Moslems in Cairo, as we know there is always
strong sympathy between that city and Stamboul.

February 2nd.—In a letter written to Mr. Alexander
this week Ahmed says he is "a prisoner at Dr. L.'s house,"
and begs to be prayed for much that he may have strength
given him to endure all.   When the first Sabbath came he
declared his intention of going to church.   There were

many fears that he would be shot before he could reach
the church, as his father *had given orders for his assassination*, Mohammed having been sent for again from Minyeh.
However he went over early with Dr. Watson, more or less
disguised—probably a dress coat and hat only, as he could
easily carry his tarboosh in his pocket, and so put it on
and appear natural in the church.   There was great joy
among the native members; *some of them kissed him.*
Neither in Cairo nor here have we heard of a single native
doubting or condemning him, even though they were so
slow to believe him at first.   They are so accustomed to
oppression, to being *driven*, that they really seem unable
to understand how *one* man could oppose his will to all
Islam with the Viceroy behind it.   While Ahmed was at
church *his mother came to bring him some clothes.*   Not finding him, she left them with the old Moslem bow-wab, and
in the afternoon sent back her servant to know if they had
been received.   Next day she came again herself to see
him.   What a comfort it must have been to him!   He
loves her very dearly, and is her favorite son.   Of course
the father does not know what she does, but it seems to me
she risks a great deal.   Ahmed seems to have been a general favorite at home, and that may make the servants
willing to help a kind mistress against a severe master.
Last Sabbath Ahmed went to church again and went home
in a company of English people, without anything hap-
pening.   But he may escape a dozen times and be taken
as he was before.   We think he does not dare to show his
face either at a window or in a balcony yet, but they say
he is a brave fellow, and no doubt he will forget some of
his caution after awhile.

Dr. Lansing says we can have no idea of the excitement and exasperation which his return stirred up in

Cairo, and that it is impossible to foresee the end. They all think Ahmed very prudent, and some one wrote that "now since they had heard all *they did not blame him.*" But it was added, "it has done us all good; Ahmed is more distrustful of *himself* now—trusts more in God, and sees better where his strength must come from."

"April 11th.—As we have mentioned Moallim Ahmed's escape from Egypt in our private letters, you will doubt-less be interested in hearing some of the details.

Several years ago there was a pious Scotch Earl who made one or two trips up the Nile, and took great interest in our mission work, always carrying Bibles in his boat and making many efforts to do real missionary work. This winter his son brought his young bride to Egypt, both of them manifesting quite as much interest in missions as their distinguished father and mother. They visited the mission in Cairo and Osiout, and took books and a colpor-teur with them from the latter place. The first of March, as they returned down the river, they again stopped in Osiout to place in the boys' school four slaves whom they had bought from a slave dealer, or rather, as Lady Aber-deen said, "they gave a compensation" for them. Three of them are small, and these three they asked Dr. Hogg to baptize, Lord and Lady Aberdeen standing as sponsors for them. The boys are to be educated, and then Lord A. hopes they will return to Soudan as missionaries to their own people.

You will see from these things how differently this young nobleman and his beautiful countess have behaved on their " Nile trip " from most travelers—seeming obliv-ious of themselves, and only endeavoring to find out how to do good. Soon after they left Osiout, the annual meet-ing of the Association met there. Drs. Lansing and Wat-

I

son of course wished to attend, but they were almost
afraid to leave Ahmed behind, and they did not dare to
take him with them. Their perplexity became known to
Ahmed's family, and suspicious inquiries began to be made
whether he was going or not. He remained however.
Then it soon became evident that the old Moslem bow-wab
was not bringing in the Osiout mail until twenty-four
hours after it was due. So, as it was the custom for some
of the missionaries to take the key of the post-office box
Saturday night, Miss Johnson resolved to test the matter.
Monday morning early she went herself and found no
letters in the box, when she knew they should be there.
She returned and sent the old servant. He suspected
nothing, and came back immediately with letters—those
from Drs. L. and W., in Osiout, appearing to have been
opened. Of course much anxiety was felt, and besides no
answer came from the wealthy Scotchman to whom application had been made for Ahmed's support in case Dr. W.
could succeed in getting him out of Egypt. Just at this
time, however, came a letter from Lord and Lady Aberdeen, saying that as they were coming down the Nile they
had read an account of Ahmed's case in the London *Times*,
and that if they could assist in any way it would give
them great pleasure. The winds were favorable and they
soon arrived in Cairo. The ladies of the mission laid the
case before them, and Lord A. went immediately to the
English and American Consuls. The former said there
was great danger of Ahmed's assassination, and the latter
said it would be a great relief to him when Ahmed was
out of the country. Accordingly, Mr. Vivian, the English Consul, proceeded to procure passports for "Lord
and Lady Aberdeen with their two men servants," for one
of which Ahmed passed. None of us knew how the pass-

port was to be secured, and neither, I think, was there subterfuge on Lord A.'s part, as he met the Viceroy and told him what he was going to do.   The English Consul has been able to influence the Government in several cases where our own could do nothing, the Viceroy seeming to be anxious to avoid difficulties with England.   When all was arranged Lord A. engaged rooms down here at a quiet hotel, and left Cairo on a night express.   When they left the carriage in Cairo at the station Lord A. walked on one side of Ahmed and the countess on the other.   She said next day, "I felt very nervous."   The passports were sent down to the English Consul here, who had all necessary arrangements completed.   By ten o'clock next morning the party were all on board the steamer.   Mr. Giffen met them at the hotel and went on board with them.   Ahmed, he said, looked very serious until they were on the steamer, then his spirits seemed to rise.   Naturally he wished to go on deck with the others, but the Consul sent him below immediately.   Lady Aberdeen expressed herself as much pleased with his manners and bearing, and said it was their intention to send him on directly to Lord Polworth, her brother-in-law, in care of their English servant, while they themselves would stop awhile in Italy. Lord A. said this Lord Polworth was one of the most deeply pious men in Scotland, and that Ahmed could not be surrounded by better influences.   Then when they reach home themselves they are going to send him to the university at which Lord A. graduated, and one of the Professors of which is a very intimate friend of Lady Aberdeen.   So the whole thing worked out so beautifully and so unexpectedly, and when Dr. Watson got back Ahmed was, I suppose, at Brindisi.   His father said once that Ahmed wasn't a Christian at heart—that he wasn't really changed, that it was just those cunning American chowagat (gentlemen) who had imposed upon him. I wonder how he enjoyed it when he learned that the American sittat (ladies) had succeeded in spiriting Ahmed away to Scotland before he could find it out, and without any help from either of the chowagat.

He wrote to his family—beautiful letters—and was so very anxious to have seen his mother, but he did not dare communicate with her. Though a brave, manly fellow, he had a good many genuine *cries* about leaving all for so long, and was very sad and quiet when he took leave, but he wrote from the hotel here to Mrs. Lansing a most affectionate letter, and also wrote from Brindisi. They reached there on the fifth day, Ahmed having been terribly seasick all the way. He said very soberly that "he never expected to see land again." Everybody laughs at seasickness, and yet who can ever forget the misery of it? No doubt the poor fellow suffered real agony in those five long days, and very likely he would wonder if he might not just as well have stayed and "died in the land of Egypt."

December 20th.—Dr. Watson and family have recently arrived from America. They spent a few weeks in Scotland—their native land, and while there, were invited to visit Lord Aberdeen. They also saw Moallim Ahmed, who had entered the University of Edinburgh. Dr. Watson says "he is holding fast to his good profession and making many friends among the sincere lovers of our Lord Jesus in Scotland." Lord Aberdeen pays his boarding bills and gives him forty dollars quarterly for books and clothing. Ahmed thinks this very liberal and writes very cheerfully and happily, except that he so longs to hear from his family. He writes to them frequently—

beautiful, touching letters, but they give him not a word
in reply.   The mission in Cairo can get no news of them
and do not dare to visit them.   When Ahmed left them
first to come to Dr. Lansing's they made "a mourning"
for him and bewailed him *as dead*, and so they no doubt
now regard him.   He is very affectionate in his disposition, and few of us perhaps can estimate the trial it is to
him never even to see the handwriting of those he loves
so dearly."

Ahmed is still supported by Lord and Lady Aberdeen,
and is in the University at Edinburgh.   In addition to the
regular literary course, he is studying medicine.   "It was
his desire to be a minister, but Lord and Lady Aberdeen
urged him strongly to be a physician, thinking that in this
way he would be more acceptable among his countrymen,
in case he returns to Cairo."   He is very highly esteemed
by his acquaintances in Edinburgh, and his progress in
University studied shows him to be possessed of decided
mental powers.   His future is largely in other hands than
his own, but "it has always been his desire, as well as the
hope of those who support him, that some day he may be
a strong Christian worker, in Egypt at least, and if possible, among his kindred who are, as he was, following the
" False Prophet."

Heretofore one of the most discouraging features of
mission work in Egypt—and indeed in every Mohammedan country—was the unapproachableness of the Moslem element.   In the wall of exclusiveness and fanaticism
which the Moslems have built around themselves, the utmost efforts of the missionaries could make no appreciable
breach.

But recent advices from Egypt assure us that the door
to the Moslem world is gradually opening—all the indica-

tions show that the bars and bolts that have held it so firmly are weakening. The Sultan at Constantinople seems to feel this and is putting forth an effort to strengthen the props and bars, but the missionaries believe that he will fail, and that the door will give way in spite of him. The opening may not be like the bursting of a door before a giant stroke, but more like the letting out of waters, through a very small opening in a dyke, scarcely to be noticed at first, but in the end irresistible.

CHAPTER XXIII.

HEAT—ITS INTENSITY—OPHTHALMIA—HINDRANCE TO MISSION WORK.

The two physical drawbacks which operated most in hindering Mrs. Giffen in her labors, was *the intense heat*, and the prevalence of long-continued *and acute attacks of Ophthalmia.* The one prostrated and enervated, and the other often shut her up, a close prisoner, for weeks. When we come to add up the hindrances and difficulties under which mission labor is prosecuted in Egypt, the aggregate makes a large sum, and we often wonder that the devoted laborers in that land have patience and faith enough to sustain them in their trying position.

When Mrs. Giffen was transferred to Asyoot (Osiout) she says :

" There was but one vacant house in Osiout in which we felt we could live, and it was so small and inconvenient and so very hot that we could not reconcile ourselves to

attempt living in it.   One of the rooms has four windows,
but the other has none, except little places near the ceiling which cannot be opened, the door being the only way
of admitting air.   Doors and windows here are always
closed by eleven o'clock in summer, and must remain so
until after sundown, as the hot air, if permitted to enter,
would be almost unendurable.   The court walls keep out
the air from us, and we feel as if we could not breathe.
So we have our breakfast and tea on the porch and sleep
on the roof.   Last week, and the preceding one also, the
heat was really terrible.   The gentlemen had to close their
eyes riding over to school, and at night they said their
nostrils smarted still from the burning.   In the coolest,
closed room up stairs the thermometer was ninety-eight degrees during the afternoon, and when we left for the roof
at ten o'clock it was ninety-five degrees.   No doubt you
often have it as high as that, but you do not have this dry
air.   There is scarcely any sensible perspiration, and you
feel all the time as if you were being roasted in an oven.
This throws you into a nervous, feverish condition, which
makes you both weak and irritable and unfits you for any
kind of work."

Yet small, hot, inconvenient as this house was, Mr. Giffen was, from the simple fact that there was no better to be
had in the city, forced to live in it until a few months before
Mrs. Giffen's death.   The air and the surroundings were
so bad that they lived in it at a continual risk of their
lives.

"August 4th.—We are still exhorting ourselves to patience in the heat.   Between five and six o'clock we went
over to church and found the air so hot that I tried to hold
my breath as long at a time as I could until we got in the
house.   I have no doubt that the thermometer would have

gone up to one hundred and forty in the street. It has been one hundred and thirty in our court, its high walls shutting out the burning air from the desert which makes the streets so scorching. The walls of our houses are built with a view to these winds. Our window sills are about two feet deep, so that when our windows are closed during the day there is a great difference between the inside and outside temperature. But still when the thermometer stands at ninety-five or ninety-eight in these closed, darkened rooms it is very hard indeed to endure the still, dry, burning heat from ten in the morning until eight or nine at night.

The rise in the river has been so rapid that as it spreads over the hot ground cracked and broken with a two years' thirst, the air is just laden with a hot vapor which keeps us from sleeping anywhere and robs us of almost all comfort. 'The world is like fire,' is on every lady's tongue, and the natives declare that such heat was never felt here before. I have been wandering about everywhere trying to find a place to sleep ever since I came. The first night or two I was afraid to go to the roof on account of ophthalmia. I carried my mattress about from place to place almost every night, and at last we were driven to the roof. Last night there was a high wind from the desert when we went up, but by dispensing with the net we could sleep. It grew higher and hotter, however, and in an hour or two we felt that we must not expose our eyes to it whether we slept or not. So we came down, and going back a little later I found a real simoon blowing. The stars, before so bright, were now entirely obscured, and the darkness, instead of being black, seemed to be grey. It produced a singular sensation, while the skin and eyes seemed to dry up in the fierce heat. The rest of the night I spent in fanning Bruce

and trying to quench my thirst.   Everything in the house
felt just as if a fire had been burning under it, and the
sand and dust drifted in everywhere.   At dawn I felt so
weary that I thought I must find somewhere to sleep, so
went back to the roof and found the hot southern wind
still, and I threw myself on a straw mat on one of the
bedsteads, but two or three minutes drove me from there.
Coming down into Mr. Alexander's house, I tried all the
unoccupied corners, but everywhere there was nothing but
heat, heat, heat."

A week later she writes :

" It is still extremely hot.   Since my last we have had
another terrible simoon.   We were awakened at dawn by
a strange burning wind.   Looking South we could see the
sand clouds coming, and as we were on the roof we made
haste to get down.   The storm lasted about two hours, I
think, the air being *yellow*—the color of desert sands.   Of
course the heat was great, indeed for a week it was almost
a burden to live.   In Dr. Hogg's house the thermometer
was from one hundred degrees to one hundred and twelve
degrees all the time.   During the recent great heat the
water was going over on the eastern shore where there was
none at all last year, and in consequence the weather was
such as the natives say *never was known* here before.   In
the house of an Italian near us, the mother died one day
and the father the next, from no known cause except heat.
Arabs also died in the same way.   This has been heretofore unheard of.

We have been trying very hard to find a house in which
we could be comfortable.   There are, perhaps, a dozen *fine*
houses in Osiout, but the remaining thousands are models
only of darkness, dirt and small rooms."

" August 29th.—The last week has been cooler, the thermometer being from ninety-one degrees to ninety-three de-

grees in the closed room. Yesterday I put it out in the porch at four o'clock in the afternoon when the sun had disappeared from that side of the house entirely, and the mercury ran up to one hundred and fifteen degrees. To-day, as it is Saturday, I went to the house of one of our rich men who bought a piano for his daughter and doesn't know what to do with it, and though I went early, the heat was very oppressive. If it were not that we are missionaries, and realize what we have come here for, it would be *very hard* to stay. We have almost no fruit, so far; no vegetables scarcely, and cannot have milk and butter until clover comes; that is, we cannot drink the milk or make butter.

We have all been sick, except Mr. Alexander; and the Moslem doctor says it is from sleeping on the roof. So we have been trying to sleep down stairs; but it is poor success. I think I have never been so discouraged since we have been here. The summers are so long, and when we cannot sleep at night we have so little energy left for the long, hot day.

Our house is very much against us. In this country it is necessity to have the air from the North in summer, and to have sunshine in winter. We cannot get either."

" April 26th.—This is Saturday, and a long, dreary, oppressive one it has been. The "South wind," which brought heat long ago, brings it still. It has blown almost like a storm all day, and the air has been like " the breath of a furnace." There is an open passage from our sitting room to the dining room and here the thermometer went up to one hundred and eighteen degrees. We shut ourselves in the little sitting and bed room by eight o'clock in the morning and all are reading, writing and other work must be done in comparative darkness, very trying to weak eyes. Once this afternoon we were startled by a loud, sudden report, as if a stone had been thrown in the room. On examination we found it was the end of my bureau— which had burst from top to bottom for the third time— the hot winds of April being harder on furniture than the steady heat of summer. These winds prevail for fifty days, but every *fourth* day is usually cool—sometimes chilly, and these constant changes produce much sickness. Mr. G. was greatly oppressed with the heat to-day and had neither strength or energy to do anything."

"August 20th.—We have been back in our places hard at work for the last ten days. It was exceedingly "uphill" work the first four or five days. The journey here from Cairo was the hardest I ever experienced. It was very hot and you can form no idea of the dust. The others would run down to the canal at almost every station and wash their heads and faces, but my head ached so that I was content not to move. You never saw so dirty a house as we had to come into just at night, without supper or drinkable water. But worst of all we tossed through the whole night with almost no rest. The hot rare atmosphere made us itch and sting so that sleep was almost impossible even outside the house. There had been very little real hot weather until that day and the natives declare we "brought the heat." The nights were worse than the days, we got up in the morning with a feeling that we could not live here. But such things happily do not last always."

If the intense heat experienced is a serious obstacle to effective work, *ophthalmia*, in its varied forms, is far more so. Happily in this favored country we know little of this Eastern scourge. All other causes combined have not done so much to drive faithful missionaries from Egypt and from mission work, and to disable them for life, as this dreaded disease. Mrs. Giffen's case proved no exception. Her experience in this particular is recorded in these words :

" About two weeks ago a violent eruption broke out on Bruce's face and soon entered his eyes, which, with the exception of *three days*, had already been sore for *seven months*. It became quite alarming, and as I was just recovering from another and more acute attack of ophthalmia, and able to do nothing either in the house or out of it, we decided that I had better take Bruce to Dr. Grant in Cairo. He pronounced the eruption contagious, and most probably caused by some diseased native having touched him. Our house is in the midst of a low class of people, and he may readily have come in contact with some one of the hundreds of such persons who are every day to be seen in the streets.

Of course with such a disease I could not ask any one else to come in contact with Bruce, and I was too weak to take care of him night and day. Neither could I apply the medicine to his face and eyes alone. So I telegraphed Mr. Giffen to meet me in Ramle, and started down the second day after my arrival in Cairo. Bruce had taken some breakfast, but could not open his eyes. I put a large sunbonnet on him, and a light shawl over that when in the light. It was a ride of seven hours, and I have not often spent more anxious ones. The fever rose again and his restlessness became extreme ; I could not keep his face covered, and it was bleeding profusely. The car was crowded with not very nice people, and everybody stared so at the sore face and little blind eyes. The tension of the last hour or two was extreme. I had besides lost a good deal of sleep and was greatly fatigued. But when I went into the waiting room at the Ramle station, and closed all

the blinds, after a while the little man opened his eyes and
sat on the divan while I took lunch and rested myself. I
think one who has not nursed a child blind from ophthalmia
—that is unable to open its eyes—cannot guess how very
pitiful a sight it is. When Bruce was four months old he
had ophthalmia very severely. Both eyes were swollen
until the lids shone like glass at night. Every fifteen
minutes they had to be pulled apart to allow the discharge
to come out, and twice a day the lids were turned entirely
inside out and *brushed* with nitrate of silver and a solution
of salt. But the eyeballs could not be seen. This was
here in Ramle when Mr. Giffen was up the Nile. I had
never seen such a case, did not know what to do, and could
not get the doctor when I sent for him. So at a venture I
got Mr. A. to help me apply a great ugly leech to each
eye lid. The doctor approved it when he came, and next
day turned out the lids and scarified them. The blood
streamed over the little face and I never can forget how his
lips quivered. After another day I could detect a slight
quivering of the lids as if he were trying to open them,
and at twilight of the *sixth day* I could see that the lids
were just parted. But I had to turn him over on his face
in a dark room to enable him to do this. It is very painful to lie on the back in ophthalmia, perhaps more so to
grown people than to children. In my last attack during
the meeting of Presbytery I could not lie down one night
for four or five hours, and the hot water from my eyes
greatly irritated my face. One eyeball felt as if a nail
were through it, and the least ray of light seemed unendurable. Drs. Lansing and Watson, who were with us at
the time, charge the greater part of the trouble to our
house, and say that if ophthalmia of that kind is allowed
to continue it cannot be cured in the Egyptian climate."

In the last year of her life, even in Italy, Mrs. Giffen suffered severely from this cause. She was attacked on the journey to Torre Pellice, and tells us of her sufferings in these
words:

"I walked slowly and not very far, having my eyes well
protected with a large drooping hat, but before I got back
I felt one of them burn a little. Monday morning after
we started to Pompeii, Mr. Giffen remarked that the inflam-
mation had increased a little, but as we were not in Egypt
we did not think of it amounting to anything. I wore a
double veil however in Pompeii, besides having an umbrella, and when we started back Mr. G. said he was glad
to see that it was no worse. However, about the time we
reached Naples it began to feel uncomfortable but it did
not amount to a pain. Still before we finished dinner I
could scarcely hold it open, the veins in my temple began
to swell, the temple to throb, and my eye to burn. By
the middle of the afternoon I was almost *wild* with
pain and nervousness, which is part of the disease. I
really wished to get up and stamp the floor. It would
have been a real satisfaction to have torn things to atoms,
in fact to have just abandoned myself to the wild feeling which completely possessed me. Mr. G. had gone to
take our tickets to Genoa, and though Bruce and Lulu
were as good as other children would be shut up in a
dark room and left to amuse themselves, yet I thought I
could not endure the noise they made until their papa
would get back. I grew steadily worse until eight o'clock
when Mr. G. began giving me chlorodyne. Dr. Mackie
had told him to use it when I had a severe attack of ophthalmia. But the dose the doctor prescribed had no per-
ceptible effect. I waited an hour and took more, another
hour and took more, but did not get relief until about

midnight. Before morning I became very sick from the
chlorodyne, the effect being almost exactly the same as
sea-sickness. We had wished to leave at eight o'clock
but I could not hold up my head, and none of our things
had been packed. We had not brought a trunk and the
valises require so much more time and care. So Mr. G.
did the best he could with them and the children, in the
dark room, and got all ready to go by a boat at noon. I
contrived to dress after a fashion, tied a handkerchief over
my eyes; put a shawl over my hat and felt my way down
stairs by the railing."

When Naples was reached she was better, and says :

"Before leaving the Custom House I had been able to
take the shawl off my head, and I walked to the station
with only my veil over my eyes. No one knows it until
he has experienced it, how pleasant it is to pull off bandages and look freely at objects around you, after an
attack of ophthalmia, and all this day I could feel my eye
growing stronger every hour, and the contraction in that
side of my face gradually relaxing."

A letter of inquiry addressed to Mr. Giffen in regard to
the origin and effects of ophthalmia, elicited the following
reply : " It is the Egyptian hydra—a many-formed evil
to which the eyes are subject in this country. I have
never seen any one book that describes all the forms even
of the first attack, and then that which has one form at
first may soon change—if not cured will certainly change
—and finally assume some chronic form ; it may be of
simple granulations on the inner surface of the lids; it
may be a cataract, opacity, or total blindness."

The real cause of sore eyes in Egypt is a mystery. The
cause, whatever it be, is greatly aided by the dirt, squalor,
wretchedness and want in which the people live, although

no amount of cleanliness and careful living can be a complete safeguard against the disease.

Some of the missionaries have suffered greatly from ophthalmia, others with apparently no better general health, or more rugged constitutions have suffered none at all. Almost all children suffer more or less from it. That it is a hindrance to mission work is apparent when we think of the precious time and strength we waste in caring for our own weak eyes and those of our children ; and that it has been the main cause that has sent out of the field nearly all the missionaries that have retired from the work in Egypt. It is the cause of most of the blindness seen among the native school-teachers, and the vast number of beggars mentioned by all travelers who have written about Egypt. You may wonder why I mention school-teachers with the miserable blind beggars. Simply because if a poor person becomes blind he has been shut up to the alternative of entering one of these classes. If he is bright, and has opportunities for learning by hearing some one read, then he may commit part of the New Testament, if a Christian ; or of the Koran, if a Moslem, and thus earns a few piasters, or a few loaves of bread, or a bushel of grain per month teaching school. Until we began to send out teachers from our college the blind teacher was the only one known in the schools of Upper Egypt. The unfortunate victim of blindness who has neither opportunity to learn, nor friends to support him, must go into the streets and beg."

A beggar—and blind—and upon the streets of Asyoot —could human wretchedness be more deep ? Verily there is weighty obligation upon the people of *this* land in regard to their unfortunate brethren in such lands as Egypt.

CHAPTER XXIV.

HER FATHER'S DEATH.

Rev. Jonathan Galloway died, of pneumonia, at his home, in Due West, on 3rd of March, 1879. When Mrs. Giffen was informed of the fact she wrote to her sister as follows:

"Your long letter about Pa came last week, and I felt sure I would hear again Wednesday night, but only the paper came. Still I hope I may hear to-night. . . . How hard it must have been. But I infer you were all reconciled to it, and could in some measure rejoice that a long life of suffering and much anxiety was over, to begin in the world of rest and glory. It was very hard, at first, for me to imagine the house without him. If I tried to see you in my mind, he was sitting, at the table, or by the fire, or out on the steps, and especially it seemed so easy to see him and Ma going to church together. It seemed hard to me, to think that you had been without him a whole month, and I did not know. But I do not feel the *separation* as you do. When I left home, I think my feelings were *just of the nature of death*—the same in *kind* whatever they may have lacked in *degree*, and now Pa does not seem any further from me than before. I do not think of him as buried, but always as in heaven, and sometimes I think of him and the ones who went before, much as I do of you; and when I read about heaven it is like news from home.

I do not grieve for myself, but it does pain me to think of you—to think how the large circle is melting away, and how lonely you will be this summer. But Pa's anxieties and sufferings are over and he is at rest now. I think I rejoice more in that than anything else. I know he would not feel about me as he would have done, had he died the winter I was in Mansoora, for I am not alone now. * * * * The night I got your letter I could not sleep. It seemed to me I was with you in the parlor where he was dying, and that I saw it all. It stays too in my mind and seems a real thing. How long was it before he died that he said he was going to Sarah?—[Sarah, Mrs. Giffen's little sister, who died twenty years before, when she was six years old, and to whom her father was ardently attached.—ED.]

I wonder if consciousness remained after the great suffering was passed? Sometimes I have thought it would be just like going to sleep. * * * * It seems hard that I could not be with you, and sometimes I feel hard-hearted that I do not feel deeper grief, but I *cannot* sorrow for Pa. He had had a long and useful life. I am sure he did not live in vain. He was *meek*—as meek as that article in the paper makes him, but he was a man of *far more force of character* than was shown there. I think he was the most self-sacrificing man I ever knew. I am sure his first wish was for us, that we might serve and glorify God, and I doubt not we have a rich legacy left us and our children in the prayers he offered for us."

In a letter to the writer referring to the same event she says: "If I could only have known at the time I would feel so differently. It seems so hard to go back and try to go through such sad scenes, when all has been so long over, and to think that our friends die when we are at school or asleep. Dr. Boyce wrote me the night Pa was buried—how terrible it seems to write those words—and yet I do not think often of him as in the grave. How much more of a reality it gives to heaven to think that our friends are

there. It seems to me now that I have *two homes*, that Ma is with one part, and Pa with the other, and each I hope has three of us children with them; and the other three of us are *so* scattered. I remember once feeling very sad and desolate, very much oppressed in the English cemetery in Alexandria. We had gone there to see the graves of Mr. and Mrs. Curry—two of our missionaries—and I wondered who of the rest of us would lie there. * * *
"How strange it seems that it will soon be two years since Pa went away. How different they have been to him from what they have been to you. Is it not a blessed thought that he has not suffered in all that you have gone through?"
* * * "This is the anniversary of Pa's death. Two years! Well, I am sure he has been made 'perfectly blessed in the full enjoyment of God,' and I hope he knows about us, and loves us yet, without feeling any sorrow in what befalls us."

Not many months after this Mrs. Giffen almost experienced another great sorrow. Her little daughter Lulu was seized with fever and brought to the verge of the grave. To her sister Mrs. Giffen writes: " We have been through a dark valley with her this week. We thought she had died in my arms on last Tuesday night, when I supposed she was sleeping. Her face was cold and waxen-looking, there was no pulse, no movement of the chest, no sign of life, and we were sure our little darling had been taken from us. How fearful it seemed, to sit there with our little dead baby between us. Our minds were in such awful confusion that it was hard to feel anything else than our great pain. I begged Mr. Giffen to let us look at her as long as we could keep her in our arms before she would be taken away to be made ready for her last resting place. In doing this we moved her and she opened her eyes. It was just like the dead returning to life. We knelt down beside her and prayed for the little life to be spared us if it were God's will, and then when the others came Dr. Hogg made a very solemn affecting prayer for us. We watched all night fearing the little life might go any moment. But by the next day she was better, and we packed up a few things, put her on a pillow and came to Dr. Hogg's, for it seemed suicidal to stay in that wretched air. Sometimes now when I take my little dear in my arms it seems as if she had come back to us from heaven. That night when we had no hope, my human heart would keep thinking about her going to Pa—one more little dear one to be with him there. It seemed so natural to think that our Saviour would take her to those so dear to us. But now I hope she is spared to us to train for heaven, whenever it shall be His will to take her."

CHAPTER XXV.

ASYOOT COLLEGE—NEGOTIATIONS—PRESENT PROSPECTS.

" I mentioned some time since Mr. Giffen's hurried return here to confer with Dr. Hogg about the purchase of a site for the college. They were not well pleased, but the owner of the land made them a very fair offer of positions for the two schools in the tract which he was reported to have just purchased. And after a good deal of conference and reflection it was about agreed to accept the offer. Just then it came to light that *there had been no purchase* and that Chowaga Weesa had no titles to the land from the government and might never get any! One of the Bashas had been sent up here after Rivers Wilson was dismissed "to get money." Chowaga Weesa had agreed with him as to the terms of the sale, but the Basha had been recalled by rumors of abdication before the sale of the land was completed. Of course Chowega Weesa still *hoped* to secure the property, but being an Oriental he would let Dr. Hogg and Mr. Giffen hurry here and would spend ten days waiting on his movements, and discussing what he would give or what they would take before he would say that he had no land to sell them. Of course it was a disappointment, but missionaries have to get accustomed to such things.

When all this failed to come to anything Weesa told them there was a nice garden in the city which he could buy for them, but he thought the owner would ask $2,500 for the seven acres. The situation is *very desirable,* but the gentlemen scarcely felt like making such an offer. Since then it appears that it might be bought for less and Mr. G. is very anxious to hasten the business. The school building now in use is greatly overcrowded and is in danger of falling down in any high wind. But nothing can be done except *through these slow natives.* Nobody will sell to us because we are Protestants—or rather because we represent and act *for the sect.* So the gentlemen *have even to look at a piece of ground secretly.* Rich Copts will run up land *thousands of pounds* to keep us from getting it for *mission purposes.* Individually they probably would not interfere with us."

"April 20th.—Our examinations came off the week before the meeting of the Association. This gave a fresh opportunity to agitate the question of a site for the college. Among others Dr. Hogg spoke of the matter to the Moslem

physician up there. A few days subsequently this
man met Mr. Alexander and told him he had been in conversation with a certain Khowaga Hanna who owned part
of the Garden near the station and who would sell it to
the mission for the schools. On speaking to Dr. Hogg he
exclaimed: " Why that is the very man that we supposed
would do everything to defeat us!" This Garden—as
they say here—is a large palm grove, and is owned by a
great many persons in bits of a fourth or half an acre.
The consent of several *families* had therefore to be obtained before land enough could be bought. Two women
especially had to be *coddled* into the matter. Their shares
were parts of their *inheritance*, and as such, were far more
valuable than the same amount of land "bought with
money." You remember Naboth was unwilling either to
exchange his vineyard for a better one or to sell it for
money—though it was a king who desired to possess it.
"Should I give the inheritance of my father unto thee?"
Well, Naboth's feelings and principles are those of every
rich old family in Asyoot and the consequence is that the
mission has been *ten years* trying to buy ground for the
schools which educate the children of almost all these
families. A few years ago Khowaga Weesa—who is from
a rich *new* family, that is a "self-made" man as we would
say—persuaded the husbands of the two women referred
to above, to sell him their shares of this Garden and had
actually paid down the money when the women heard of
it and compelled their husbands to rescind the contracts.
"Must we women put on the *mantaloon* (pantaloons) and
maintain the honor of our houses! Sell our inheritance to
a man who has made all he has! Has he grown so rich
and we become so poor that he can buy and we need to sell!
Never!" Selling to the mission, however, is a little dif-

ferent from selling to individuals. They know that it is
not for ourselves, that it is for a religious use. There is
therefore no shame in selling to us, only it is *selling land*,
and people in Asyoot would almost as soon sell their children. No further results were obtained during the meeting and the members all settled down into the belief that
the college would have to be taken to some other town."

After months of weary waiting and fruitless negotiations, she writes:

"No advance has been made in the matter of the Garden. Even our own members, who volunteered to do the
buying, are evidently working against us, to facilitate
their own purchases. The *greed* for land in Asyoot ex-
ceeds anything I ever heard of. What we have bought is
not sufficient and is yet undivided—that is, the "shares"
in the Garden are not yet located so that each owner can
say this, or this is my part. We hoped to be able to buy
more and then to exchange one piece for another outside
the Garden, more desirable for the front of the lot, but
one difficulty after another has been thrown in the way,
until the feeling is becoming very strong that we will be
compelled to sell what we have and go to some other town.
The rich men of Asyoot do not want us to leave, and do
not believe that we will. The college, if built near the
railroad station, would greatly increase the value of the
property of many of them, both Copts and Moslems, and
besides they know that they would be compelled to send
their children from home to be educated if we left Asyoot.
But we have waited and waited for ten years nearly, and
they think we will continue to wait until they get as much
land as they wish for themselves.

At present the gentlemen are trying to negotiate with
the Government for another Garden. If we could get

that, what we now have could be sold. After a month Dr. Hogg will return to Asyoot and then I hope we can all unite in special prayer for guidance and direction in this matter.

October 26th.—Wednesday and Thursday nights of this we had a concert of prayer with reference to the site for the college. We bought land in good faith and paid for it. But those who sold it now refuse to divide the garden, and give the amount for which we have paid—that is they won't agree to anything we propose. They say "it is not their custom" to be in a hurry about parting with land. The influential one among these men is the old uncle of that little Frooza who married Khowaga Wasif's nephew last winter. And his greed for land is something amazing. Our gentlemen cannot get these men to meet them except for Kh. Wasif to send for them to come to his house. Then one will come, and another send word that he is sick and another busy, etc., etc. And even when they do come they just sit and count strings of beads or smoke in your face. So we thought we would all meet and lay the matter before the Lord, beseeching him to show us why he had a controversy with us, and to show us plainly what he would have us do. Our meetings were solemn and we tried to empty ourselves, and to plead with our Heavenly Father to guide us. It really does seem sometimes that every indication of Providence is that we must sell what we have bought and go elsewhere.

November 20th.—We have at last secured a division of the Garden, and that of course brings up the building question again. After our concert of prayer the gentlemen got the heirs all together and worked a whole day to get a suitable piece or indeed any piece, but the one who owned the most would do nothing at all until the Garden

was divided into thirds and "the lot" cast for his third.
And he got just what we wanted. After that we could
only get ours in *three pieces.* The largest is one and one-
fourth acres and does not please us very well as a site.
Besides it is so much smaller than we wished. It is still
possible though to effect an exchange and get an equivalent for our three pieces in one piece outside of the Garden. But it may take half a year longer to do this. In
case we succeed in this we could have the girls' boarding-
school on the same lot, and that would be a great advantage in many ways. Dr. Hogg and Mr. Giffen were to
have gone this afternoon to survey our largest piece, so
that they may be able to determine upon plans for
building. If they see that they can put the kind of
of house they wish on this piece they will then most
likely begin collecting materials and making up esti-
mates, etc., etc. By the time the brick and lumber are
ready it will probably appear on which piece of ground
we must build and the work will then go on.

December 28th.—They are cutting down the palm trees
on our lot, and are bringing earth and stones. One thous-
and cubic metres of stone are to be delivered within two
months at a cost of about one dollar per metre. That is
five times as expensive as around Cairo. In consequence
they have had to abandon the idea of building entirely
of stone, as was desirable in order to have the house cool
in summer. Only foundations will be of stone, and it is
thought these must be *two metres broad,* (seventy-nine
inches), but they will not require to be more than a metre
deep."

Most of the foundation for the main building has now
been laid, and the workmen are busy erecting the walls of
the other minor buildings. The entire work is being

pushed forward to completion as rapidly as circumstances will permit. In the meantime the college is flourishing as never before. The dormitory, for the poorer classes of students who must live as cheaply as possible, accommodates ninety, and is full, and some have not been removed from the old building. Soon room will be made for one-third more, and then with little expense rooms for as many more can be constructed on the second floor. The pupils now in attendance number one hundred and sixty-nine. The future of the college seems very bright.

In a recent letter Mr. Giffen says:

"The college is now doing a great work in the way of furnishing teachers for village schools. At least twenty of our undergraduates are at this time engaged in teaching, and of course every one copies as well and as faithfully as he can the only model he knows anything about. If Mr. Pressly of Monmouth, Ill., (a brother of Rev. James P. Pressly, D. D.,) could only pass up and down the Nile and see these teachers at work—nearly all of whom have been helped by the fund which he so generously provided it would certainly rejoice his heart, that he had been the chosen means for placing money where it is doing so much good."

CHAPTER XXVI.

The repeated and severe illness which Mrs. Giffen experienced just at this time seemed to make it imperative to seek rest and recuperation in some other climate. During the absence of the gentlemen at a session of the Presbytery, Eddie Alexander was seized with diptheria and soon fell a victim. Watching and nursing the little sufferer had greatly enfeebled and prostrated Mrs. Giffen, and on the day that he was buried she writes:

"That day I had a good deal of fever, but Mr. Giffen came at sunset and I felt comforted. The fever kept up, however, until Thursday, when I felt *obliged* to get a girls' school ready for examination before the commissioners, on the next Monday. That gave me hard work for the rest of the week. Monday we were all day in the church, Tuesday the commissioners, Drs. Barr and Stewart, with all our mission circle dined with us. That night we were invited to Kh. Wasif's to a dinner of fifteen courses. It was eleven when we left the table and midnight when we got home. Next morning I went to the college. About night I took a chill, was very sick all night and continued to grow worse and worse with severe pain in my chest. By Saturday hope was almost gone, but they decided to telegraph to Cairo for a doctor. The telegram reached Dr. Grant just barely in time for him to dispatch to a town not far from Alexandria for a German doctor to come to Cairo on that night's express and go next day to Asyoot. He arrived at sunset Sabbath night, but all I suppose had then quite lost hope. When Mr. G. heard the train coming he thought it was of no avail, but after a careful examination the doctor began "cold water" treatment very vigorously and at ten o'clock left me better. Next day however I was worse, but he kept up the treatment, wrapped me in a thick wet sheet, fanned me and gave me wine of ipecac and after I began to shiver, removed the sheet and applied twelve leeches to my side, the wounds of which bled all night. No one who knows of the case doubts that he was the means of saving my life. Five or six days after Lulu was severely attacked with fever. By the time she was out of danger, I took another disease, which seemed half East India jungle fever and half scarlet fever, which greatly prostrated me, and just as soon as I could get out bed from that, we had to get our things together to leave the house we were in. We decided that I should take the children to Cairo. There Bruce took dengue and when he got better I went to Ramle. That night Lulu was attacked with the dengue also, and was very sick for a few days. So much loss of sleep and general weariness began to tell badly on me, and to make me long to be away from Egypt for awhile.

Just then too it became apparent that Mr. Giffen could not go on with the building during the summer, as there was necessity for finishing the business of the titles before the Cadi or Moslem judge. So we decided to go to Italy for a short time and try to gather up strength and energy for next year's work and responsibilities."

Just at this time the intelligence of the death of Dr. Bonner reached her, and to Mrs. Bonner she wrote: "We have been afflicted and tossed, but I need not tell you that we have spoken and thought much of you. I am sure that I can sympathize with you, since we were almost certain that our time of parting had also come. The first time we had prayers after I was able to sit beside Mr. Giffen, he selected the 116th Psalm, and while we sang it with full hearts I longed that you and yours also might live to rejoice in singing it together. But it was not God's will. How sad it is, how sore it makes one's heart to give up the greatest blessing we ever enjoyed. How different home will seem in some respect, if I am ever permitted to see it. So many are gone, and perhaps many more may go before I am there. But last spring in Asyoot I supposed that I would meet first the dear ones "gone before." It is comforting that it is the All Knowing, the Ever Kind one who holds all in His hands."

The journey to Italy was made without any noteworthy occurrence, and from Naples she wrote:

"We had not been long in the city until we learned that Vesuvius was in unusually active condition, and that many persons were hurrying out to see it. On inquiry, however, we learned that it was both an expensive and fatiguing bit of sight-seeing, so fatiguing that I could not think of going even if we had felt able to pay a Napoleon each for the trip. So Mr. Giffen went alone. At the Lower Station he met with a party of good United Presbyterians from Allegheny.

There are *two cars* only on the railway. One is descending while the other is ascending. They are moved by *endless wire cables*, worked by an engine at the Lower Station. The cars run on a *single rail*, which is about a foot in height by ten inches across. There is a wheel at each end of the coach running on the top of the rail, while from each side of the coach there are arms, which pass under at an angle, are furnished with wheels at their lower extremities, and run in grooves *upon the sides* of one rail.

Should the cable break, these *side wheels* clasp the rail automatically and hold the car still in its place. In consequence of running upon a single rail, there is no jolting but a smooth, even motion, at about the rate of a man walking on level ground. From the Lower to the Upper Station it is nine minutes by the car. From there you walk up to the crater, which is about fifteen minutes distant; and it is for this part of the trip that one requires a guide. On leaving the car the guides were in readiness, and Mr. G. fell in with the Allegheny party.

In some places they were almost suffocated with the sulphurous fumes rising from crevices in the cooled lava beds, even though they held their handkerchiefs over their nostrils. A large stream of lava was running down the side of the mountain to the left of the railway, while every few minutes, perhaps every three, there was an explosive burst in the crater, which threw up a great column of vapor, smoke and melted matter. The latter fell in showers all around, and of course sight-seers needed to watch to avoid being struck by the pieces. Mr. G. brought home a bit as large as my closed hand which fell at his feet. It is black, and very porous and brittle. He also brought some pieces of sulphur from the crater.

Some ladies who had paid for their railway tickets had not the courage to make the ascent to the crater, or even to go as far as the Upper Station, and Mr. G. thought that no one really *enjoyed* the ascent. There was too much thunder, too much hot lava, and too many Plutonian vapors to make one feel content to stand and gaze over the grand panorama always in view around Naples, and especially when seen from such a height as Mount Vesuvius. Just now he was saying that if he were going out there again and were in good health, he would take the ordinary railway to Pompeii as far as Portici, and then walk across to, and up, Vesuvius alone. He says it would be fatiguing, but could be done in a day. When he and his party reached the lower station, he heard some one call him, and turning round he found himself face to face with Miss Linn Pressly, of Allegheny, who was just about to take her place in the ascending car. She was greatly surprised to meet any one she knew in Vesuvius, and could hardly believe *Miss Galloway* was in Naples. Mr. G. inquired why she wasn't going to Egypt. "O," she said, "the Atlantic was *so much* that I cannot think of crossing the Mediterranean." I *guess* she pays tribute to Neptune, too. Her party were going to Rome early the next morning, and she said they would not get back from Vesuvius until night, when she would be too weary to come to our hotel. We would have gone to see her at theirs, but I had no one with whom to leave Bruce and Lulu, and I knew they would be too sleepy to take out calling at that time in the evening. So we did not meet.

It was a great disappointment to me that I could not ascend Vesuvius. But as soon as I understood the situation I knew I could not make the trip, no matter how much I wished to, as I would not risk my health for any sight-seeing in Europe. Indeed, sight-seeing to Missionaries is a *very different* thing from what it is to travelers. When we are going out, what is *beyond us* in Egypt, the unknown, untried life, takes most of the interest out of what would be otherwise all engrossing; and when one is in search of rest and recuperation there is nothing worse than sight-seeing. So now I do not care about Vesuvius, do not regret not having been to its summit; and sometimes I think I would not have endured the fatigue of the journey, which Drs. Barr and Stewart have made, for a great

sum. It is, especially, mental fatigue which I have in
mind. One gets weary of *sights* and looks at and tries to
fasten them in memory, not because it is pleasant or enjoyable at the time, but only to think about them and tell
one's friends afterwards. And that soon becomes very
weary work.

We had arrived in Naples Thursday morning. I staid
quietly upstairs until Saturday morning, when I felt almost like myself, and thought I should like to go with Mr.
Giffen to the Museum. It is a very extensive building,
but most of it is on the ground floor, and we could see
things pretty well without much fatigue. Lulu and Bruce
ran about and amused themselves, while we looked at
objects of interest. I had supposed that no museum would
be very interesting after seeing that of London, but it is a
mistake. In Naples there are rooms and rooms, the walls
of which are entirely covered with paintings and frescoes
from Pompeii. They are well preserved and show that art
was quite well understood in those old days. There are
also very fine mosaics from the same place. One is on a
raised space in the center of a large hall, and is surrounded by an iron railing. It is oval, about 18 feet long
by perhaps 12 feet in width, and is a very fine picture of the
battle of Issus. Alexander, on horseback, is one of the
prominent figures. The bits of stone, of which the picture
is formed, are almost as large as the point of my little finger, but it is wonderful how bright and clear the picture
is. In the rooms lined with these scenes from Pompeii
there were many artists at work, making showy copies of
gods and goddesses, of cupids and their victims, but especially of handsome women, who were nearly all dressed in
pink or sea-green. One of them begged us to buy some
of his copies. We were amazed that he only asked 2
francs for them, and yet many of them were very pretty.

In another room we saw the clay copy of a beautiful statue, the first time I had ever seen clay modelings. There were many long galleries of bust and full sized statues, not only of gods and goddesses, but of almost all the great Roman and Grecian heroes and heroines. There are all the Cæsars, I think, and some of their wives, the mother of Nero, the Ptolemies, Homer, Dante, Representatives of the Nile; while there are *four* Apollos, and perhaps half a room full of life-sized, standing Venuses. But there was only one Apollo and one Venus which pleased me. This Apollo was of immense size, in sitting posture, lyre in hand. The head was grandly crowned with laurel, all in beautiful white marble, as also the hands and feet, while the graceful robe was of *fine red porphyry*. The effect of the two colors was very striking. The Venuses are merely handsome women, or intended to be such, but to me, some of them had real simpering countenances, while others had wicked-looking mouths. Yet all of them were done by great Greek and Roman sculptors. Beside the galleries of Marble figures there are perhaps half a dozen filled with bronzes. One of these is a magnificent figure of Nero on horseback, found in the forum of Pompeii, from whence also were brought a great many others of the finest pieces in the Museum. There is an immense statue of Hercules by Glycon of Athens, found in the baths of Caracalla at Rome. The sinews are wonderful, and the appearance of *strength* so striking that one did not need to be told for what it was intended. In the same Hall is a group called " The Farnese Bull." It is cut from one piece of marble, and represents a beautiful woman bound to the horns of a wild bull by two men, but I think there are five full-sized persons in the group, beside the magnificent animal in the center.

J

The second story is devoted to painting principally, at least on one wing. There are separate halls for all different schools, and every hall was filled from floor to lofty ceiling with magnificent pictures. Here, as down stairs, there were many artists copying, but these were grand pictures, and one could not buy them for two francs. One Hall is called the Hall of the Venuses, and was far more revolting than the same ideal in marble. Art in Europe, holds nothing sacred, and one has *to become accustomed* to what people do not look at in America. This feeling of "getting used to it" is the only way in which one can excuse European taste; but I hope it will require a long time for Americans to get so "used to it," as to tolerate nude art to the extent that one sees everywhere here.

By far the most interesting apartment in the Museum was the one which contained "Comestibili" (Provisions) from Pompeii. These were in glass cases running round the room. There was first a row of about a dozen *perfect loaves* of bread, all carbonized, found in the houses and bakeries of Pompeii. They are in the form of an ordinary loaf cake, and have indentations on the top, made with a knife before baking, as one cuts a pie. Then there were dishes of dates, figs, cherries, coffee, rice, &c., all of perfect form. In a case by itself were glass tubes containing olives *and the oil which had been pressed from the fruit since found.* It was clear and of a natural color, but the olives were a little dark. On the other side were cases containing charred cloths, silk and thread, lamp wicks, corks, sponges, needles, bones, eggs, of natural color, only a little yellow, almonds, grapes, nuts, wheat, &c. The texture of the cloth was perfect, and the large skeins of thread unbroken. There was also a sauce pan containing meat and a purse containing three coins of the time of

Vespasian. In a hall on the other wing were cases of the jewels found at Pompeii and Herculaneum. There are handsome rings, bracelets, and earrings, and some immense gold chains, not very unlike the present fashion of articles, the endless ones I mean. Among these jewels are the chain and bracelets found on " Julia," Diomed's daughter. It made one feel very sad to look over these things, these witnesses if I may so speak, of that great catastrophe, and when I had seen these I did not care to see other things, though there were many other halls besides the great library. As we came out, however, we stopped and looked a second time at quite a number of beautiful marble columns of many different colors from the buried cities. Some of them were ten or twelve feet high, and of the finest polish. We both came away far from satisfied, feeling that we would like to come another day and just go over what we had already seen, which was a different feeling from anything we have experienced before or since.

Early Monday morning we took the cars for Pompeii. It is an hour's ride from Naples. As we came in sight of the Station of Pompeii, the first thing which met my eyes was " *Hotel de Diomede.*" It gave me a strange sensation— a feeling that it *was almost* sacrilegious. From the Station you walk through a cultivated field which is quite low and level, up the hotel and offices which is situated on the foot of the hill of Pompeii. Tickets of admission cost 2 francs each, but this includes a guide. These guides are in uniform, and ours at least was a very civil sort of a fellow, never once hinting at buksheesh. He spoke English, very brokenly however, and from the manner in which he pronounced or rather mispronounced his *h's* I decided that like the Belgian *attachee* at Washington, who did not like to talk English with Americans, he must have learned his

English in London.   It was always *halters* for altars, and
orses for horses.

Passing up the hill about 100 yards, we came first to a
great strong gate or street door, and entered an arched
covered way, paved with very heavy, rough stones, which
conducts to the level of the city.   This gate is called the
"Sea Gate," and I suppose from the strong manner in
which the covered way and the gate are made that the sea
may once have come up near to this entrance, though now
it is at some distance.   From this street we entered the
Museum, which consists of a long hall.   In the center in
glass cases were *the petrified bodies* of six persons, just as
they were found.   Three are men, one a single woman, and
one case contains what is supposed to be mother and
daughter, the latter apparently a child of 10 or 12 years.
Some of them had apparently died in great agony.   One
is lying on the face with the arm under the forehead.   One
man had a belt of money, or at least what appears to be
such a belt, around the waist, and one woman would soon
have been a mother.   Besides these skeletons, or forms
rather, there is that of a dog, which had died in a half
sitting posture, and in the utmost agony.   Its writhings
are as plain as if you had witnessed the death.   These
were sad sights.   They made you realize the feelings and
enter into the sufferings of those who were overwhelmed
in the great eruption as nothing else could.   You felt you
were in the presence of the dead, in the presence of those
on whom God had laid his hand in a terrible way.   Beside these bodies there were specimens of all the articles
we had seen in the Museum of Naples, except the jewels
and the olive oil.

Passing up the remainder of the street we soon found
ourselves in the still vacant city.   Oh, it is a strange experi-

ence! All the houses are there, and most of them have
the number and name of the owner marked upon them.
They are all one story, and that not very high, except one,
which seemed to have been built with some limited ideas
of two stories. Those of the rich are much on the style of
Egyptian houses. There is first a general entrance then a
court for the men, and behind that a larger court for the
women, in the center of which was a fountain, with often
beautiful marble steps over which the water fell to form a
little cascade. Beside one of these fountains was the faucet
for turning on and shutting off, and it looked just as if one
might use it still. Some of the fountains had a kind of canopy
over them with a back piece very handsomely designed in
mosaics, and in the recess formed thus, in some houses,
were fine pieces of statuary. Around these courts were
the dining and sleeping rooms. One could easily imagine
what a nice, cool place one of these large courts must have
been, and after seeing Egyptian women, it did not stretch
imagination much to infer that plenty of gossip and side
talk had echoed round these walls. Many other things
reminded us of Egypt. The water jars, kitchens, wine
shops, oil stands, mills and bakeries, which were sometimes found in the same house, and also the public
bath. In the latter was an artist sketching. Many of the
streets were marked at the head with various devices to
show the craft or calling. There were streets of wine shops
only, of oil shops, of masons, carpenters, &c. In one of
the back streets, the guide called it, as we thought, " the
street of the *brothers*," and before we knew had unlocked
a door to a room, the walls of which were covered with
bright, well executed pictures of *the most obscene* character.
In an instant we knew he had said *brothels* instead of
brothers. And he said a vast quantity of such paintings

and other objects found in this street were kept in a hall
in the Museum at Naples, and never opened to women and
children—a statement corroborated by the guide books.

In Diomed's house we were shown the spot where the
skeleton was found wearing bracelets marked " Julia " and
always spoken of as Diomed's daughter. The guide said
there were *seventy* skeletons found in that house, but afterwards I wondered if he really intended to say seventy, as
I have always understood that there were comparatively
few persons who did not escape. Just now I have looked
up the matter in a guide book, and the number is given
" as seventeen women and children furnished with provision,
but who are supposed to have been suffocated by the torrents of ashes and water which rushed in after the eruption." Diomed himself, as was supposed, held a key in
his hand, and near him was a slave bearing money and
other valuables. *I sat down and rested awhile in Sallust's
house.* It is considered one of the finest. In it, as in
many others, the mosaics of the floors are covered with
earth to prevent the rains from destroying or injuring
them, as the wooden roofs of the houses were almost all de-
stroyed early in the eruption, or else fell in with the weight
of ashes, lava and pumice stones. The house of Sallust opens
into three streets. In the court of the men are some fine
frescoes covered over to protect them, and which are still
very bright and distinct.

One is Acteon watching Diana in her bath, and on the
other wall is Phryxuson, the ram, and Helle, in the water,
Europa and the Bull, followed by cupid, &c.

There are many temples, among them that of Venus,
Mercury, Jupiter, Augustus, or that of Vesta, the Temple
of Fortune, &c. The most interesting to me was that of
Isis. We saw the grand altar and the pit into which the

remains of the sacrifices were thrown, and also a small cell with an underground entrance for the priest who stood behind the figure of Isis and delivered her oracles for her, when the people inquired of her. There are also two or three theatres and an amphitheatre with barracks for the Gladiators. The streets are generally very narrow, many of them not being more than ten feet. Nearly all had a narrow raised path on each side, while the chariot way was paved with rough lava stones, into which the traces of the wheels were sometimes pretty deeply cut, while at little distances there were stepping stones, generally three, for crossing in rainy weather. These were often a foot high, and would just admit of a horse passing between them. After we had seen most of the city, which is not large, there having been about 12,000 inhabitants only, and the great majority of the houses being small and near together, we went up upon unexcavated ground and looked over the whole, as well as at the grand amphitheatre, in the centre of which Pompeii seemed to lie. It is hard to realize that lazy looking, idly smoking Vesuvius could do so much damage. The unexcavated parts of the city are not very extensive, but where we went up on the bank there was quite a field of corn and beans growing greenly over what the guide said was unexcavated ground, being, I suppose, within the walls.

The eruption took place in August, A. D. 79, and lasted three days, Vesuvius pouring out torrents of boiling water, mixed with ashes, as well as great masses of inflammable matter and pumice stones. Much glass was melted, though a vast quantity of rain is known to have fallen, perhaps, during the three days. The stratum of earth, pumice stone and ashes is about four metres deep. At the place where we went up on the top, we seemed to climb up a bed of ashes only.

Excavating was not begun until 1748, when some valuable objects were discovered by accident, but it is only since 1863 that the work has gone on regularly. Skeletons have been found crushed in the houses, others buried under the stones and ashes, and others apparently sleeping in the streets, it is supposed, from inhaling the peculiar gases. In a locked room, with a slatted door, we saw a skeleton embedded in the ashes, though enough had been removed to give you a good idea of the manner in which the person had been covered up. After we left this house, I sat down in the street with the children and rested, while Mr. Giffen and the guide went farther on. There were pretty little blue and pink flowers growing along the side walks, and I sat and indulged myself in a good many reflections, while Bruce and Lulu's little fingers made sad havoc of the flowers. What would I not have given once for the assurance that one day I would see Pompeii! And now without such thought or design, in leaving home, there I was with my two little ones beside me!

When we were satisfied with looking at streets and houses we went back to the offices, and into a large room filled with pictures, photographs and albums.

There were many tempting things, but we only bought four photographs, and then went down to the Station, sat in the shade and waited for the train. Only think of the railroad running along beside Pompeii! What a change from the time when its poor frightened citizens went flying along over the same ground! We had an hour to wait. So we sat on the stones in the yard, and listened to the wind making Æolian harps of the telegraph wires, until the train came along and took us back to Naples."

In a few days they reached their destination in the Waldensian valleys. Here they remained nearly two months,

in sight of the mountain snows; and with the comparative
freedom from care and labor which they felt, the long
rambles among the hills and the pure cold springs on the
mountain sides, Mrs. Giffen and the children soon seemed
to have recovered their full health and strength; but Mr.
Giffen was soon prostrated with ague and rheumatism, and
so continued much of the time during their stay, and here,
doubtless, were soon the seeds of the disease—acute rheumatism— which, in a few months after, terminated Mrs.
Giffen's life.

But the harvest was so great and the labors in their
mission field so few, that we soon find them on their return voyage to Alexandria. The events of the journey are
given by Mrs. Giffen.

"As you see we are back in our old place again. I had
hoped to write regularly after I got started again in Italy,
but I could not. We received letters one morning in La
Tour that there would be a meeting of the Association on
the 26th of July. We had walked down to the Post together, so we sat down at a restaurant, made the calculation and found that we could reach Egypt in time for the
meeting, if we were in Turin next morning at 9 o'clock.
So we went home, got dinner, saw a young gentleman
whom Mr. Giffen wished to engage as French teacher for
the college, explained everything to him, and packed up
our valises. We intended to go Pignerol, the railway station, that night, but when we paid our boarding, we were
charged with the nights lodging and breakfast, whether
we staid or went, and as it is not pleasant to move about so
much with two children, we decided to stay in La Tour for
the night, and leave at daylight next morning. Two
members of the family had done this during our stay, and
we heard the lady say she had ordered coffee for us. But

she was not in good health, and her husband was away. It was a very warm close night, and when we took Bruce and Lulu up at 3 o'clock both began begging for water. There was none in the room, and the little fountain from which we had been drinking had dried up only two days before. Neither of us knew where the other one was, and we thought we could get it at breakfast, but when it was time to leave the house no one had stirred. The omnibus was down in the town, and when we got in, we asked the attendant for water, and we thought it was coming every moment, but the omnibus drove off before it came. O well, we thought, we can get the best of water in Pignerol, but the driver stopped at grog shops so often that when we got out of the omnibus the manager urged us off, saying we would be late for the train. There was just time to get tickets and get in the cars, and then the guard locked the door. We went third class, and the car was terribly crowded, and the heat very great, Lulu crying most of the way for water. We had but little time in Turin, and as the ticket offices are only open a few minutes, Mr. Giffen was obliged to attend to that first. Meantime Lulu had seen a man go along with a bucket of dirty water, and she was nearly frantic. I knew where there was a restaurant, but I could not leave the baggage, and thought there would certainly be time for Mr. Giffen to get the water after he would put us in the car; but when he jumped out with the bottle, the guard peremptorily ordered him back. and we were obliged to submit. The heat was fearful, and the dust as bad as in Egypt. None of us had anything to eat, and Lulu seemed wild with thirst. We were on the Express, and we flew past station after station without stopping until nearly noon. At last the door was opened, and Mr. Giffen came back with a bottle of about as bad

water as I ever tried to drink ; but it had been iced slightly,
and the poor little thing seized the cup as if she would
like to swallow it whole, and would not let it go even
when she could drink no more. In southern Italy the
water is almost universally bad, so much so that it is not
safe to drink much of it. It must always be iced, and
they generally add to it a syrup of anise seed—on hygienic principles, I suppose, but to me it is very disagreeable. It is never brought to the car windows as here, and
as all the buffets or restaurants are at the back of the railway stations, one can only get water when the guard
chooses to open the car door. Indeed there is little comfort in railway travel in Europe without you can take
everything you may wish with you, and *happen* to get a
compartment to yourselves, which, of course, can be but a
rare occurrence. We found that we could overtake the
Italian boat at Naples by leaving the next night at midnight.

After supper Mr. G. told me to take the children and
go to sleep, and he would wake us in time to get off. But
Bruce had got so nervous over our oft-repeated going and
stopping without ever getting back home, that he had become fully persuaded that sometime we would go off and
leave him asleep, and he therefore decided that he would
watch for himself. But at last his determination failed
him, and we all slept.

We left Genoa at 11 o'clock at night the 19th. There,
as everywhere else in Europe, you must wait in the station
until the porter unlocks the door, before you can pass to
the train. Then, of course, there is a great rush for seats,
though ordinarily the compartments are not overcrowded.
But this time there were a great many second-class passengers, and very few second-class compartments. Some of

them were filled with soldiers, who would smoke and drink wine the rest of the night; but after going the length of the train, we found we could do no better than just to pack in as others were doing. Most people carry so much baggage in Europe that it becomes a question how to dispose of it when there are many passengers. While we were putting ours in order, we sat the children down in our places. Instantly a man next me began to growl about babies taking up grown people's places. I did not answer; but in a few minutes a young man on the other side took up his own things and helped Mr. Giffen to a seat, where he could hold Bruce in more comfort. It was refreshing to find a man who remembered that little people have some rights as well as grown men and women. The dust and heat were very great, and the passengers next the window resolutely kept them closed. Then one or two began to smoke and I wondered how we would get through the night. But to our great joy two passengers got out in an hour or two and a little further on we got rid of the wretched grumbler who sat by me and kept pushing Lulu's feet off his pants whenever her slippers touched him. Towards day there remained but one passenger beside ourselves, and we got one nice little sleep. But as the morning advanced a little, Mr. Giffen grew very ill and suffered extremely. Had we not had medicine with us I do not know what we should have done. His face had such a queer look and he was so flushed and hot that I felt greatly alarmed, especially when we found that we had been misinformed about the time of reaching Naples. We saw we would miss the Italian steamer by a couple of hours and would have to wait two days for the French. We supposed it would be hot, and not very safe to remain in Naples two days at that season. But there was no help for it. We reached Rome at noon. There we had to wait three hours. The station hall is very large and tolerably cool. As soon as I could I got out our spirit lamp and made Mr. G. some strong tea. He was very nervous and could not sit still a minute, but the tea relieved him apparently, and when we left we got a half compartment at the end of the car to ourselves. You don't know how thankful we felt for it. Mr. G. continued to feel better and the air grew cooler and fresher. By nine o'clock we were in sight of the light of Vesuvius, and once I saw a very brilliant explosion, just as the volcano is represented in some of the night views of Naples and Vesuvius, except that the lava streams had then ceased to flow. By midnight we had reached our hotel, and there we spent two very pleasant days. Naples was just full of fruit and it was all so good and cheap. O how we enjoyed the peaches! They were so much more like home fruit than anything we get here.

When Mr. G. took our tickets they told him at the agency to be on board of steamer by eight o'clock Saturday morning. So we hurried as much as we could, but when we reached the harbor and had got into the little boat which was to take us out to the steamer the boatman said the latter was not in, but to sit down, and it soon would be, as the French boats were not often late. Our baggage was in and the carriage dismissed before we knew the state of affairs, and any way we supposed it was a matter of no moment. But the minutes went round and the sun grew hot and we still had to sit there on the water and wait. After a time I took the children and walked up the street where we could at least walk in the shade and get some air, but I was afraid to stay long, lest the boatman might go off with Mr. G. and the baggage and leave us behind. Fortunately we got some water and fruit, and the children were just as good as they could be. But there we had to sit *until noon*. At last the flag was run up from the agency and we started. When we were quite out of reach of all other other boats the owner of the one we were in and which we had taken for *three francs*, turned around to Mr. G. and said in bad English, "This boat has to have twenty francs to take you out to the steamer." And when Mr. G. would not agree to it he stepped the rowers and let us sit there. It was so provoking, but by dint of a good deal of talk and keeping quite cool and quiet, Mr. G. got him to go on for ten francs—$2.00. From all we have learned I guess there are no meaner boatmen in the world than Neapolitans, and yet after all perhaps they are no more than Pyramid Arabs. Still I think the Neapolitans would have to work hard to catch us in the same trap again. It was one o'clock before we were on board, and you may guess how tired and sunburnt we were. Bruce was wearing a Scotch cap only, and the little fellow was almost in a blister, but neither he nor Lulu cried once the whole morning.

Having at last succeeded in reaching the steamer, we were soon comfortably arranged in a very nice state-room. The day was fine and all the accommodations much nicer than by the Italian line; so we promised ourselves a pleasant trip. But we were not an hour out of port when Bruce, Lulu and I were all on our backs in a row. There were an unusual number of lounging places on the upper deck, and Mr. Giffen brought up our rugs and blankets and kept us up there all the time in daylight. Lulu got up before night the first day and had a great romp over the deck, but Bruce kept to his back most of two or three days. He seemed to think things were not equally distributed, frequently remarking, "Poor *mamma*, and Bruce have cough very much; papa and Lulu not." And yet there was very little rough weather. Most of the sea was as calm as a river, but the steamer was an unusually long, narrow boat, and it rocked unmercifully when there seemed to be neither swell nor waves. I remember that I still felt sick when the pilot came on board in Alexandria harbor."

Here the record ends—the pen laid down when these sentences were finished was never again to be taken up. The familiar "Letters from our Missionary,"—letters which had brought instruction and rare enjoyment to so many thousands of readers for half a score of years, were to be seen no more. The oft-repeated question, "Shall we see her face again?" was answered—not until the earth gives up its dead and we all stand before the judgment seat.

CHAPTER XXVII.

SICKNESS—DEATH—BURIAL—SUMMARY OF MRS. GIFFEN'S CHARACTER AND WORK.

In a short time after their arrival in Alexandria, they went on to Asyoot their old home, and resumed work as usual. In a few weeks they moved into the new building, for a mission family, that had been erected on the lot containing the College building and dormitories. But meanwhile they were forced to go into the old, tight, hot, miserable house in which they had lived for years, and in which they had suffered so much, and which so nearly

proved the death of the entire family. When Mrs. Giffen
at length found herself in a new, clean, comfortable house
for the first time, her contentment and happiness seemed to
know no bounds. She felt that all their former troubles
and sufferings were happily ended; that she was now fully
equipped for effective work in any department of mission
labor, that before her lay a future bright with hope and
promise,—she was just entering upon the work her heart
had so longed for all her life, and for which she had labored
so long to fit herself. But alas! for human hopes and expectations, how soon they are blasted. She was permitted
to live in this pleasant home but three weeks, and when
she left its threshold, it was to enter upon the last journey
ever made in Egypt.

Shortly before her last illness she went to Cairo, because
there were none but native physicians in Asyoot who were
but little skilled in the management of patients, or the expert use of medicine. On the 9th of October Mrs. Giffen
gave birth to a son, and all went well for a time, but on
Tuesday, the third day she complained of a pain in her left
hand. The physicians pronounced it rheumatism caused
by cold. But the pain became sorer, and by next day had
extended to the other hand and was felt in the side and
ankles, and soon became almost unbearable. That night
she slept some from an injection of morphia, and for the
same reason was easier through Wednesday and Thursday.
Her husband and friends knew little of the nature of acute
rheumatism, and as she seemed quiet and easy were not
alarmed as to her condition. Friday she had little fever,
but complained through the day of oppression and slept in
a fitful way. But that night the heart action became very
strong, and this violence continued through Saturday and
Sabbath to the end. At daybreak on Saturday her mind

became confused and so partly remained. Indeed it is almost certain that she was either partially unconscious during most of her illness, or was not aware of her condition, since she left not a message, even for her mother, and her's was not a nature to die and give no sign.

On Sabbath in one of her lucid intervals she was heard to say, "O dear Saviour come to my help." It was Communion Sabbath, and she had asked to be remembered in the services, and when Dr. Watson came in he told her that he had reference to her in all the morning's services; she answered that it was well. In the conversation which followed she said, "I am ready and willing to die, but Oh! it will be so hard for Mr. Giffen and the children." That night after dark vomiting commenced, and immediately a great change passed over her face, and they knew that the end had come. Mr. Giffen was in an adjoining room and was called: He quickly came, but to his question "Do you know me?" she answered, "no." This was the only reply she ever made to any of his questions. The physician came but could give no help.

At 10:20 o'clock on Sabbath night, the 16th of October, 1881, her spirit passed away, and was conducted by ministering angels to that mansion prepared in the Father's house.

When her father died some one stood over his body and said, "the battle is fought and the victory won," and who will deny to her, though she fell earlier in the battle, the same pean of victory. After his death heaven and his spirit always seemed so near. Who shall say that his dear face was not the first that rose upon her glorified vision, when she entered the world of the dead? The busy, teeming brain cold and frozen by the touch of death, the active hands folded for the long, long rest, "the church's brightest star," vanished, from earth and risen evermore in the firmament of heaven.   But she had gained a "good report," fell at her post, "died upon the field of honor," and when " her spirit passed the portals of light, it was doubtless met by an array of the noble army of martyrs and confessors, that would do honor to any reception in the universe."

On the day following, the interment took place.   Her countenance was calm, peaceful and sweet like one who had lain down to pleasant sleep. At 3:30 o'clock the body was borne to the church, and Dr. Watson, the officiating minister read the 90th Psalm in English. The 46th Psalm, 1–4, was then sung to a very plaintive tune, in Arabic. The reading of I. Cor. 15th chapter, was then followed by touching and affecting remarks.   The little band of Missionaries and friends wound their way through the crooked streets to the new American cemetery, and there the dust so precious was laid to rest until the time when " the voice of the Son of Man" shall call it forth, and "fashion in like unto his own glorious body."   Hidden always from our human eyes—but not lost—only gone before. She will sleep as well as if she rested beside the dust of her father, under the sound of the church bell, and the Master will be as near to guard her lonely grave in that dark land, as among us.

The tablet erected in her memory by her husband bears the following inscription:

In Memory of
MARY E. GALLOWAY,
Wife of Rev. John Giffen.
Born in Newberry County, South Carolina.
The First Missionary of the Associate Reformed Presbyterian Church of the South.
She Sailed from New York, February 10th, 1875.   .
Died at Cairo, October 16th, 1881.

"Be thou faithful unto death, and I will give thee a Crown of Life."

Mrs. Giffen left three children:

Bruce Johnston Giffen, born in Ramle, Egypt, March 5th, 1878.

Lulu (Margaret) Speer Giffen, born in Cairo, Egypt, February 24th, 1880.

Marion Galloway Giffen, born in Cairo, Egypt, October 9th, 1881.

The death of Mrs. Giffen was a most unexpected shock. Only a few days before, letters received from her husband contained the most encouraging reports, so that her friends perhaps felt happier and better satisfied as to her future, than ever before in her mission life. Then without a word of warning they were overwhelmed by the terrible blow. And so throughout the entire church. It was believed by all that her visit to Italy had fully restored her health, and that she was never better prepared for effective labor. The fondest hopes of the church were centered in her and her work, and the probability of her untimely death was not even regarded as among the possibilities. The surprise and sorrow of the church, therefore, was profound when it was known that Mrs. Giffen had passed away. There was a universal desire to see her face, and take her by the hand. "I do not think there was a member of the church so universally beloved, or one in whose behalf so many prayers ascended to the Lord. Her correspondence was the first thing read, by old and young here in these mountain fastnesses. In her the church has lost her brightest star." No one in the church was better known, and in none was there more interest. It was not surprising, therefore, that her death was the occasion of a spontaneous outburst of sorrow and sympathy, through the entire church, and brought letters of sympathy and condolence to her sorrowing friends from every part of our common country.

The day after the tidings of her death reached this country, a memorial service was held in Due West, her old home. "The bells were tolled one hour before the exercises began. On entering the church one was struck with the impressive decorations of the pulpit and the walls in the rear. There was a floral cross and crown most beautifully devised. Beneath this there was a large, well executed picture of the deceased. Underneath this again, was the word in illuminated letters:

FAREWELL.

The exercises throughout were of solemn and tender interest. As the first missionary of our church, Mrs. Giffen, has won a prominent place in its history, and her name and memory will ever be precious to those who appreciate unselfish devotion, high moral heroism, and the consecration of eminent gifts to the cause of God."

When one dies in the Master's service in a good old age, and is gathered home as a shock of corn in his season fully ripe, has contended in the battle for God and man, until age has dimmed his sight and unstrung his sinews,—we feel like saying:—"Servant of God well done," enter the rest. But when we see one who has just girded on the armor, has just perfected himself in the use of "the sword of the spirit," and whose soul and body are both aflame with zeal and love, and has just stepped to the front a recognized leader in God's host—when we see such a one fall in the very beginning of a struggle where their help seems to be so much needed, our human hearts are rent with conflicting emotions and questionings. Why this strange providence? Why are the strong and valiant taken, and

the spent and useless left? To the human eye it seemed
that a wide and effectual door was just fully opened, and
her step was upon the threshold, when the messenger arrested her, "the Master hath need of thee," and bore her
away to the portals of light. But the Father knows best.

But this is not the first instance where a life that was
brief, but full of glorious promise, has brought inestimable
blessings to the church. The influence of such lives are
not measured by days and years, or material results. The
public ministry of Jesus was ended in three brief years.
The zeal of Martyn and Brainerd wore out their frail
bodies in a few years, but when will their influence perish?
There are some blades so keen-edged that they soon cut
through the sheath.

After all there is a sad side to the thought of living till
one's work is done. Whatever is *incomplete* is of course
but partial, and the incomplete has always more in it by
its possibilities and its suggestions than the finished has by
its actualities. As a rule those whose work is best and
longest in the world, are those who were cut off with their
work unfinished—what they did do was so full of suggestions and expectations of what they were to do, that their
glorified memory remains an example and an inspiration
beyond all that their completed work could have been
" It is the broken column, rather than the capped one that
marks the grave of him whose life is still a power in the
world."

It only remains for me to give a brief summary of Mrs.
Giffen's character and work, as a woman, wife, mother and
missionary.

Those who have read these pages attentively will have
seen that she was distinguished for *an intellect strong, comprehensive and piercing,* almost masculine in its robustness ;

yet she was never unfeminine. To this vigorous and acute intellect she added all the tender and attractive graces of a pure and refined woman. Her mind was full and well rounded—developed in every direction, and symmetrical in every part, enabling her to excel in whatever she undertook. It was so thoroughly under the control of her will that she could fix it on any given subject and hold it there for any desired period, and to the exclusion of other thoughts and subjects. This habit, gained early in life proved of great value, enabling her to concentrate every energy upon the work just in hand, and ensuring speedy and thorough work.

She seemed to *read character* by intuition, whether in in man or woman. Her first judgment of one's character rarely needed revision. Her warning, often given the writer, " beware of such a one," generally needed only time to vindicate its correctness. By the same faculty she was enabled to discover those whose qualities fitted them to become the truest and highest type of a friend—and of this latter class she could count very many.

That she was a very *close observer* is manifest in her varied correspondence. Whatever claimed her attention was grasped even in its minutest details, and when her pen was taken up for its description, every linament and feature stood forth as faithfully and vividly as on the painter's canvas. In this faculty lay one of the elements of her power as a writer.

In *power* of *will* and *high resolve* she was very superior. Of this trait of her character an abler pen has said: "Difficulties which would have appeared insuperable, even to adventurous man vanished before her unconquerable resolution. She was ready for every emergency, and she allowed no disappointment to check her ardor, or quench her zeal. Her whole life reveals this element of her character. Whether she is solving some problem in mathematics, or traveling in the wilds of Texas, or mastering the forms of idioms of the Arabic, there is the same detertermination never to yield."

There must be *thoroughness* in all that she did, if it could approximate her standard. Half-work and half-way measures found no favor at her hands. Of that monstrous language—the Arabic—" a steep and high mountain," and one rarely climbed by a woman, she said, " I am *determined* to get it with *the best of the men.*" Where there was such a will there was a way.

Her speech and actions were the very embodiment of *frankness* and *candor.* Direct and transparent in all her motives and aims, deception and evasion constituted no part of the means chosen by her to gain an end. Double-dealing and deceit in others, she heartily despised. To what was low or even questionable in its tendency, she never stooped. Hence her standard of a man or woman was very exalted—so exalted that few ever attained it,— yet that standard she ever tried to attain.

Her temperament was ardent and hopeful, and at times almost sanguine. This disposition served as a buoy, even in the most depressing circumstances. The hope of ultimate success was ever strong within her, and the anticipation of coming happiness took away the sting of present grief and failure. The motto of her life might well have been "trust in God and hope for the future."

To one thus variously gifted, it would only be natural to expect that her feelings and emotions would be quick, vivid and powerful: nor are we disappointed. If she ever hated any one her friends never knew it. But of the existence and power of every other feeling and emotion which noble natures may have, there was abundant and almost daily evidence.

She was *generous* and *large-hearted* almost to a fault. To be doing some kind act for another, seemed to be a necessity of her being, and her warm and affectionate nature was shown in the many ways she tried to make others comfortable and happy, and she seemed able to create ways in which to accomplish this. She lived for others : of herself she thought little and spoke less. There were few things which she possessed that were too valuable or too precious to be withheld from a friend. If she enjoyed a rare privilege and it could be shared with a friend, the pleasure was doubled. When she was crossing the Continent, and was permitted to visit the famous galleries and museums of London and Paris, to see the ruins of the Colliseum and the priceless treasures of the Vatican in Rome, she says, " It hurt me so, that none of you could see them all with us, so I brought some pictures that you might gain some faint idea of what the real sight was."

But it was when these feelings and sympathies were turned upon the members of her own family, that they found their freest scope and most intense activity. For their comfort and happiness all the resources of hand and brain were exhausted. She was never too busy, or too tired to sit down by brother or sister, and help their little puzzled brain and unravel some—to them—great difficulty ; and not of constraint, but willingly, and in such a sisterly way that remaining difficulties seemed half lessened. In every way, nameless here, because innumerable, her pure and single-minded devotion manifested itself, until her love for them had kindled in them an affection inferior only to her own. As the heart of the Jew turned to Jerusalem. " If I forget thee, O! Jerusalem, let my right hand forget her cunning. If I do not remember thee, let my tongue cleave to the roof of my mouth." So turned her heart to her father's house, and when the hour of parting came she said, " I experienced what it was to die." Few brothers ever had such a sister, and few parents, a more loving and affectionate child. After the law of the God, their wishes were the guide of her life.

The writer would be unjust to the memory of a devoted sister, and false to his own feelings, if he did not here put on record his own obligations to Mrs. Giffen. Not many months before her death he wrote to her in these words: " I do not know how long you or I may live, but before the end comes, I wish to tell you something of how much I owe to you. I know that father and mother did all for me that parents could do for any child. But I now feel that if I ever succeed in life, or do any thing in life, either for myself or others, that I owe much of it to your efforts and your inspiration. I want to thank you for it."

To all this she simply answered, " If I was ever of service to you, you may be sure it was a willing and loving service,—and that was all. But he is glad that the acknowledgment was made while she was on this bank of the river and could make answer.

Doubtless the happiest period of Mrs. Giffen's life was the five and a half years of her married life. The love of a husband, whom she honored and revered, and the sweet prattle of her own children, filled up every vacant niche in her great affection, and completed the sum of earthly happiness. A few months before her death, when she was teaching in the girls' school, and superintending two day schools, she said, " I am never so happy as when after a day's hard work and I am on my donkey going home to as good a kind husband and loving little children as I have, even if it is a poor shabby home I have to go to."

How well she filled the position of wife and mother will

be seen from this extract from a private letter of Mr. Giffen's: "No one could read her letters without knowing that she was giving her whole soul to her duties; that she was as loving and devoted a wife and mother as it was possible for a woman to be; that she was self-denying, entirely forgetful of personal comfort in trying to comfort and help others. She never had a fear for herself. Her care was always for me and the darling children. How she worked and prayed for us. It seems hard that the little ones, dearer to her than life, can never know what an unbounded wealth of affection has been taken away from them. A truer woman never loved a man; few are capable of loving like she did; few are capable of helping like she helped. She had become my ideal of a woman before we were married; but the longer we were together the more of her true worth did I feel."

"As you say, I always had a feeling of *safety* when in her presence. She was one in whom I could repose all confidence. When I was doing what she approved, I felt that I was acting a prudent part. When I would be cast down and everything seemed to have its dark side turned toward me, she was the one to cheer me up, and that without appearing to try to do so. We both seemed to feel that so long as we had each other, we had enough with which to be satisfied, so far as this world is concerned. I never before so nearly felt that the shortness of life was a thing for which to be thankful."

Her children, like herself, had most affectionate dispositions, and in their measure returned their mother's devotion. Bruce, a child of three and a half years at his mother's death, often lavished his kisses and caresses on his mamma in an extravagant way. Whenever he entered the room in which she was, he would run to her and place his hands about her neck and say, "Mamma, I love you, do you love me?" over and again.

In the last attack of ophthalmia, through which she nursed him, he lay for days in a darkened room, and perfectly blind, his mother sitting by him. He could not see her, but he could talk to her, and twenty times a day he would say, "Mamma, I love you," as if he so longed to hear the response, "Yes, my child, I love you."

When she started to Cairo on her last journey, Bruce was left behind, and did not know for three weeks that his dear mother would never caress him again. Once in a few days after his father's return, he sat very still for some minutes, and then turned to his father with the heart-rending question, "Papa, where *is* mamma?" He answered that "the Lord had taken her to a nice home He had made for her," "I go see her some day?" "Yes, if you are a good boy," and Mr. Giffen adds, "I hope to be able to teach him, in a practical way, before I leave Egypt, what death and heaven mean, and what that lone grave by the river is.'

It is a commonly received opinion, and one often founded on fact, that a woman of high literary abilities and tastes, is apt to be so engrossed in such pursuits, that the ordinary prosaic duties and drudgeries of domestic life are neglected. But Mrs. Giffen was as distinguished for "sound common sense," as for, perhaps, anything else. When the engrossing cares and duties of mission labor were not pressing, her time and energy were devoted to her household affairs. These were carefully superintended, and in all details managed with economy and energy. Her early training had given her a thorough knowledge of domestic economy, and "she looked well to the ways of her house." She was a most accomplished needle-woman, and there was no article of dress, either for herself, her husband or children which she did not or could not manufacture. But at the same time it must be understood that she regarded *mission work* in all its branches as the supreme duty of her life, and to this all other things were made subservient— even the duty she owed to her husband and children being no exception.

In mission circles in Egypt, her industry and worth seemed to have been fully appreciated.   Dr. Hogg, one of her associate missionaries, and of whom she often wrote, thus speaks of the high promise which she gave of her future usefulness: "From what I saw of Mrs. Giffen and her work, first during the two months that I had the pleasure of assisting her in her first lessons in Arabic, and afterwards during four years of associated labor at the same station, it is my earnest conviction that had her life been prolonged and leisure been granted her in the midst of her increasing family cares, to devote herself in the future—as in the past—to the work so dear to her heart, the record of her life-work would have had few to match it in the history of modern missions."

"Her heart was in her work and she gave herself wholly to it.   Prostrated from an excruciating headache, as she often was after an exciting and protracted mental effort or strain, she must be up and at work as soon as the crisis was over.   By an act of self-determination she seemed to be able to shake off all languor and exhaustion, and resume her full quota of work, from the first day of her convalescence.   Not only did she forget herself in the ardor of her zeal, but sometimes she seemed to forget those who were dearer than self. Loving her children with a doting affection, yet the cases were very rare in which she allowed the sickness of a child to interfere with her daily work in the school."

"She was prepared for useful and efficient service in almost any department of missionary work.

To instruct a native audience, one must not only know

their language, but also their mode of thinking. Unless you are able to take their standpoint, and look at the subject through their eyes, you will fail to throw much light on it although your remarks may be made in the purest Arabic.

Mrs. Giffen seemed to me, to be gifted with a special aptitude for putting herself *en rapport* with a native audience. Her nature was sympathetic, and her power of perception was such that she seemed to guess at the tenor and color of your thoughts by a kind of intuition."

" She not only loved mission work, but by dint of intense application became qualified for taking a leading part in it. She also had very enlightened ideas of mission policy, and above all, was possessed of a strong faith in the ultimate success of missions in the world. Like most missionaries, who have been blessed with success in their efforts to extend the kingdom of Christ on earth, she based her confidence of the ultimate success of the cause, on the fact that this is the very thing which God the Father pledged, when He exalted His Son in human form to His own right hand. " I will give Thee the heathen for thine inheritance, and the uttermost parts of the earth for thy possession." Believing this your sister *expected* success in her labors in this land."

When the church, here in America, sent Mrs. Giffen forth—its first messenger to the heathen world—it had high hopes centered in her and her work. It felt that it had no worthier daughter to send upon this mission, and that in giving her, it had offered its choicest treasure, and this feeling continued, without abatement, to the end.

Prof. E. L. Patton, in a recent missionary address, thus voices this universal sentiment: "It was the remark of a distinguished Carolinian, that if the South Carolina College had done nothing more than educate one such man as

George McDuffie, the State would have been amply repaid for every dollar expended in establishing and maintaining that institution. And I do not hesitate to say that if the Due West Female College had sent forth from her walls only one such woman as Miss Mary E. Galloway, this institution would have been entitled to the lasting gratitude of the Associate Reform Church, in the South, of which she was the pioneer missionary in the foreign field.—*'Dux femina facti.'*"

While we are filled with keen regrets, when we think of the splendid possibilities which Mrs. Giffen's future seemed to warrant, still the review of her life shows us much for which we can thank God, and take courage. We see in her case a signal proof of the fact, that " the stuff of which martyrs are made" is still in the church.

To those who appreciate unselfish devotion, high moral heroism and the consecration of eminent gifts to the cause of God and humanity, her name and memory will ever be precious. Her character and example will ever serve as a model for the woman who would cast her life in a high and heroic mould.

Her husband is still left the memory of a true and loving wife, her children the legacy of a Christian mother's prayers, and the church the inspiration and power of a noble self-sacrificing life.

For her own sake—however sharp the pang to the living—we would not grieve. For hath not the Master said, " Every one that hath forsaken houses, or brethren, or sisters, or father, or mother, or wife, or children, or lands for my name's sake, shall receive a hundred fold, and shall inherit everlasting life." If God fullfills his promises, then surely hers will be no mean crown.

THE END.

SONNETS.

A TRIBUTE TO THE MEMORY OF MRS. MARY G. GIFFEN, THE PIONEER MISSIONARY OF THE ASSOCIATE REFORMED PRESBY-TERIAN CHURCH IN THE SOUTH.

Dux femina facti.

—*Virgil.*

Chi vuol veder quantunque puo natura
E'l ciel tra noi, venga a mirar costei.

—*Petrarch.*

Hearken, O daughter, and consider, and incline thine ear ; forget also thine own people, and thy father's house.

—*Psalm* 45 : 10.

I.

Another name is added to the roll
  Of noble women, who with faith sublime
  A father's house forget in some strange clime
Beyond the sea, and with undaunted soul
  Explore the trackless waste, or forest drear,
Bearding the lion in his very den,
Or tiger fierce, or still more savage men,
  To bring the tidings of salvation near :
Though weak, yet strong, a glorious sisterhood,
  In body weak, but strong in faith, and love,
  And bright-eyed hope ; as when the timorous dove,
Back to the ark, across the rolling flood,
  Sped like an eagle hastening to the prey,
As in her mouth she bore the olive leaf away.

II.

Not dead, but sleeping! and thy silent power
  The world shall own, when yonder stately pile,
  Which towers in solemn grandeur o'er the Nile,
Shall vanish like the pageant of an hour;
  When she, whose beauty dazzled every eye,
And lured the haughty Roman to his fate,
A willing victim, robbed of all her state,
  Shall unlamented and forgotten lie :*
Then take thy rest, our honored pioneer,
  All undisturbed amid the deafening roar
  Of hostile guns that shake the neighboring shore,
And blanch the cheek of swarthy Copt with fear;
  For thou must sleep until the Bridegroom come,
And open wide for thee thine everlasting home!

E. L. P.

July 24, 1882.

         * Cleopatra, queen of Egypt.